RISE
OF A
PHOENIX

P.S. SYRON-JONES

Rise of a Phoenix By P S Syron-Jones

Copyright © P S Syron-Jones 2014
P S Syron-Jones has the right to be identified as the author of this work.

Cover Art & Interior Designed by Indie Designz

This book is a work of fiction and, except in the case of historical fact. Any resemblance to actual persons, living or dead, is purely coincidental.

TO MY MOTHER.

WHO'S STRENGTH, COURAGE AND FAITH
IS AN INSPIRATION FOR US ALL.

Acknowledgments

I would like to thank

My Wife Ani, family, friends, and Tina Death

for all their support.

Also: Julia Gibbs my Proofreader.

Geoffrey West my Editor.

And Indie Designz for the art work and interior design.

Without these people this book would have never have seen the light of day.

ONE

THE WARM AUGUST NIGHT air was still, and above the bustling streets of New York city, the cloudless sky gave a wonderful view of the sparkling heavens and a moon that shone as brightly as the morning sun. Traffic flowed smoothly, and the bright illumination from stores and streetlights served as a contrast to the dark. City folk hurried on their way, and tourists stopping to capture memories as they stared in awe of the immense structures and breathing in the pleasant aromas from restaurants and delis and wallowing in awe by such a great city.

From her open office window Karen Lane could hear the sounds of sirens wailing and the blaring horns of angry taxi drivers, but she had no time to take a moment to look out upon the fantastic view below her; no, she had work to do, a mass of paperwork to write up for the meeting tomorrow. She had already typed page after page, stopping only to take a sip from the water glass next to her computer.

Her hands cupped her long blonde hair and combed it through her fingers so that it fell on her back. She found that this had a calming effect, it was almost better than drinking alcohol, but didn't always do the trick.

She was tall, with an hourglass figure, and even though she was in her forties, she still had the face of a much younger woman, with the looks of a model. Looking at the computer monitor she blew out a lungful of air, as she knew there was still plenty to do in the limited time. The office was large with a glass-topped desk on which there was her monitor, telephone and other useful items. On the left wall was a large oak cabinet, which stored various books and photographs of places around the world where she had been.

The white painted walls to her right were adorned with diplomas from Columbia law school, Harvard and various other educational establishments she had attended, and below these was a long black leather sofa. Its soft fabric and comfortable padding had been a good companion to her after so many late nights.

A miniature bar sat in the middle of the wooden cabinet; this had a selection of **beverages** ranging from scotches and bourbons to brandies and other liqueurs. These were more for her clients than for personal consumption but she had her moments, such as tonight.

"God, I could do with a drink," she thought, eyeing up the bottles. However she resisted temptation, aware that the work was her priority.

Maybe I'll have a drink later, she promised herself. When everything was finished, she decided that she would go home, slip into a hot bath, relax with a nice glass of fine wine, and soak the night away. With that, a little happiness edged into her soul and the side of her mouth rose slightly as if to give a secret smile. Karen worked for another hour, and then finally with a triumphant 'yes!' she pressed the 'save' key on her keypad. Then, as she listened to the printer churn out the pages, representing her hours of typing, she picked up the glass in her right hand and swivelled in the black leather office chair to face the large window. As Karen stood up, the leather creaked with age: it was old, and in fact, she had owned this chair all through college. Her lucky chair, she called it.

Walking towards the window's view, she stopped, raised her glass as if to salute the city below, and knocked back the contents, at which moment the office printer completed the operation, with the sound of tiny gears grinding to a halt. The abruptness of the silence shocked her slightly.

It took her around half an hour to put the document together and pack it away into the presentation folders for the partners of the law firm. She raised her wrist to look at the watch on her slim wrist. The gold-faced Rolex showed half past two in the morning. Letting out a silent curse, she found it hard to believe that she had really been working until this time.

Powering down the computer and switching off the lights she locked up for the night, stepping into the hallway that contained a mass of booths and desks on the firm's floor. She realized that everybody else was long gone, tucked up in their beds hours ago; she scanned the floor and found the janitor buffing the floor next to the elevator.

"Hi, Karl," she greeted him with a smile of relief to see another person. Karen struggled to close the office door behind her, as her arms were full with her coat, handbag, files and, balanced under her chin, her thermos coffee cup.

"Hi, Miss Karen, working late again?" he said, almost disapprovingly.

"Young lady like you should be out having a good time,

not cooped up here on a Friday night, no sir," he added, shaking his head. Karen gave him a grateful smile for being concerned about her, and most of all, for being considerate enough to press the call button on the elevator. The doors opened and Karen stepped inside.

"Good night, Karl," she said.

"Good night, Miss," he replied.

The doors closed and she nudged the button for the garage with her elbow, hoping she had hit the right one. The button illuminated and Karen sighed with relief. Then she felt the slight shudder and the elevator started downwards towards the underground garage. She observed the panel displaying the numbers, watching the downward count.

Finally, the elevator reached its destination and with a DING, and the doors opened to reveal the grey, dark parking lot. She stepped out, noticing the temperature change. Just now the air had been cool from the building's air con, whereas now it was warm and dry.

Karen headed for a group of parked vehicles at the end of the lot. She began to hum a tune she had heard earlier that day which was repeating in her head. She walked past the large round pillars that supported the roof. She began to notice shadows dancing in front of her, contrasting with brightness from the hidden wall lights. Her car was in sight, but the uneven light played tricks on her, conjuring up all kinds of imaginary apparitions at the edge of her field of vision.

Her ears pricked to the sound of the elevator, and, as she turned, Karen noticed a silhouette of a large hulking figure stepping out of the elevator. She started to walk quicker, and her humming began to match her steps in an attempt to calm herself. Then there were pounding footsteps from

Rise of a Phoenix

behind her. Too fearful to look around she made for her car as fast as she could.

Who was following her? What did they want? Her pace quickened until it was almost a jog, until she was a few feet from her car. Behind her the pursuer had also broken into a jog to keep up with her.

Nearly there now, she thought, her eyes set on the vehicle before her. Her baggage of coat and coffee mug were flung aside as she ran. Her heart pounded in her chest as she searched through her bag for her keys.

"Where the fuck are they?" she screamed, as she reached her car. Fear drove her into panic as he fingers scrabbled though her bag's contents. Her pursuer's footsteps became ever nearer as she dug deeper, cursing and throwing items from her purse in her frantic search.

Suddenly a large shadow cast over her. She screamed,

"Don't kill me, please!" as she cringed against the cool metal of her blue BMW awaiting the inevitable.

Nothing happened. She heard a calm voice, slightly out of breath from the chase, but nevertheless calm and somewhat familiar. Karen chanced a peek from under the arm that was raised to protect her face.

"Hey I'm sorry to startle you, Miss Karen, but you left these in the door." Her arm dropped down and she stood up from her cowering pose as if nothing had happened, quickly taking the keys from his large dark hands. She playfully smacked his right arm with her bag, and giggled.

"Karl, you scared the crap out of me." They both laughed and he helped to retrieve her belongings. Opening the car door for her, Karl waited until she was safely inside, then closed the heavy door; she rolled down the window and smiled at the old man.

"Good night, Miss, and I'm so sorry for scaring you," Karl apologized. "You have a save journey home now." And with that he turned and headed back towards the elevator.

Karen blew out a deep calming breath, looked at herself in the rear-view mirror, she stuck out her tongue and made a "blaahh" sound as if to make a self-examination. *God I look like crap*, she thought. Then she let out a small self-indulgent smile as her mind strayed to the thought of a hot bath and a large glass of red wine—after all that had happened tonight, she deserved it. Karen started the engine, at which the radio burbled to life. Music bleared from the speakers as she sped away towards the exit.

As she approached the barrier to the private parking lot, she noticed a large wheeled garbage bin blocking the exit.

"You have got to be kidding me," she responded to this latest annoyance at the end of her day. Whipping the seatbelt out of its fastener, she exited the vehicle. Walking up to the barricade, she grasped the handles of the bin, and with a heave she pulled but to no avail. She looked down, and noticed that the brakes had been activated; she clenched her fists and looked up, making a muffled scream, as if to ask someone up above for help.

Why me? Karen thought as she bent down to release the device. Suddenly she was grabbed from behind, and a sweet smelling rag was placed over her nose and mouth. She fought her assailant, kicking and clawing, but it had no effect. Whatever chemical that had been on the rag was starting to take effect. As she slowly started to drift into the darkness, a tear rolled down her cheek and fell into the darkness.

TWO

JOHN AND SUE MITCHELL walked down the main street laughing and joking like a couple of teenagers. After leaving the restaurant they had gone to the bar where they had first met, the hours had drifted into the early morning as they just wandered happily back home. These lovebirds had just celebrated their three years of blissful marriage, and it was the first time in years they could be alone together without work or the kids to interrupt. Even though it was now a Monday morning, they thought *what the hell* and had palmed off the kids to Sue's mother's place the night before and so they had the night for themselves. No, the night they'd shared was about them and nobody else.

As they walked for a couple of blocks, John suddenly grabbed Sue by the arm and pulled her into the nearest alleyway. Pushed her against the hard brick, he kissed her passionately as his hands moved all over her, caressing her slim body underneath the black velvet dress. She responded to this lustful moment by kissing and biting his ears and neck. The two locked in a passionate embrace, an almost animalistic lust for one another came over them, and they forgot where they were and who might hear or see: they did not care.

They moved down the alley, away from prying eyes. He pulled her over to a bricked-up window of an old wall and pulled up her dress. As he lifted her onto the window ledge, she pulled open his trousers and they fell around his knees. Slowly, he carefully entered her, and as he did so she groaned with pleasure and gripped onto him, then used her legs to pull him closer. Entwined in the moment as they felt and enjoyed one another, the world around them just disappeared. As their passions drew them closer to a mutual climax, Sue began to bite him in the left side of his neck, whispering,

"Oh God yes, *yes*!" This turned him on, making his actions more intense. But at that moment something made her to look up the alleyway. As she did so her screams of passion became shrieks of terror. Backing away quickly, John thought he had done something wrong. His gaze followed hers, and he joined in with her chorus of dread.

A gang of heavily built college students who had seen the happy couple dive quickly into the alleyway, came rushing towards them, assuming that the woman was in distress, and to their surprise they were greeted by the sight of the woman and the man, his trousers around his knees, both cowering like babes. They ran up to John and Sue, unaware of what was behind them.

"Hey man, you two OK?" said a large African-American kid.

"Hey what's up? You look like you all seen a ghost or something," joined in the other large skinny white kid. Then, catching on that John and Sue were intent on something behind them, they tried to see what it was. When they did, they yelled:

"Oh shit man, that's fucked up!" The kids froze for a moment, then they made for the entrance of the alleyway, where their friends lay in wait. "Hey man, call the cops," ordered the black kid to one of the others, who whipped out his cell phone and dialled.

"Hello, police department, what's your emergency?" asked a female on the other end of the line. The skinny blond kid grabbed the phone.

"There's a dead body in an alleyway," he informed her, then burbled the address.

"Please stay at your location, we will send a unit to your location as quickly as possible." The kid hung up, passed the phone back, and then he threw up.

Detective Samantha McCall woke to the sound of her alarm. The high-pitched 'BEEP BEEP BEEP' was irritating enough to do the job of getting her up after a short sleep, and she leant over and checked the time on the digital display. It read 05:00, then, giving a quiet moan of disapproval, she slapped the off button then collapsed back to her sleeping position.

Just a couple of minutes, Sam thought to herself, but then she changed her mind and got up. She left the bedroom and made for the kitchen, where she reached for the coffee machine and clicked the button to bring it back from its slumber. Heading to the bathroom she prepared to shower, and the steam from the hot water filled the air, misting over the mirrors and small window in the six-foot-square room. She stepped under the torrent of water and just let the cascade run over her for a while.

Switching off the taps, stopping the warm flow, she stepped out of the shower unit, and wrapped a large towel round her slightly tanned body. McCall used her dry hand to wipe the fog from the mirror that hung above the white porcelain sink, then she looked at herself in the mirror. Staring for a moment, she smiled, and then left for the kitchen.

Coffee in hand, Sam headed for the bedroom, slipped on some jeans and a t-shirt and got ready for the day ahead. Grabbing a bowl of cereal and the freshly filled coffee mug, she entered the sitting room. As she approached the couch that was housed in a cut-out section of the floor, McCall stepped onto the cushions and sat down cross-legged, grabbing the remote for the TV, and clicked the ON button. With a burst of light and sound the set came to life and showed a tall man telling New York the weather for the day. *Great, another hot one*, she thought, then switched channels, looking for something less depressing than a news station.

Breakfast done, she switched off the TV set and headed for an antique desk at the back of the room, next to the entrance to her bedroom. Opening the left hand drawer she took out her service 9mm Glock 17 pistol and slipped it into the rear holster that nestled in the small of her back, then carefully picked up her police badge. Sam gave it a quick brush with her hand then clipped it next to the handcuff pouch above her right-hand trouser pocket and gave it a friendly tap.

As she reached the front door, the police officer grabbed her short leather jacket and slipped it on, checked the keys were in the pocket and left for the station.

It had taken her longer than normal to get to the station, but now she was sat at her desk with the reminance of a fresh coffee ready to begin typing up the mundane paperwork that followed the closing of a case. However, she did not mind, it gave her some time to reflect on the crime. In addition, she found that going over what had occurred during the investigation of a particular case, often taught her useful things to use for the next one. Her fingers danced over the keyboard like a pro: if anybody had seen her they might easily have taken her to be a secretary or typist, not a homicide detective.

She needed coffee. Standing up, she reached for the stained coffee mug with the faded police badge symbol on the side and walked towards the coffee room that was adjacent to the Captain's office. The space was small with a couple of chairs and a square table next to the far wall, and a counter below a large window, which housed around four coffee peculators and a number of unclaimed mugs for visitors. In addition to offering refreshments, it was also a good place to go to unwind. Sam picked up one of the steaming hot containers and poured herself a mug of the dark liquid, the potent aroma of cheap coffee filled her nostrils. Fetching the milk from the small refrigerator she sniffed to see if it was still drinkable, and then topped up her brew.

As she looked out and surveyed the 'shop floor' before her, a bustling array of cops talking on phones, chatting to each other about the game, she smiled. *God, how I love this*, she thought to herself.

Taking a sip from the coffee she looked over to the desk in front of her, and the two detectives there beckoned her over. Joshua Tooms was a large African-American man, well over six-three tall with a ball players build and a van dyke beard that covered his heavy jaw. The other was Antony Marinelli. A well dressed Italian / Irish cross bread that was around two inches shorter than his massive black colleague, but his a medium build fitted well in his Italian suit. Tony was huddled over a desk writing down an address that was been given over the desk phone.

"Yeh, I got it," he said. "We will be there as soon as we can." He finished scribbling and put the phone down.

"We got one on the east side," he said, waving the bit of paper in his hand. "M.E is already there."

The two men grabbed their jackets and headed for the elevator at the far end of the room. "I'll meet you guys downstairs," Sam said, swigging the remains of the coffee down. She grabbed her jacket and waited for the return of the elevator.

The street was full of onlookers, press, and TV, she thought to herself. McCall had purposely parked quite a way from the scene, she knew that stretching her legs would do her good and it gave her time to get her head straight and her senses tuned. She parked, and then slipped out of the cool of the air-conditioned vehicle to the raging heat of the morning. Shutting the door, she then combed her shoulder-length brown hair through her fingers. Then, with a confident tap on her service pistol, slipped on a pair of sunglasses. She was ready.

Walking up the barriers, she noticed the large crowd of people shoving each other aside to get a look, and some press photographers trying for the shot that would make them big money. In the corner by the walled entrance to the crime scene stood a tall broad-shouldered officer that on Sam's approach smiled, tipped his cap and lifted the tape for her. She ducked under the yellow police barrier, and as she stood up on the inside, McCall thanked him and smiled.

Stopping for a moment before venturing down, she viewed the crowd then turned once more to the veteran cop.

"Tom, can we get these people back?" she asked "A long way back?"

Tom chuckled then proceeded to move the barriers back further.

"Come on, folks, show's over, come on now, let's go." The other officers followed suit, getting rid of the crowd.

Detective Sam McCall walked up to her two colleagues, who were busy questioning witnesses. As she approached Detective Tooms he looked up from the notebook which he was busy scribbling in, and met her gaze. She stood for a moment, letting him finish up. He thanked the two students he'd been talking to, and as they left McCall walked up to him.

"So what we got?" she asked him.

Tooms pointed out the couple who sat huddled together on the steps of an ambulance.

"John and Sue Mitchell, both thirty years old, just celebrated their wedding anniversary when they decided to go up the alley. Next thing these guys are hearing screaming and the students called 911."

She regarded the couple, registered their fear.

"You been down there yet?" she asked him.

Tooms shook his head, "Been waiting on you. You want to talk to them first?" McCall nodded while she watched John and Sue cling tightly to each other.

"What the hell is down there?" McCall thought. She thanked Tooms and headed for the ambulance.

John and Sue Mitchell sat there, still shivering with fear as a result of what they had witnessed, their shoulders covered by blankets as they each grasped a cup of steaming coffee. As she approached them, she nodded to the paramedic who was attending to them; he immediately knew that as a, Give us a minute gesture. As he left them she gave him a quick silent thank you. He just smiled.

She took a minute to jot down the time, date and location in her notebook, then proceeded to start the interview:

"Hi, I am Detective Sam McCall."

"Hi, I'm John Mitchell and this is my wife Sue." The woman gave a slight nod.

"I know it's difficult but I really need you to go through what happened."

Sam gave them a sympathetic smile. They both looked at each other and nodded. It was Sue who started talking: "Well we had just had dinner at some Italian restaurant around two blocks away."

Her voice was as shaky as the rest of her.

"You see it's our anniversary and it was the first chance we've had to go out alone without the kids," John explained, making an effort to keep his voice calm.

Sue continued after giving his hand a little squeeze. "Well we were just walking, enjoying the evening when John pulls me down here to well … to be alone." She looked down to the ground and blushed.

"Why?" Sam enquired, then she figured it out. "Oh OK, sure I got it." McCall felt embarrassed for the woman. "Go on Mrs. Mitchell, but I think you can leave out those details," she added, trying not to smile.

"Well we got down here to, well, you know, and it wasn't until we got to the end before we saw it—her." Sue Mitchell broke down in tears and Sam waved to the paramedic to take the couple away.

The woman detective seemed puzzled; she called over the other two officers to join her.

"What we got, guys?" she asked.

Rise of a Phoenix

Tooms flipped open his notebook. "Well, those guys over there," he pointed with the end of his pen towards the group of students sitting on the doorstep in front of a newsstand. "They saw the couple go down the alleyway and thought nothing of it till they heard screaming and thought the guy was doing a special on her and ran over and saw the body." He closed the pad and returned it to the inner pocket of his short brown leather jacket.

"Well, we got nothing over here just some passers-by, didn't really see anything." Tony, the other officer, pointed to an elderly couple standing beside an ambulance.

McCall noticed that it was still the early hours, dawn hadn't yet broken, and the alleyway was still in darkness.

As they moved deeper into the dank and filthy alleyway McCall moved quickly out of the way, as a fresh-faced uniformed officer almost bowled her over. *God-damn rookie*, she thought, watching him heading for a mass of large heavy-looking wheeled garbage bins. Sam and her colleagues rounded a corner to find a slim African-American woman leaning over something; she wore blue medical overalls that had the words Medical Examiner in yellow print on the outside. Her back was towards them, which obscured their view of the body.

"Hi, Sami," she said without turning round. "Well we got a mean one here."

"Hi, Tina," McCall replied, always happy to see her friend. "What are you saying? A mean one?" she asked Sam's eye gazed past the back of the ME and the sight before her made her want to lose her breakfast.

"Jesus, what the!"

The other two covered their mouths and turned round.

A young female lay on the cold ground, her naked body lay

as if it had been posed, and her clothes lay folded next to her. All seemed relatively normal, apart from the body.

"Yeh, like I said, this person is nasty … Brilliant but nasty," said the ME, instantly regretting calling him brilliant.

"Why, what do you mean?" McCall asked curiously.

"As you can see," Tina pointed with a gloved finger towards an area where the front of the torso should have been,

"The area here has been completely removed." There was a large space, once occupied by a chest and stomach. All that remained was the upper and lower parts of the torso and the flesh and bone structure of her back. The lower section of the ribcage and raw naked flesh and muscle held it all together.

"Till I get her back to the lab I won't know any more, apart from the fact that she wasn't killed here."

Sam looked puzzled for a minute then added with a confirmatory nod,

"There's a lack of blood."

The pretty M.E looked up at McCall with saddened eyes and nodded.

"'Lack of' isn't the word. I mean I found no blood anywhere, it's as if she had been completely exsanguinated. But, hey, don't shout vampire just yet," she said, looking up and giving Tooms and Tony a *Don't think about it* look just before they could make a comment.

Tina waved at two orderlies to come and take away the 'Jane Doe', and the two men, both in their late twenties, brought over the body bag and trolley, then, taking great care, placed the corpse in the bag and took it back to the coroner's wagon.

The three officers waited for CSU to finish their sweep. Sam watched impatiently while the team started to take photos and collect fibers and prints.

RISE OF A PHOENIX

"OK, detective," called a familiar voice. The grey-haired man was in his late forties but still had the style and bearing of a much younger man.

"You're clear to go in," he said smiling, treating her just as a grandfather might treat his granddaughter.

"Did you find anything?" McCall was hoping that the killer had left something, but she already had a bad feeling about this case.

"Not really. Son-of-a-bitch is smart, put her in an alley, put it like this we have too much data." the newcomer gave her an uneasy smile.

"Thanks, Jim. Oh say hi to Denise for me, will you?"

He waved and left with the rest of the CSU.

"OK." McCall turned to her two colleagues. "We need to do a canvass of the area, I want to find something that this bastard may have left." She motioned for her colleagues to go to the further end of the blocked alleyway, while she went back to try and mentally reconstruct how he may have got 'Jane' there. She reached the entrance of the alley and realized that all the onlookers had gone, obviously leaving once the body had been taken.

Looking round the entrance, she imagined a vehicle pulling up and stopping, then went though the movements of a person getting out and walking along the alleyway, assessing what he may have touched or banged against, trying to envisage the scene, and what he might have encountered.

"Why here?" she thought aloud. "What's so special about here?"

As Sam stared down the breadth of the dark brittle-stoned passage she took a deep breath and closed her eyes. As she slowly opened them she was ready, taking her time, checking for something, *anything*.

"Sometimes things are in plain sight," her father used to say. So she stopped for a second as the thought of her dad brought a small unwelcome distraction to the moment. She shook off the memories and proceeded down the alley.

There was nothing.

Damn it, she thought. Who was this guy? Suddenly she had this feeling of not being alone. She turned to find at the alley's entrance there was a tall dark figure, silhouetted by the bright sun behind him making an identification impossible. All she could make out was a long coat that flapped in the breeze of the large truck that powered past. Moving towards the figure, she drew out her badge and held it up.

"Hey excuse me can I talk to you?" she yelled out. "Hey you!"

But the figure remained motionless. Something seemed wrong about this guy, whoever he was. Suddenly something jammed up against her leg, and there was a loud screech as she kicked a ginger cat who had only been trying to be affectionate. She looked down, shocked at what had just happened, but when her focus returned to the figure he was gone.

"Stupid animal!" she screamed, running in pursuit of the man. Reaching the mouth of the passage, she burst out, half expecting to see him running or a car speeding away. But there was nothing, just passers by suddenly turning at the sight of McCall. He had completely disappeared. Who hell was he and where did he go?

THREE

THE MIDDAY SUN WAS hot and stifling, which caused the bustling traffic to crawl across the city, ice cream vendors worked hard to supply the needy crowds that had gathered in the streets. Within the coolness of the Grand Central Station thousands of commuters hurried to find their platforms. As she headed for the exit, Susan Black nudged her way through the endless wash of motivated people. Pushing the brass door rails of the wood-and-glass doors Susan was suddenly taken aback by the sudden change in temperature, as the startling heat slapped her in the face.

Stepping into the street, she headed for the coffee shop that sat under the Park Avenue Viaduct. She smiled to herself as she noticed a few heads turn, and detected appreciative glances. She was a sexy forty-year-old woman, her long blonde hair flowing attractively in the wind, her grey business suit hugging her neat slim body, accentuating the alluring curves. Men's mouths dropped open, even some women stared in admiration, and she lapped up the attention. As she entered the coffee shop one man paid her special attention. This blond-haired man readjusted his sunglasses to get a better view, then picking up his cell phone, he pressed the speed dial and waited.

"Yes," the voice on the other end of the line was soft but the tone was like nails on a chalkboard. The dark haired man shivered at the sound of the voice in his ear.

"I have just seen something I think you will like," he said. There was a pause.

"Can you bring it?"

The blond man smiled,

"Sure, I'll pick something up for you." He disconnected the call and put the cell phone into his jacket pocket and waited.

Susan lived only a couple of blocks away so she decided to 'walk off' her long journey, and the hours of sitting; it was good to be back after a two-week business trip to Canada. As she waltzed down the busy streets, the sound of the wheeled suitcase rattled on the hard concrete, warning people to make way for her. She was not far from her apartment building when she stopped at an alleyway and listened: a faint sound emanated from the depths of the dirty alley. Moving slowly closer, she strained to make out the sound.

What was that? An injured animal? She moved nearer to the noise until she realized it was the sound of a crying child.

"Hello, are you hurt?" she asked. Releasing the grip on her case she edged in further until she found a little girl sitting in an old cardboard box, which was large enough to hold a freezer or some other large object. Susan knelt down just in front of the child, and at her.

"Hi, are you lost, do you need help?" She didn't reply. "Where's your mummy?"

Rise of a Phoenix

Before Susan could turn round, she felt her body seize up as the taser bit into her back and she passed out.

The next day Detective McCall headed to the precinct, still wondering whose body it was at the entrance of the alleyway. The day before, after examining the scene of the crime, the rest of the time was spent chasing missing persons files and hoping Tina, the Medical Examiner, had come up with something. McCall hated to drive in the mornings as the traffic was its usual nightmare, but what else could she do?

Suddenly her radio crackled to life.

"Hey, McCall, if you are on the way to the precinct, don't bother, we are needed at Central Park. We are at the Bethesda Terrace." It was Tony and he did not sound happy.

"Why, what's up?" McCall was almost afraid to ask.

"We got another one, the son-of-a-bitch has struck again."

This time another voice spoke, it was rougher, deeper and more authoritative: the Captain.

Bethesda Terrace was a late 1800s wonder, the two-level courtyard displaying a mix of red and white brick, beginning with the smaller forecourt on the upper level, to which on either side two large sandstone staircases came down to give entry to a weathered underpass. This made the place look as if it had once belonged to a castle or a cathedral. A magnificent fountain loomed at the other end of the fantastic courtyard. This was intended to be a place of dreams, a place for people to come and lose themselves in another time.

The park was awash with police putting up crime-scene tape and barricades, the press in their droves setting up tripods and getting video cameras ready to go on air: a media circus.

Sam pulled up her car as close as possible and surveyed the chaos.

"Well, so much for keeping this one under wraps," she said to herself, getting out of her car. McCall gave her gun a reassuring tap and then moved forward towards the tape.

Cameras flashed and microphones were thrust in front of her face, and people were begging her for a statement, but she just shrugged them off, treating them like an unwanted infection.

Passing the cordoned-off area, she moved freely, checking to make sure nothing out of the ordinary stuck out. A voice called out for her as she walked down the weathered sandstone steps, and looking round McCall saw the rest of the team and headed towards the crowd of plain-clothes officers, two of whom were Tony and Tooms. They were speaking to a very tall African-American man. This man was well over six feet with broad shoulders, wearing a blue suit that fitted tightly enough to advertise his large muscular arms but not tight enough to constrict his movements.

As she approached she nodded to Tony and Tooms, and then acknowledged her superior, saying

"Morning Captain."

"McCall." He returned the greeting. "This is getting out of hand."

She noticed a blue cloth covering something on the ground by the large sculptured underpass opposite the large fountain near where they stood. The group moved over to where they found Tina crouched in front of a covered corpse.

"Hi, Doc," They all said to her. Concentrating hard, she just raised a hand and waved in response to their greetings.

"So, Doc have you got a cause of death?" the Captain asked causing Doctor Franks turn round to face him.

"Well, I'm not sure how she died," the attractive M.E replied,

Rise of a Phoenix

"But I know ID is going to be a bitch."

As she said the words, she unveiled the corpse to reveal a woman. Her naked body looked trim and athletic, and unlike the last victim she was intact except for one small detail.

"Well, it's definitely your guy," Tina continued.

"Blood drained from the body just like last time but as you can see the head has been removed, and not just the head but also the neck all the way down to the collarbone."

Even the unflinching Captain had to look away.

"We need to catch this bastard and fast," Brant almost growled the words, "Before we have a full blown panic on our hands. Come on, let's move, people."

"OK, Tony, you check for CCTV footage, they must have picked something up," Sam McCall instructed.

"Tooms, can you grab some uniforms and talk to as many people as you can, someone may have seen or heard something. Thanks, guys." She looked round at the layout. The detective had to admit it was brilliantly staged: no buildings for miles and a road that ran right next to the steps. Getting witnesses would be nothing short of impossible.

The two men gave each other a quick knuckle-bump and left. Sam walked over to Tina, who was just finishing the location paperwork.

"Hey, you OK?" McCall asked the ME.

"Yes, I'm fine." Tina paused as McCall gave her friend a meaningful look. "Well not really, something's bothering me about this case."

McCall was puzzled. During all the years they had known each other this was the first time see had seen the ME spooked by what she had seen.

"What's up, Tina? It can't be getting to you, you're tough as nails."

The ME smiled at her and placed a reassuring hand on McCall's left arm.

"No it's not getting to me, I'm just thinking, how he is doing this? Now we have seen some sick perps in our time. But when sick meets brilliant, then we got a problem."

McCall gave her a quick smile.

"We will catch this guy, don't worry," and with that the M.E left for the morgue.

McCall waited an hour for the CSU to complete their normal crime-scene evidence collection; once they were finished, Jim Burke- the lead investigator of the team, strolled up to McCall with a clipboard in one hand and a sandwich in the other.

"Hi, kiddo," he said with a smile like a granddad greeting his granddaughter.

"Hi, old man." They hugged like old family friends who had not seen each other for years.

"How you holding up?" he asked, a concerned look upon his face.

"I'm doing great, it's just this case is tying everyone in knots." He nodded in agreement.

"Yeh, this is one smart SOB," he said, trying to be polite but failing.

"Both crime scenes we have found nothing! Don't get me wrong, we found stuff, but nothing out of the ordinary. Lots of tread marks, millions of fibers, I'm just hoping the smart bastard gets too cocky and slips up—they normally do."

"I hope so too, old man," she said in response, unable to prevent the doubting tone in her voice. They embraced once more, and then she was alone to walk through in her mind the events immediately prior to the body drop. She looked around. The best entrance point was definitely on the road by the large steps she had entered by. At the top, beside the road, she ran through the events, acting them out as best she could.

"OK," she spoke to herself. "Stop the car, get out. I look around, make sure everything is clear." She accompanied the thoughts with appropriate movements, using her imagination to lead her.

"OK, coast is clear; I move down the steps, I'm nearly at my goal."

She reached the bottom of the steps and turned the corner. To her surprise she found a man crouched on the ground where the body had been.

"Hey, can I help you?" she shouted to the figure.

The man rose up and turned towards her. He was tall and wore black from head to foot. She noted that he was handsome, and his clean-shaven chiselled jaw was curved into a smile, and his eyes were masked by a pair of dark Oakley sunglasses that hugged his face. He did nothing at first, then simply put his right hand over his chest and gave a small bow. Then he left.

She was too stunned by his brashness to follow, instead shouting:

"Hey! No! You stop right there, Mr.!" But he just carried on up the steps to her right on the other side of the courtyard. She started to follow him but even though his pace had not quickened he remained well ahead of her.

"Hey, you! Get your ass back here!" Sam yelled after him, but he carried on as though nothing was amiss. Suddenly, just as she was in reaching distance of him, apparently out of nowhere a horse and carriage darted between them, blocking her from her quarry.

"Police, move ... NOW!" she yelled, holding up her badge. The carriage driver quickly whipped at the steed and they took off. McCall looked around, but the mystery man was nowhere to be seen.

"OK, this guy is really starting to piss me off," she thought to herself.

Detective Sam McCall clenched her fists and screamed to the sky, as if to blame someone up in the heavens for sending this man to torment her.

FOUR

IT WAS ANOTHER WARM cloudless night and the stars in the heavens glistened like the millions of lights of the city below them, and the moon was full and massive, its brightness beamed upon the city, giving it a shade of icy blue. People went on their way to-ing and fro-ing, cars easing their way down the busy streets, but all had the same agenda: going home. A shadow passed down the street and slipped unnoticed into an alleyway. Silent as a whisper the man made it to a point in the darkness of the passage. He knelt down and scanned the area. Suddenly he rose up with the same ease as before, and moved to the row of large, heavy-looking garbage dumpsters. Something caught his eye and, slipping his hand between two of them, he grasped something; it was two dirty pairs of gloves, perhaps once owned by a homeless person. He examined them for a brief moment and slipped them into his jacket pocket.

From down the far end near the entrance, two beat cops with flashlights approached the white coloured outline of a figure on the ground. The pair were discussing how in a couple of years they would be detectives, busting heads and getting rid of scumbags like the fella who did this murder. All of a sudden, they looked up to see a shadowy figure in front of them.

"What the?" one of them yelled.

"Hey you aint meant to be down here, buddy!" He reached for his pistol. Right at that moment the moon's minimal light faded as a cloud covered it, rendering the alley pitch dark for a few seconds. The cloud passed and the alleyway was once more lit up like a winter's morning. However the policemen were alone, the shadow of a man had disappeared.

"Frank, let's not tell anybody about this, right?" The larger of the two men said. His colleague just nodded and they both got out of there as if they had seen the Devil himself.

FIVE

THE MORNING BROUGHT A red sunrise that blazed across the sky as if the heavens themselves were on fire, and a multitude of colours filled the canvas of the early morning sky. Sam rose and started her normal morning routine as if it were ritual: get up, make coffee and hit the shower. As she sat and had her usual large bowl of sugary cereal, McCall scanned the news for what the media were giving away on this case. Luckily they had nothing, just some babble about a serial killer. *Fine*, she thought, the less that these vultures knew the better, for the moment at least; there were too many times when the press had messed up a case because they were too eager to put out information. She dressed and headed for work.

The main hall of the precinct was full of people, some waiting to report something, others to get booked. McCall passed the desk sergeant, who waved to draw her attention.

"Hey, Sam," the large white-haired officer said, handing her a post-it note,

"The Doc says she wants to see you."

"Thanks, Sarge," she replied, then headed for the elevator.

"Morning, Tina," McCall greeted her friend.

Tina Franks was slightly shorter than McCall but had more of an hourglass build. Where McCall had a more athletic look about her, Tina had more the build of a cheerleader. Her father was a marine whose family had come from the Jamaica's and her mother had been a Brazilian law student studying in New York; her parents had met at a mutual friend's party many moons ago.

"Well it's about time, girlfriend," Tina replied jokily.

"So what we got?" asked McCall, eager to get some news.

"Well the blood was drained from both vics so we couldn't get a tox screen but we have other ways, don't worry, the guy's just making me earn my money," she mumbled. "We got nothing from prints, so looks like they were all good little girls. We're waiting for dental records on this one." She used her pen to point to the slab behind her.

"I wish I could tell you more, Sam, but we are backed up at the moment. Soon as I get something you'll know."

Sam thanked her friend then left to go upstairs. *God, I need coffee*, she thought. McCall was soon back at her desk in the bustling chaos of the homicide department. Phones were ringing madly, there was the sound of computer keys rattling, certainly it was a maddening melee of noise and confusion, but to her ears it was a perfect melody.

The rest of the morning was spent going through personal records and walking round the buildings surrounding the crime scene to try to get some sort of idea of where the latest victim came from. From what they could gather, she had plenty of money, judging by her almost perfect appearance, with her manicured nails, flawless teeth, and stylish dyed hair, all indicating wealth. Unable to find anything from the neighbourhood, Sam returned exhausted from the walking round.

She sat on the edge of her desk, and one arm crossed her waist, while the other was bent upwards at the elbow. In her hand she held a black white-board marker, with which she was tapping her bottom lip in thought.

The large shiny white board was filled with photos and scribbles of ideas and information on the vics. It had two thick black strips of tape running down, dividing the area into three parts, each of them allotted to one of the victims. McCall stared at the board intently, her eyes scanning to try to pick up something they all had in common, but the harder she looked, the more she worried that she might be missing something.

Tooms joined her, while Tony Marinelli was busy on the phone.

"We checked database for prints, came up nada, we also checked FBI, got nothing there either," Tooms announced.

Suddenly Tony put the phone down and quickly scribbled something on a bit of paper as he stood up and came over.

"Well we may have a lead on the first vic," Tony announced, sitting down on the edge of McCall's desk, beside her. "It appears a young lawyer in the Brookman building never showed up for a big meeting the other day and they haven't been able to reach her."

"Good, it may be our first lead, you two go there first thing in the morning," she answered, still looking at the puzzling information board. "OK, guys, go home, get some rest, God knows we could use some," she said, standing up and stretching.

"See you all tomorrow," Tooms announced as he headed for the elevator. Marinelli said his goodnights, and left, flinging his jacket over his shoulder, as if he was some kind of superstar.

She finished her paperwork, swigged back the remains of her coffee and prepared to leave. Entering the elevator, all she could think about was going home and having a nice hot bath, and a large glass of the red wine she'd bought the other day.

SIX

THE PARKING LOT WAS dark with just a few hints of light dotted here and there.

She had parked here for years; in fact, it was the only one in walking distance of the station. The collection of cars scattered all over looked more abandoned than parked, but it was cheap and secure so who gave a damn. In the distance she saw her car, it's strange faded paintwork glinting under the light of the spot lamp, which gave it an almost welcoming glow. Walking towards her beloved 1966 Mustang, her mind was focused on the case, not on the darkness of the lot; hell she knew she could take care of herself and she was armed, so if anyone screwed with her, she could sort it.

Stopping at the door of her car Sam reached inside her jacket pocket for the keys. Suddenly she felt cold steel of an automatic being pressed up against the back of her neck as she was pushed forwards against the car. There was a slam as her face met the glass of the door. She heard laughter from behind her.

"Well boys, lookie what we got here, my, ain't you a purdie little thang!" said the vile-smelling man behind her. She was overwhelmed by the rank smell of his sweat, and it made her want to gag.

"OK, darling, put your purdie little hands on the car and spread 'em."

She heard other men giggling like school kids, assessing that there were possibly two others behind her but precisely where they were, she had no idea. McCall stood rigid, refusing to budge. She got a smack at the side of the head with his large fatty elbow for her disobedience.

"I said, put your goddamn hands on the car and spread 'em, bitch!"

Under duress she obeyed, then she felt his hands moving slowly up her legs towards her crotch.

"Now we gotta search ya just in case yer packin."

He jammed his hand between her legs and moved it back and forth. Sam kicked backwards and caught the man in the face. She heard him let out an agonizing, "Oomph," then, turning quickly, McCall took aim with another blow, only to receive a belt to the head. She was thrown head-first against the car's roof. Despite seeing stars, she forced herself to stay standing.

"Listen, I'm a police officer," she yelled. "So I know you don't want to do anything rash, so if you all leave now we can avoid a situation. So now just put down the gun and—"

She was answered by a punch to the kidneys.

"So we got us a cop, well that just sweetens the deal, don't it?"

Sam tried to lash out again, but, once again he banged her head against the car.

"Well boys, we got a feisty one here, I'm gunna luv breakin' her in," he said, laughing.

But his was the only laughter to be heard.

"Hey, where you fuckers gone too?" He turned round to look. "What the?" His voice betrayed his surprise and shock. She felt the pressure from the gun loosen, so she span round. As she moved, she punched with the heel of her hand, catching him full in the stomach. He grunted in pain and, as his large frame bent double from the impact, McCall delivered another mighty upwards kick, sending a fountain of teeth and blood into the air. Before her lay three unconscious hillbillies and in the distance there was a figure masked by a bright light. All she could make out was a long coat that carried in the wind like a ship's flag.

McCall called the precinct, and assistance soon came, in the shape of five burly officers. But all the while, she was thinking, *Oh I can't wait to explain this.*

Thinking of all the shit she would get from her colleagues at the department, at least the three morons would spend the night in lockup until morning, and then she would show them that it is not wise to mess with this gal.

McCall climbed into her car and drove home, the thought of that bath becoming ever more blissful. When she arrived at her apartment Sam threw off her jacket and shoes, went to the bathroom and drew a bath, ensuring that the water was laced with plenty of foam. She slipped into the deeply filled tub as she listened to the sounds of jazz emanating from her stereo system.

SEVEN

THE SUN ROSE IN a blaze of colour, the city was ravaged by hordes of commuters heading off to work and the streets heaved with the morning traffic, and subway stations were packed with jostling inpatient people. Men and women moved in a long processions, going in their different directions whilst carrying coffee cups with logos plastered on them or cell phones pressed hard against their ears, as they pushed through the chaos to get to the safety of their offices or other places of work, keen to escape the mayhem of Manhattan in the morning.

Marie-Ann Talbot was a businessperson who bought and sold real estate and had various fingers in many other pies. For her pursuing her business interests was not so much for the money as for the thrill of it all. After she finished her 'daily shock' workout at the gym, she was ready to get to work. Coffee in hand she waited at the side of the road for a cab, when at that moment her cell phone rang. She pressed the activation button on her earpiece to answer the call.

Rise of a Phoenix

"Hello?" she said. Her voice was soft but had a slight gravelly tone to it.

She wore grey sweat-suit bottoms and a white t-shirt that clung to her ample breasts, and her tall athletic figure cast a pleasing shadow in the morning sun. Her secretary, Jenna, was on the other end of the line, and they spoke for a while about a property that had just come on the market. A yellow cab came screeching to a halt next to her, she climbed into its rear, and the lock clicked as she pulled the heavy door shut, engaging the dead bolt.

"Forty-second, please," she instructed, and the cabbie just raised a hand to confirm he had heard her and proceeded to drive. Marie-Ann continued her conversation and flicked through a magazine she had purchased earlier that morning.

"I tell you, Jenna, the place was huge and the view was," she broke off her conversation to call to the driver. "Hey, buddy, where the hell you taking me?"

She looked up and saw that they were going over the Brooklyn Bridge. Fear set her heart racing.

"Hey, fella, I am not some tourist, I live here! Take me back, you asshole!" She pounded her fists on the security glass between them till they were red raw with pain. Mary-Ann grasped at the door handles and banged on the window in the hope that someone would see her plight, but no one came. After a while she stopped. She felt so tired, so very tired.

A new fear swept over her as she realized that her tiredness was not natural, but before she could work out what had happened, she fell into blackness like no other, a sleep from which she felt as if she'd never wake from.

Marie-Ann woke up; she blinked several times so that her eyes could adjust to the brightness or lack of light. She tried to move but, to her horror, she was unable to. What was wrong, she wondered? Where was she?

She struggled but found she had been bound: her arms, legs, and her head were all tied up. Why was her head secured? From somewhere in the room Marie-Ann could hear a faint sound, something distant; no not distant, *small*. She strained to hear what it was and where it was coming from.

The noise got louder; it was music, a kind of chiming, from … maybe from a music box or watch, she concluded.

"Hello? Hello? Is anyone there?" she called out, not so much for help, for she realized that nobody was likely to hear her. Calling was a way of ascertaining if there was someone else in the room, she didn't care who it was.

The chimes seemed to be moving round her, not getting closer, just circling round. She almost felt like a zoo animal being stared at. Around and around the direction of the sound seemed to be travelling, but not quickly. She listened harder and could almost hear footsteps mixed with strange breathing. The music stayed in place for a moment, it seemed to be near her head. Suddenly she felt something moving across her hair. It was not an animal, no, it was more like fingers gently brushing across the top of her scalp.

She started to shake uncontrollably, and sweat began to pour across her brow as a mix of the fear of not knowing who her captor was, coupled with the terror of not knowing what was going to happen Her imagination was going wild with images of what this maniac could be capable of. This was too much for her to bear.

"Please don't hurt me," she begged. "I'll give you whatever you want, but please don't kill me."

She sobbed uncontrollably, hoping that this stranger might feel some sort of compassion for her.

"You will give me whatever I want, is that correct?"

Rise of a Phoenix

The voice that filled her ears sent shivers down her spine. His tone was calm and lucid, while the pitch was a missmash of highs and lows, like nails running down violin strings. But most of all she sensed the pleasure in the eerie murmur that filled her ears. Whereas before she longed for someone to speak, she now yearned for the previous deathly silence.

"Now, now, there is no need to cry, my dear," said the stranger.

His sickly sweet now high-pitched voice rang in her ears; she tried imagining the face that belonged to this monster but nothing in her worst nightmares could conjure something that obscene. Something deep inside her wanted to see his face; something in the darkest reaches of her soul wanted him to look her in the eyes. A tear rolled down the side of her face and she felt a gentle hand brush it away. As she stared up at the dimly lit ceiling, she could make out a shadow here and there, then a shape in the distance coming closer. She blinked for a second or two, just so her eyes could adjust to the light conditions but as she opened them, she was greeted by a face with large maniacal eyes and a smile that froze her with terror.

"So you would give me anything I wish?" he repeated. His smile widened and his brow creased with a scowl.

"I like your eyes my dear, so blue I have never seen the like."

"Th...Tha...thank you," she replied, somewhat shocked by the change in mood.

"No, I am afraid you don't understand. I really like your eyes."

For a brief second she saw the strange instrument come into focus above her right eye then there was blackness. Her ears filled with the sound of her own screams until she passed out, while all the time the chimes from the pocket watch played in the background even after her screams had faded into the shadows of the room.

EIGHT

A SLIGHT BREEZE BLEW through the streets of little Italy, but that just cooled the warm air left over from the scorching day's sun. People sat outside on the tables and chairs that lined the streets outside the many restaurants scattering the well-lit streets, the reds, greens and blues of lights reflected in windows and from vehicles. The night air was filled with music and laughter, and everyone was happy and having a good time, bar one.

A shadowy form crept into an alleyway, carefully clinging to the shadows as it went. It stopped just before a group of stacked boxes and observed someone at the end of the passage. The stranger looked at a large man who was watching a TV that was somehow plugged into the local power, and light from the set lit up the alleyway but also created convenient shadows—convenient for the stranger.

Vince Carbone was a large bald man, his giant form seemed almost too large for his blue hand-stitched suit, and he danced up and down as he watched the ball game on TV.

"Come on, God dammit!" he barked in a gruff, almost gravelly voice.

"Where is Santini?" asked the figure bathed in the darkness.

"Well, well, my mystery guest is here," answered the large man, whose name was Vince.

"We have been expecting you, didn't think you would show, but hey…"

The man turned halfway round just so he could lay eyes on the idiot who was disturbing him, but all he saw was shadows and a form that was bathed in darkness. The form did not move at first but then stepped into the middle of the walkway. As the newcomer moved all light seemed to disappear from around him, as if he was himself a shadow.

The mysterious figure stood upright, almost alert. From behind him, several large brutish-looking thugs in jeans and t-shirts appeared, brandishing weapons of all descriptions.

Vince turned fully, not wanting to miss this confrontation. His suit was matched with a white shirt that was opened wide enough to show off his bronzed barrel chest and a gold chain with a large crucifix that hung amidst the grey hair.

The light from the TV set caused flashes of light that danced up and down the alley, but still the stranger was hidden.

"Take this bastard apart, boys."

The fat man nodded to his counterparts who were behind the mystery man. The shadowy character felt a man coming up steadily behind him. The thug swung a baseball bat, brining it downwards with such power that it splintered on the ground as the 'shadow' sidestepped. The thug let out a painful, "Ooff," sound as the other man spun round and elbowed him in the back of the neck; this motion knocked the bat-wielder off balance and he then received a knee to the face as his head travelled downwards.

Rise of a Phoenix

The air was filled with an eruption of blood and bone as the man's nose exploded from the impact. Another guy rushed forward, slashing blindly with a large blade. Instantly the Shadow blocked the hand wielding the weapon, dragging his attacker's arm underneath his own armpit so that the outstretched arm was in a lock. There was a brief moment before the stranger pulled down on the arm, and snapped it at the elbow. The thug screamed and the knife fell straight into his adversary's hands. "Stick around, we haven't finished yet," called out the fight's winner. The newly-acquired blade whistled through the air and embedded itself into the back of Vince's knee, the fat man creaming in agony as the steel cut through muscle and met bone. Vince hit the ground with a crash, reeling in pain.

The Shadow turned, only to be met by two more men, one with a bat and another with a pistol.

The bat was swung at head height, but The Shadow leaned back just as the business end sailed past so close that he felt the displaced wind tickle his nose. As he came back up, he used the full force of his body, to drive his forehead crashing into the face of his attacker. There was a sickly crack, like snapping twigs, as he shattered the man's nose. The thug stumbled, but not too far from reach, as The Shadow used the falling man as a shield from the remaining attacker, who had a gun. The armed man bobbed and weaved, trying to get a drop on him, but The Shadow pushed the batsman towards his mate, then rushed him. There was a scraping sound as The Shadow slid across the floor, knocking his enemy to the ground, then in the blink of an eye, using one swift punch, the man was out cold.

Vince scanned the alleyway, still lit by the flickering TV images, but saw nothing. He called for his crew but there was only silence. Crawling forward, leaving a trail of fresh blood on the dirty ground, Vince went to see if his boys had got the man shrouded by shadow, but all he saw were bodies lying motionless across the passage, bodies that were all familiar to him.

"Where the fuck are you, jerk off?" he screamed, his head dancing backward and forward checking everywhere, except…

Behind him, a shadow loomed over him like a phantom, a long coat moving with the wind, like some beast clawing at the breeze. "Now where were we?" The Shadow said. "Oh yes."A scream filled the alley but it was drowned out by the nearby festivities of the night. The TV flickered on, lighting up the alley and after one more scream, it flickered no more.

NINE

THE MORNING TABLOIDS WERE packed with tales of a psycho killer at large in the city, and the police had released a statement but had supplied only enough detail to feed the press's appetite, rather than satisfy demand.

Sam McCall read the article and chuckled to herself, wondering how long the vultures had waited before printing, but she was more interested in the sports page to be bothered about what was fact and what was fiction. Today was Saturday, and tomorrow she would be at her mom's for the usual family get-together, Saturdays were her 'kick back and recharge her batteries days', and she was going to enjoy her relaxation time.

Why not, she thought? The bad guys were not going anywhere and her two colleagues were more than capable of handling things; on the other hand she had left instructions for someone to notify her if she was needed.

McCall sat down on her brown fabric sofa and flicked on the TV, her finger pressing the remote's button as she tried to find something decent to watch. *Not quite a breakfast feature*, she thought, but then her choice was better than nothing: an old Basil Rathbone Sherlock Holmes movie came on. She watched cross-legged, eating her milky cereal slowly, savouring the quiet of the moment.

As she sat watching she noticed her cell phone dance across the table in front of her, driven by the vibration alert of an incoming call. McCall leant forward and noticed the caller's ID: it was the precinct.

"Yes, what's up?" she inquired, trying to sound annoyed but feeling somewhat relieved. A day off, who needs one, she thought? There's too much to do out there.

"Get your butt back here, Detective, we got another one. The bastard's back."

It was the Captain on the other end of the phone and he did not seem happy. In fact, there was something different about his tone that she could not put her finger on.

It took but a moment to shower and change, and before she knew it she was at the door of her car. The address she had been given was the Pier 15. She knew that it was going to be a nightmare of a drive but she blue-lighted all the way. Finally reaching a safe parking area she parked up under the viaduct next to a public parking booth. This was a short walking distance from the scene. It was a beautiful sunny morning and she wanted to walk towards the crime scene, it gave her a moment to look at things that may have been missed or try and see the scene through the killers eyes. The police tape confines the scene at hand but a sometimes thing outside the box gets missed.

McCall sat for a moment, composing herself for what they would find. She got out and began to walk, looking back to see her car's bodywork being stained by the red of the sunrise, as she headed for Pier 15.

Rise of a Phoenix

The scene was chaos, with camera teams, and reporters of all description pushing and shoving to get the best shot, and microphones waved about in the hope of finding someone who would answer their questions. Heading for the tape, McCall was immediately engulfed in a frenzy of press people.

"No comment," was all they got from her as she pushed through the masses. Finally, as an officer lifted the tape, she ducked and went through, followed by a couple of shifty-looking photographers who tried to dodge the wire, only to be caught by the large stocky built officer.

"Get your ass back over the wire, people." His tone was loud and aggressive, and the two men backed away sheepishly. McCall looked round and smiled at the performance, then carried on to the end of the pier.

On the way, she saw the crowd that had gathered in the food court peering through the sun-kissed windows, flashes from cell phones and cameras lit up the glass that separated them from the crime scene.

"Captain, Guys" she greeted them with a nodded.

"McCall," the Captain returned the greeting.

"Okay, so what we got?" McCall asked, putting on her sunglasses.

The Captain pointed to a group of CSU officers huddled round a railing at the far end of the wooden boardwalk; they seemed to be pulling on something. McCall looked at her Captain with a searching look, but received a shrug and an equally puzzled response.

The four detectives crept forward until they reached MD Tina Franks, who was waiting with her crew and a dolly ready to transport whatever it was they were all waiting for.

"Doc," the Captain spoke softly.

"Captain," she replied, and just nodded to the others. "Well, I must say this is a weird one. All we were told was that there was something hanging from the balcony." She pointed with her head towards the congregation of CSU guys in front of them.

"So," said the Captain, puzzled, "maybe it was kids messing around." His look was slightly annoyed, as if he was afraid that their time was being wasted.

"Well, that's what we thought," Tina agreed, "at first. Until we knew it was bleeding."

"Bleeding!" McCall had a disgusted look on her face as she spoke.

"Yeh, two fishermen this morning tagged it by accident and they said they saw blood in the water."

They were interrupted by shouts from down in the water:

"We are ready here, you ready up there?"

"Yes, OK, cutting now."

The CSU had cut the rope holding whatever was hanging over the side, and another crew below in a patrol boat caught it. McCall and the others made their way to the other side where the boat was about to dock so they could see what all the fuss was about.

As they got to the dock they noticed a crowd of people in blue overalls with CSU lettering on the back of their uniforms. Some were taking photos, others just acting as a barricade against prying eyes.

McCall and the other three drew near the scene to find Tina bent over something; it was around three feet long, wrapped in what appeared to be brown-stained bandage wrappings. The MD cut the fastenings open carefully, using a scalpel from her medical bag. When it opened, the audience standing behind her, suddenly reeled away holding their mouths.

Rise of a Phoenix

The open sack contained what used to be a woman; both her arms and legs had been removed, but unlike the other bodies there were small amounts of blood visible, that had found their way to the bottom of the cocoon. Taking out a small white device that looked almost like a pregnancy testing kit, Tina dabbed some of the blood on to it and waited. She searched the body and sack for any evidence that may have been left behind, but she knew there would be nothing. She was only too aware that the killer was too smart to leave anything incriminating, unless he put something there to deliberately mislead them. The CSU team began to take photographs but would have to wait until they took the remains back to headquarters before they could look for fibres and fingerprints.

Tina examined the corpse painstakingly to see if there was any evidence, but came up empty, working from the lower part and slowly moving up the body until finally reaching the head. Carefully, she opened the woman's mouth, noting that everything seemed normal. Then she opened an eyelid to check for any signs of eye dilation or other unusual signs.

"Uh, guys, we have a problem," said the doc, sounding confused.

"Why? what's up, doc?" asked the Captain bracing himself against the sight and trying to hold on to his breakfast.

"Her eyes are gone."

"What do you mean, gone?" replied Tooms, horrified at the thought.

"I mean gone! Not there anymore." Tina stood up and waved the two orderlies to bag the body and take it downtown. The atmosphere was tense, as the Captain looked as if he was about to explode.

"OK, people, I have had enough of this dirt bag taking our city apart! We are going to find this son-of-a-bitch." He clenched his fist and shook it at them, more as a gesture of anger and promise than a threat.

"Call in all shifts," he announced angrily. "We work round the clock if we have to, but I want this guy."

The teams in front of him were New York City's finest and if anyone could get the killer, it would be these men and women. McCall knew it and felt the surge of energy that the Captain gave off just in those few words, words that inspired everyone to think that they could do the impossible.

From behind them came a voice that broke the silence, like a soft breeze on a still morning. It was softly spoken but had a hard tone to it:

"Maybe I can help."

The group turned as one, to find a man dressed all in black; he was sitting on the backrest of a bench, his black shiny boots that rested on the seat of the bench were glinting in the morning sun, and the long black jacket he wore that had fallen behind the backrest was flapping in the breeze.

"Who the hell are you?" asked the Captain, shocked not just by the arrogance of the suggestion that they required help, but wondering just how the hell did he get there and when?

"You have got to be kidding me." McCall's jaw hung slack at the sight of the man who had caused her so much trouble and kept eluding her. Now he was finally within her grasp but why was he coming forward? And why now? No, the only question she had, and it was a simple one, was not 'Who are you?' or 'What are you doing here?' No! The question she wanted to ask was much less complicated. It was, 'Can I shoot him?'

Tina Franks was busy checking over what remained of the female from Pier 15. She scanned the remains carefully inch by inch, taking photographs of any distinguishing marks such as bruises and scars. In the background there was music coming from her MP3 player that sat happily on top of the stereo; its blue lights broke up the sterile whiteness of the morgue.

McCall entered, her footsteps sounding loud and aggressive. Her expression could have frozen the very depths of hell.

"Hi, what we got, Tina?" asked McCall, trying not to think about the events on the pier, and the details of their ghoulish discovery.

"Well, I have got a Caucasian female with lots missing. What I heard too, is your white knight in black armour put in an appearance." Tina gave McCall the look that said 'more information please'.

"Oh really, and what else did you hear?"

"I heard he was British and kind of cute."

McCall's glare stiffened. Why was he here, she wondered? Was he following her? It was strange that he always showed up just in time; she shook off the temptation to work out theories. The mystery guy would have to wait—the case came first.

"Are there any similarities with the two other killings?" McCall was desperate for a clue. This guy was good, but in her experience the more comfortable they got as they killed more and more, the more likely it was they would eventually mess up.

Tina stopped what she was doing and took off her slightly scratched eye protectors. "Well, what we have is a man who, for some reason, drains all of his victims' blood, and removes not just body parts but *whole chunks* of body parts." She walked between the tables on which lay the remains of the first two victims. "What I don't get is the kind of parts that have been removed. Most of the 'trophies crew' takes a finger or an ear. This is way too extreme."

"Maybe he is fussy about what he eats." McCall smiled, trying to lighten the mood, but she couldn't budge the look of worry on the pretty ME's face.

"This guy knows how to use a scalpel," Tina pointed out. "So we're probably looking for some kind of surgeon."

McCall looked puzzled. "How do you know?" She moved closer to the most recent corpse, unable to resist her curiosity.

"If you look here, you can see the cuts that were made are straight and even, not jagged and ripped. No, the guy took his time and by the look of the others I would say that this surgery was done with respect more than out of brutality." Tina shrugged. "You see McCall, the person who did this, did it for a reason. It wasn't so much about the kill itself like we see so many times, no, the parts he took *meant* something to him because of the way they were removed. And our last vic, the blood wasn't even hers—it was animal blood, added maybe because he wanted the body to be found more easily. I still don't understand why he is draining them." Tina shook her head in apparent disbelief.

McCall sat at her desk when Tooms and Tony returned from interviewing the boss at the law firm where one of the victims had worked. They strolled in, and Tooms sat in the spare chair at McCall's desk and flipped open his notepad as Tony crashed into his chair and picked up his phone and started to dial.

"So what did you get?" she asked her sweating colleagues, who had been busy.

"Well, we scored," Tooms told her. "We got the place of

work and a name, Miss Karen Lane, aged forty. She had an apartment on the East Side, we are just about to go there once we get a warrant."

McCall nodded, grateful that, at last, they had a lead of some sort. "Do we know who may have seen her last?" She was hoping to establish a time frame.

"Yeh, we got a Karl Buntee, he is the janitor there, and he reckons he saw her in the parking garage at around three on Saturday morning."

"Why was she working on a Friday night?" McCall asked suspiciously.

"Well, it turns out they had a big meeting on the Monday, all to do with some high profile case. Seems she had to get the briefs typed up in time for that."

"OK, so we have a time frame for vic number one," McCall said, getting up and writing the numbers on another board, this one for time frames; she drew a line from 03:00 hours until the end of the mark that covered Monday, when her body was found.

"So what have we got?" McCall said, perched on her desk. "Vic One, Karen Lane, went missing on Friday and was found Monday night, so on that basis I guess we can presume he only keeps them for a few days."

The other two joined her at the time-frame board and stared at the puzzle, hoping something would reveal itself.

"Vic Two was found in the park on Thursday, so if he is holding to his time line she must have been taken on the Tuesday. That's in theory, but until we find out who she is, it's only speculation. Same with Vic number three." McCall looked puzzled. "What I can't get is, the others were posed but Vic Three was hung off a pier. It doesn't make sense."

McCall stood and picked up her coffee mug. She needed

caffeine, and was hoping that some strong coffee would blow away some cobwebs. She went into the rest room, followed by Tooms and Tony.

The smell of strong coffee hit them with an awakening jolt; picking up the glass beaker she poured herself a cup then offered it to the others, who responded by putting their cups on the surface next to hers. She filled the cups and put back the half full coffee jug into the coffee machine.

"I don't get it; there is nothing that connects these women," she began. "We need to find out who the other two vics are, or this isn't going anywhere."

The others agreed and they all moved out of the room and made their way back to their desks. As they turned the corner, there by the board stood the mysterious stranger whom McCall had last seen at the crime scene, his hands behind his back. As he studied the board, he couldn't help but feel he was being watched.

"Nice board," he said without moving, in an unmistakable British accent.

"Can I help you?" Sam McCall's voice almost growled with disapproval at just the mere sight of him, let alone the idea of him staring at her information boards.

"Simple but effective," he continued, but this time he turned slightly just to acknowledge she was there.

"BUT?" she prodded him to continue, almost as if she was waiting for some 'British' sarcastic remark, which never came.

"No really, I like your boards, that's all. I'm sorry if I have offended you in any way." With that, he moved away from the boards as if he was trying to be conciliatory.

"Thanks," she spoke, but the words were somewhat hollow and she was unsure how she should react to him.

Rise of a Phoenix

She grabbed her cup and headed for the restroom to get a coffee, forgetting she already had one. She felt that she just had to get away. However, he followed, just like a lost child on his first day at school.

"Are you following me?" she growled, eyes blazing.

"Coffee," he replied, holding up the coffee-filled jug.

"What?" Her expression went from anger to bewilderment in a second.

"I said, do you want a coffee?"

McCall stood like a deer in headlights, then remembered the full cup at her desk and left him in the restroom to make himself a drink. The other two detectives, somewhat bemused by this whole display, just sat back and observed this strange behaviour with pleasure.

She was busy typing something on the computer and had failed to notice the British guy standing beside the empty chair next to her desk; he coughed politely just to arouse her attention; she looked out of the corner of her eye and saw him waiting.

"What now?" Her tone was one of weariness and irritation.

"May I?" He indicated the battered looking chair. Its brown coloured fabric lay loose on the cushioning, yet it did look comfortable, somehow homely. She raised a hand as if to say 'whatever', but continued to look at the screen in front of her.

Taking a swig of the brown liquid, his face winced almost immediately as his taste buds were assaulted by the worst coffee he'd tasted in years.

"What's the matter, coffee too much for you?" she said with a grin, taking a swig from her own cup, trying to ignore the foul taste in her own mouth. "I thought a big strong man like you could handle it," she smiled again.

Even though she was laughing at him he couldn't resist enjoying this tiny chink in her armour. "You know, you have a nice smile, you should use it more often, it suits you."

She stopped and looked away, embarrassed she had let her guard down.

He stared at the board over and over, but could not make any sense or connection; hell they did not even know who the other victims were, so a connection at this point was almost impossible.

The British man looked at the photos and the timeline associated with the first vic, but nothing was coming to him. He gave up and he raised his sunglasses and rubbed his eyes. They had been there hours and it had all blurred into one big mess,

"Would you like a coffee, detective?" he asked, rising from his chair.

"No but thanks," McCall replied. "Hey, one thing, when you use a cup you need to check the ones with marks on, they belong to people." She had pointed it out because he had used a cup belonging to one of the detectives on another shift.

"Got it, look out for marks," he said, going into the coffee room. Seconds later he rushed back and started looking at the photos. "It can't be—can it?" He spoke softly as if nobody else was present, then shot off towards the elevator.

"What's the matter, coffee get to you?" she called after him, making detectives Tooms and Tony laugh.

"No, the marks did," he said, bolting for the elevator. McCall just stared at the other two, who were just as confused as she was. Tony made a crazy person gesture with his index finger, and seconds later, they all got up and followed him, just in case they'd missed something that he had picked up on.

TEN

DOWN AT THE MORGUE Tina was in the back room checking some files. It had been a long day and she longed for the weekend to begin, because she and some of her girlfriends were planning to go to a new club and it sounded good. She started to dance to a little tune that had come up on her MP3 player and the mood just took her over, so she continued to boogie straight into the operating room where she saw a tall man dressed in black leaning over one of the bodies. She immediately stopped dancing and resumed her professional demeanour.

"Hey, excuse me, can I help you?" Tina's voice was calm and steady despite the sudden shock of seeing this unexpected stranger.

"I'm sorry, doctor, I'm working with Detective McCall upstairs and I noticed something. It may be nothing, you see—" he was cut off in mid-sentence.

"It's OK, Tina, he is sort of with me," McCall explained as she entered the room with Tooms and Tony.

Dr Tina nodded towards the stranger and grinned to her friend McCall. Sam let her eyes roll back in their sockets in disapproval, but Tina made a 'No problem' signal with her fingers.

"OK, English guy, what's up?" McCall felt she had to sound as if she wasn't impressed, but deep down she hoped he'd found something, anything.

"You said about the marks, what marks?" McCall asked him, was stumped by what he may have seen, something they might have missed. Even Tina looked confused.

"There were no marks on the body, only those he made himself," the ME growled, furious at the accusation she had missed something.

"What I mean is, all the areas of body remaining had some sort of mark or fault," the Englishman said. "Vic One had a tattoo on her back—that's why he only took the front part of her body. Vic Two had scars on her one leg and one arm, also she had piercings and, well, Vic Three was pretty clean so—"

"That's why the most was taken from her," Tina finished the sentence, catching on to his theory.

"What, you mean our guy is seeking out women for body parts? For what?" McCall's patience was thin and this guy was stretching it to the limit.

"Look, you said you could help," McCall continued. "But frankly if all your ideas are as half-assed as this we are better off without you. I'm sorry." And with that she stormed out, not because the idea was wrong, no. It was more maddening than that.

Rise of a Phoenix

What *really* annoyed her was the possibility that he could be right and she had failed to see what he had.

The newcomer walked up to Tina and took her right hand. "I'm very sorry for the intrusion, Madam," and, so saying, he gently raised her knuckles to his lips and planted a small kiss there, then left. Tina grabbed for the side of the table as her knees gave way. All she could say to herself was "WOW!"

As he got out of the elevator he saw the chaos of the office. Phones were ringing, computers flashed with information, and detectives were running here and there with documents in their hands. He stepped off and looked round to find McCall attacking a vending machine. Tooms and Tony were going through paperwork and arguing about what should go in a filing system, while the Captain was on McCall's phone yelling at some poor SOB about press at the crime scene. A smile crept over his face, as he nodded to himself reassuringly, deciding that it was time to tell them who he was.

The stranger walked up to the Captain and whispered into his ear, and the other man stood bolt upright as though a sudden shock of electricity had been passed through him. He said something in return and beckoned the others to follow him into a small briefing room. The tall mysterious man was already inside, and as they came in, he asked them to sit down. Shutting the door, he moved to the centre of a wall on which there was a large map of the city.

He took stock of the situation and held his two pressed-together index fingers against his lips, as if planning what he was about to say. Describing him as nervous and uncomfortable would have been an understatement.

"My name is John Steel," he began. "At this present

moment I am assigned to your department to assist with these homicides. Unfortunately I cannot disclose any more information than that at this time. I understand that my presence will cause some issues with our working relationship, however details about what I am working on is classified information. Thank you for your time."

He waited for some comeback, a snide comment or remark, but there was nothing. Everyone just left the room as though nothing had happened, simply nodding in acknowledgement, leaving a somewhat puzzled Englishman.

Steel walked over to McCall's desk with a sheepish look on his face, that turned into a smile.

"Look I'm sorry. We got off on the wrong foot, but—"

She cut him off in mid-sentence by raising a hand. She shuffled through some paperwork, searching for something, then standing up they both moved across to the information boards.

"He isn't done yet, is he?" She looked at him with saddened eyes; John Steel shook his head, the bright fluorescent lights in the room glinting on his sunglasses.

"No, he's not finished. But we will catch this guy," he said, turning back to the board. "We have to."

This left her with an even more puzzled look on her face. This time it was over the mystery man Steel. Who was he and what was his connection with the killer?

Dr. Colby Davidson sat in his black leather office chair jotting down notes as his patient rambled on about how life was meaningless without her little 'Candy'. The elderly woman was clutching a photo of her dearly departed Chihuahua in one hand and a pink diamond studded collar in the other. The doctor, who was in his early forties, listened patiently to what she was saying, appearing to be interested, touching her shoulder to comfort her, while he heard about the dog's grand funeral that cost more than he had paid for his Mercedes. He was a tall thin man with black greased-back hair and small black-rimmed glasses that covered his large dark eyes. He did not require spectacles, no, the ones he wore were more for show, to give him an intellectual air. His face was long, and a large Roman nose supported the unnecessary spectacles.

"Please go on, Mrs. Burnett." His voice was soft and sickly, like honey. He crossed one leg over the other, resting a three-thousand dollar shoe on the knee of an eight-thousand dollar suit trouser leg.

He smelt of money and so he should, for he was in fact one of the top psychiatrists in New York, if not the country. His clothes and the furnishings in his office spoke volumes about the man. How had it come to this, he thought? How had years of training and hard work led him to a life of put him with listening to the ramblings of tired old women? He looked towards his *wall of fame*, where trophies and diplomas filled shelves, photos of him shaking hands with famous people, even the President himself, and a cabinet full of trophies.

An antique gold-and-black clock chimed in the background, signalling the end of the lady's session. She slowly got off the leather chaise longue and dried her eyes with the corner of a white embroidered handkerchief.

"Now, Mrs. Burnett we are making progress." He held her gloved hands.

"Don't worry, these things take time, dear lady, now if you speak to Beatrice she will make you another appointment." Mrs. Burnett thanked him and left. As he shut the door, his back rested against the cool oak timber, and he raised his head and closed his weary eyes, and thanked God that the session was over.

Moving to the drinks trolley next to a large dark wood cabinet, he could not help but think: was this it? *Is it over, is there nothing more to challenge this brilliant mind?* Stopping, he poured himself a drink of whisky and downed it in one.

He sat down on his heavy-looking office chair, and turned to look out of the huge windows that revealed a magnificent view of the park. He took a sip from a freshly poured drink, and he sighed as he watched the people walking carelessly in the midday sun then he smiled just for a moment until the intercom broke his concentration.

"Sorry to disturb you, doctor. But you have the police on line one."

"Thank you, put them through, Beatrice." He was confused. Police? What on earth could they want? He had done nothing wrong!

He picked up the receiver gingerly and placed it slowly to his ear.

"Hello, this is Dr Davidson, how may I be of assistance?" His voice slow and tentative, but still ringing with his usual treacle tones.

"Yes, hello, doctor. This is Captain Alan Brant of the New York Police Department. I wondered if you would be so kind as to come down to the station. Sir, we could really use someone of your expertise to help with a case we're working on."

Davidson's face cracked an eerie smile. "I would be delighted to help you with your little case, Officer." He preened himself, arrogantly wallowing in this sudden recognition.

"Um yes thank you, and that's Captain, not Officer."

Davidson was suddenly taken aback by the policeman's correction; *he must think a lot about himself,* thought the doctor, admiring himself in the reflection from the window.

"Yes, yes whatever you say," They agreed on a time.

"Till tomorrow then," and he put down the receiver before the Captain could reply. He sprung up out of his chair and raced to the door. Swinging open the heavy panel he stuck his head round the corner to see his secretary, a pretty young thing dressed all in black, apart from a white frilly blouse which left not much to the imagination.

"Oh, Beatrice," She looked up with a start as the fringe of her long red hair fell over her blue eyes. "Yes, doctor?" Her voice was slightly bouncy, with the tone of a young teenager.

"Listen, I will not be available as of tomorrow, so could you cancel my appointments for the week? Thank you." He gazed at her from head to toe.

"Nothing the matter, I hope, doc," she said, the gum in her mouth clinging between the upper and lower molars.

"No, no, just consulting on a little case for the police, that is all."

He was back in his office. *At last*, he thought, newspapers, press; he would be back up there again.

The caretaker , a friendly, plump woman with large brown-rimmed glasses, had let Tooms and Tony into Karen's apartment. The place was large with lots of windows, and the white walls enhanced the natural light in the sitting area, and as they looked round there appeared to be a kitchen next to this space with only a breakfast bar to separate the two. As they went through Karen's belongings it became apparent to them that she had little social life: pretty much everything she had appeared to be work-orientated.

Tony went through her fridge while Tooms checked her mail; they both came up empty.

"This girl was super clean, I mean the fridge is laid out in some sort of order, even the stuff in her cupboards is labelled where it should go, nah, this is freaky, bro," Tony said, shutting the fridge and joining Tooms in the sitting area.

"Why is it whenever we come to a victim's home we try and find some dirty secrets in their life, or something to try to make sense and explain the bad things that happened to them?" Tony continued, going through her sock drawer. He found nothing.

"Human nature, bro," Tooms replied. "We can't really accept bad things happen to good people, there is no social justice in it, but if bad things happen to bad people, well that's all right. Unfortunately we know that aint always the way it works and it sucks."

"Yeh, I guess you're right. I got nothing, just her diary and planner, let's get back."

The two friends left for the precinct, leaving CSU to check for any more evidence about the girl.

Charlene Walters had had a long day at the club, the wives' meeting had gone on forever. The society ladies meeting only met once a month and it was a chance for her to get out of the house for a bit. She had mingled but it was time to go, so she said her farewells and made for the door.

The grey suit she wore clung to her body. Even though she was in her late fifties she had the looks and body of a hot forty-year-old, and she knew it.

A young twenty-something guy brought round her car; she observed him closely as he got out and held the door of the Mercedes for her, and she slid into the driver's seat of the sports car, pressed a hundred into his hand, and winked. He shut the door and she sped off into the distance. As he opened the folded note her business card fell out, and he picked it up and stuck it into his vest pocket with a grin.

It was a long drive from the Hamptons; however, it

could not be helped, it was that or stay home with him. And it was a beautiful night, the stars shone like diamonds in the dark of the heavens, shards of light smudged across the windshield as she sped past the streetlights guiding her path towards the city. As Charlene got into Manhattan, she was aware it was not as late as she thought and decided to do a little stop-off.

The park house was almost empty but she still decided to park as she always did, near to an exit or elevator and close to another expensive car if at all possible; she found the perfect spot next to a black 911.

The new Porsche' paintwork glinted in the light as she stopped and put on some lipstick. Fluffing her short brown hair Charlene exited the vehicle.

Looking round she saw a couple of people here and there, parking or getting ready to depart. Pressing the small transmitter on her key, the lights flashed and the horn emitted a *meep meep* to confirm the operation of securing her car. Charlene opened her brown leather bag and placed the keys in it; reaching inside she pulled out a compact, and a stick of lipstick. She removed the cover and twisted the lower part of the stick, exposing the deep red lipstick's business end. With her other hand she flicked open the compact and stared into the mirror. Charlene stopped for a brief moment, staring at her own reflection, but all she saw was a sad middle-aged woman. A car sped past, shocking her back to reality. She regarded her face once more, then shrugged at the reflection and smiled. After freshening up her make-up, she put the lipstick and compact back into the bag, then closed the flap using the gold-coloured crossed CC buckle. As she approached the elevator in silence and pressed the call button, Charlene watched quietly as the small round disks above the sliding doors illuminated, showing which floor the elevator was on. The light held position on the floor below, as her foot tapped impatiently on the hard concrete.

She smiled as the light went out and she could hear the faint rumble of the heavy metal box that was heading upwards through the shaft towards her. Just as the elevator approached, her bag gave off a faint tune as her cell phone played the theme from the musical *Cats*. As she looked down to answer it, the elevator's door slid open and a bright stream of light shone out. She looked up, shielding her eyes from the blinding torchlight. A powerful hand reached out and dragged her in. As the doors closed and the elevator made its way upwards, a terrified scream filled the shaft, then abruptly it stopped.

Tooms and Tony had returned from their trip to 'I haven't seen anything and I don't know anything' land that was Karen's apartment block.

"What's up, guys?" asked McCall, who was busy looking to see where John Steel was.

"Well, as usual, nobody knew her apart from some guy in 4c who said, and I quote: 'she was really smoking'," Tooms replied, putting down the notepad he was reading from, and his voice carried an '*I'm not surprised*' tone.

"Nobody saw her and she lived in a block with over thirty people in it. Apart from that she was clean living, quiet, always paid her rent on time." He put the pad into the pocket of his thick unyielding brown leather jacket.

"We didn't find pictures of family or anything, no boyfriend pictures, nothing." Tony added, sitting at his desk as he started to dial a number on the desk's phone while McCall worked on the white board, which was now covered with photos and scribbles.

She spun the whole thing round, revealing three long black strips, one on top of the other. Each strip had several vertical lines coming off at the top of the base lines: this was her timeline board for each of the victims.

"McCall, you may need another stripe. We got us another one." The Captain had a worn tone in his voice, he was tired of not having a single clue or anything to work on. This guy was good, and the knowledge of it was getting to him.

McCall didn't try and find Steel—in fact she didn't want him around her; yes, fine, he had saved her from Jabba and his gang but something about him was wrong, something was not quite right. She couldn't put her finger on what it was, but he made her nervous.

The detectives made their way to a dirty alleyway near the meatpacking district; the press was all over the area, reporters tripping over each other to get a glimpse or an interview. As she pushed forwards, microphones were thrust into her face as requests from the press for any information and comments such as 'was this one connected to the other killings?' She sighed with incredulity at how quickly the media people had got there.

Moving through the hordes of police she found herself with the ME, Tina, who was kneeling holding a clipboard looking over the remains of what appeared to have been a woman.

"Is it the same guy?" McCall asked her friend, afraid of the answer.

"Well, hi to you too!" Tina snapped at her without turning round.

"What? Oh sorry Tina, Hi" McCall quickly apologized, with a 'naughty puppy' look on her face. "But is it the same guy?"

"Well, our vic has had both arms removed and she has no blood present in her body, but until I get her back to the lab I can't say for sure, although it has all the hallmarks of our boy, but till then…" Tina suddenly looked worried as she noticed something.

"Strange thing, is this fresh?"

McCall looked puzzled. "What do you mean, fresh?"

The M.E stood up and called for the waiting orderlies to take the body away. "The others were at least a couple of days old, but this was done recently and quickly."

A chill went down McCall's spine.

"You figure that he's stepping it up?" Tina nodded.

McCall waited for CSU to do their sweep of the area, taking photos and searching for fibers and prints. Once they were finished, the female detective and her team went in. Tony stopped at the entrance and looked around.

"Where's Steel?" he asked.

The others stopped and looked up and down the street to find no trace of the most recent addition to their team.

"I don't know and I don't care." McCall's look was stern, she didn't have time to babysit: if Steel wanted to be there he would have made the effort.

"Screw him, that brother smells like trouble if you ask me," Tooms's voice bellowed. He didn't give a damn about this John Steel, the case was his priority. The team made their way into the alleyway taking it inch by inch, searching for pieces to the puzzle.

Each of them had spent at least an hour scouring through drains, under boxes, in fact anywhere a clue might be. Tony was doing door-to-door interviews to try and find someone who may have seen anything unusual in the last few hours, but turned up nothing.

Rise of a Phoenix

"God, sometimes I hate this city," Tony grumbled. "I can't believe nobody saw anything."

"Hey, that's New York, man, if it don't concern nobody, no one is interested." Tooms had had enough, they all had. The case was burning them out, and the sooner it was finished with the better, but McCall had a bad feeling about this one. This was trouble.

"OK," she told them. "We can't do any more here, so let's head back to the station and pick it up from there." The others nodded and they moved off. *It's going to be a long night*, thought McCall, great, that was all she needed.

High above them a figure knelt on the edge of a rooftop, his gaze following them to their vehicles as they made their exit. He stood up and his coat took to the breeze like some mythical bird, his shape silhouetted by the moon that shone brightly creating a long shadow on the rooftop. A cloud crept across the sky, briefly blacking out the moon, causing everything to go dark. In those seconds he was gone, as if he'd been carried off by the darkness.

ELEVEN

THE NEXT MORNING AT the station there was an air of panic as the news of yet another killing spread through the precinct, and it wouldn't be long before the newspapers and TV stations had the grim information plastered all over the place, instilling panic throughout the city, a panic that the Captain was trying to avoid.

The team searched through missing persons records, and took calls from possible witnesses as well as doing their best to fend off the press.

McCall spied Steel heading for her as he got out of the elevator. She braced herself for the inevitable question of

'Why did you not tell me about the latest death?'. But if he wanted to be included, she reasoned, he had to be there all the time, not just when it suited him. He arrived at her desk and sat down without a word.

"OK," she felt the urge to apologize.

"I'm sorry we didn't come and find you, but when it all kicked off we had to leave quickly." The speech was quick and speedy, as if what she had to say was too embarrassing to say slowly.

"No problem," he said. "In your position I would have done the same, if I want to be included on this case I have to be here all the time, and not just when it suits me."

She looked at him with a look of utter disbelief. Had he just read her mind? Confusion had knocked her off balance, as she stumbled through a quick briefing on what they had just found. He just smiled and handed her a coffee he had just bought from a coffee shop nearby.

"Thanks." Shocked by his kind gesture, she took a sip of the coffee, and a burst of aromatic goodness flushed through her system. *Oh my God, that's good*, she thought, but did not wish to let on.

"So what have you been up to—?" she stopped herself in mid-sentence, not wanting to go on.

"Do you really want to know or are you just saying that?" he asked.

"Not really." Her eyes shot back to the paperwork as he smiled to himself.

"Well, you may want to know someone has just filed a missing person's report which may fit your vic's description."

Her gaze shot up to his face. "Where? When?" He pointed to Tony, who was approaching quickly with a slip of paper.

"You won't believe what I just got," the other detective said smugly.

"Oh, I don't know about that," she said, looking at Steel, who was busy sipping his cappuccino.

TWELVE

THE WALTERS' RESIDENCE WAS a penthouse in a massive complex of old stone and large arched windows, a monument to bygone days. The view of Central Park was breathtaking through the large windows of the lounge area. All over the place, marble floors glistened with the touch of the midday sun. McCall looked in awe at the fine furniture everywhere, most of which was probably the same age as the building, if not older. A pretty girl who appeared to be in her late twenties had let them in; her maid's uniform was a black-and-white all-in-one short dress, the lacy white collar fluffed up around her neck. Her long blonde hair was styled into a bun then crowned with a small white maid's tiara.

"Mr Walters, the police are here to see you," she said, as she ushered them into the large sitting area. Benjamin Walters was sitting on an old heavy-looking chesterfield armchair, its dark leather encrusted with shining brass studs.

"Please come in, sit down," he said, rising from his own chair, his hands pointing to the long sofa of the same design.

They all sat, and he waved at the girl, asking her to bring them some coffee.

"I'm Detective McCall and this is Detective Steel," McCall began.

"We are here because you reported your wife missing." Her concern was genuine, fuelled by the very real possibility that she could be the next victim.

"Yes, she left for a damned wives' meeting in the Hamptons yesterday and has not been seen since," Benjamin Walters muttered in a strained voice.

"I phoned the club to see if she could have stayed over but they said she left early." He broke down, sobbing into his hand.

Ignoring him, Steel got up and walked to a marble mantelpiece which surrounded a spectacular fireplace, lifting up a silver-framed photograph that showed Mr Walters and the victim. Steel showed it to the female detective, and she nodded in response.

"Excuse me, sir, is this your wife?" The English officer said.

Walters looked confused at first at the question, then he realized why Steel had asked it.

"Oh my God, is she the latest victim of this killer that's been in the papers? What will I do now? She was my whole life!"

The coffee had arrived and the girl placed it down onto the large coffee table between Walters and the officers. She carefully poured coffee into the antique bone-china cups. It was the kind of valuable chinaware that most people would keep in a glass cabinet, hardly something to be actually used. But what was money to this guy?

"We can't be sure of anything, sir," McCall said tactfully, "but we'd be grateful if you could come downtown and identify a body…"

He nodded, with his head in his hands.

"I'm sorry to ask, Mr Walters," she said gently, "But where were you around the time your wife went missing?" This was the question she always hated to ask a loved one, but sometimes it hit the right chord.

Walters composed himself and picked up the cup and saucer from the dark wooden antique table.

"I was out at my club. I was there until midnight. We had a port tasting on that evening so our driver had to bring me back." He sipped the steaming liquid.

"And which club would that be, sir?" She took her notebook out, ready to write down any new information.

"The Harvard club, it's on West 44th." His hands shook slightly.

"When did you see your wife last?"

"Around midday, just before she left for the club."

"And when were you expecting her back" asked McCall, watching as Steel circled the room looking at photographs on the walls and shelves. She wondered if he was even paying attention to her questioning, or if he cared whether he was here or not.

"It's hard to say, I never really expect her back when she has been to the club." He placed the cup and saucer back onto the table. "You see, it depends what sort of day she has had."

McCall looked puzzled and Steel turned slightly, clearly surprised at his response.

"What do you mean?" Steel exclaimed, turning back to look at a rather colourful Rembrandt painting on the wall.

"If she has had a good day she will stay until late, sometimes may have to stay over. And if she has had a bad day, well, she normally shops." A lonely look fell upon his weary face. He was not particularly old, but it seemed as if something had worn him down, making his features careworn and weary.

"Did she drive herself or was she taken to the club?"

"No, she took her car; it's a black Mercedes SLK." His mind shifted, a faraway look came into his eyes, and then, with a start, he was back again.

"I bought it for her birthday last year and she goes everywhere in the damn thing." Bitterness swept over his face, causing the wrinkles in his skin to crease further.

"I will get you a copy of the registration and the other details," he said, standing slowly. "Please wait here, I won't be but a moment."

He left the room to go across the long hallway. From what the two detectives could see, he entered a dimly lit room with some sort of maroon velvet wallpaper and heavy looking oak furnishings. Steel continued to look at the art and paintings that were dotted round the large luxurious area, which felt more as if it was part of a stately home than a lived-in home.

Walters returned holding a piece of paper in his hand, his suit shining in the sunlight as he headed towards them. "I hope this helps." His words were almost sincere as he spoke them, but Steel picked up on something in his demeanour that suggested he was hiding something. McCall looked at the piece of heavy office paper the older man had handed her, and scanned the contents. The paper contained the licence plate and GPS number of the car. In addition, her cell phone number was amongst the main details on the list.

"Perfect, Mr Walters, thank you, this will really help."

As McCall spoke Steel turned and gave her a look of disbelief. Was she really buttering him up? He knew that if the killer had been through this kind of trouble before, then the cell phone and car would probably be at the bottom of the Hudson. Unless he actually wanted the phone and car found, he was being too thorough.

"Just one thing, sir," asked Steel as they were making for the door. "If something happens to your wife, what happens to her money?"

McCall's face dropped in shock, not because Steel had asked such a question, but because he had thought of it, and she had not. And that stung. She flashed him a quick glance of annoyance, which merely seemed to amuse him.

"Sorry, but you do understand, Mr Walters, we have to ask certain questions for the report, it's so we can eliminate you as a suspect." Her words were sympathetic, which reassured the older man.

"Well, I suppose I do, hadn't really thought about it." His eyes glazed over but he said nothing.

"Well, if that will be all, detectives, I have arrangements to make." He raised his arm as if to beckon them to the front door.

"There needs to be a formal identification, sir," McCall said.

"Of course, but you've just seen her picture, so there's little doubt, presumably?" he asked them.

"We still need you to come to identify her as soon as you can sir," she replied.

He nodded, barely registering her words.

"We will do everything in our power to catch these people, I promise you." McCall looked him in the eyes as she spoke, her face deadly serious. Steel thought it made her seem even more attractive.

Mr Walters thanked them as they left, closing the heavy door behind them; McCall took out her cell phone and pressed the contact number for Tooms.

"Well, we just left the husband, he seems genuine enough, where are we at on the car?" she said to him.

"Nothing yet but her credit cards haven't been used, so it's not robbery unless they're waiting until things cool down." Tooms was sitting at his desk hitting keys on the computer keypad, bringing lists of information onto his screen.

"This may help," McCall told him. "We are looking for a black Mercedes SLK licence, plate number is Yankee, November, one, four, two, one, her cell is 555 12 412."

Tooms read it back to her so they both knew the information had been passed on correctly.

"So where you guys heading now?" Tooms asked, his phone tucked between his broad shoulder and large head whilst feeding the information into the computer.

"Well, Sherlock, where to next?" McCall asked the Englishman beside her, purposely trying to insult him.

"I would say a trip to the Hamptons to this mysterious club, wouldn't you say, Watson?" throwing it back at her, wiped the wide grin off her face.

"We are off to the Hamptons, let us know when you find anything, will you?" She hung up and scowled at Steel, making him chuckle to himself.

"You know, you were quite rude in there just then," she told him. "I mean the guy just lost his wife."

"Are you mad with me because I asked the question, or are you mad at me because I thought of it?"

She couldn't stand his wide grin, not because his amusement was annoying. It was because he was right.

"Do you know you can be a real asshole?" she said, stomping past him like a grounded teenager. When he was out of view she gave a little satisfied smile.

THIRTEEN

MCCALL AND STEEL HAD spent most of the afternoon at the Hamptons club talking to middle-aged women; the club was a large building of sandstone and glass, a true testimony to nineteenth-century architecture. The building was swarming with badly dressed women whose only lot in life appeared to be to drink and talk badly about one another. The interviews seemed endless and pointless due to the fact that nobody knew anything.

McCall rolled her eyes as the last of the egotistical women got up and left, and she spotted Steel outside on a stone balcony looking over the view of lush green fields that was spread out before them. He was leaning against the worn sandstone wall, and his black suit and sunglasses matched their surroundings.

"Well, that was the last of them," he muttered. "God, what a waste of a day." He turned and looked at her as she joined him leaning against the wall; he smiled and turned back to admire the view.

Rise of a Phoenix

"It's so beautiful here, so quiet," she commented. He nodded in agreement.

"Pity it's wasted on them, though." He looked back at the gaggle of women parading themselves like flocks of flamingos.

She laughed and, as they took a final look at the tranquil sight, McCall sighed deeply.

"OK, let's go back." He clearly didn't want to, but they had a case to solve and it would not solve itself.

McCall had received a text that the Mercedes SLK had been discovered in the garage and that CSU were all over it, searching for prints and fibres. Tony was checking the security cameras for any shots of that evening. McCall and Steel pulled up in her Mustang, running the gauntlet of the press, who were out taking photos and shoving each other every time a person worth interviewing came close.

McCall headed for the tape at the far side, hoping to make it without the hordes of newspaper people noticing, but she failed. One of the press hounds spotted her and dashed, causing the others to follow like sheep in pursuit. She looked behind her but Steel was nowhere to be seen until she got to the car. She stopped, startled for a moment as he stood next to one of the CSU team member who was busy dusting the passenger side.

"Seriously, how did you get here ?" McCall stood there, her arms stretched out in a sign of wonderment and disbelief, but she wasn't as surprised as the guard next to the car.

"Hey, how the fuck" the officer demanded, pushing his chest out to make himself look more intimidating as he headed for Steel, only to be greeted by a badge held up in his face.

"Oh sorry, sir, I didn't recognize you," He apologized. Steel put the badge away, his attention had not even deviated from the CSU tec, who was just lifting the powdery cast using a kind of clear tape. The technician folded the two halves of tape, sealing the evidence in a bag, then labelling it.

"So cool," Steel murmured to the man, and the CSU nodded in reply.

"Just hope we get something from them!"

Tony and Tooms were examining the car so McCall dropped Steel at the precinct, because she had someone to see. McCall entered the well-lit corridor of the morgue; the white-tiled walls enhanced the brightness of the 'cutting room' as some of the M.E's liked to call it. She could make out soft music in the background and the smell of fresh coffee tingled at her nose.

On entering the room, McCall found John Steel giving Tina a cup of coffee. "What the hell is going on?" McCall was mad, so mad that she felt the veins at the side of her head throb.

"He brought me coffee, you never bring me coffee, girl, it's not like it would kill you to." Tina gave her friend a stern look then broke into a smile to lighten the mood.

"No what I mean is," McCall stumbled on. "Oh never mind." She had lost momentum and her chance to give him another friendly scolding. "Steel, you told me you had to check something." McCall took the coffee that Steel offered up in his other hand. "I didn't know it was here you had to do the checking or with whom."

"What? Yes right, I had to see Tina, that's if I may call you that," he said politely, turning to the M.E with a small bow. Tina blushed and tapped him on the shoulder.

"Well, if everyone has finished!" McCall was now losing patience with him. *If only he would stop flirting with the ME for a moment,* she thought.

Rise of a Phoenix

"Yes OK," Steel continued. "Now Tina, did you find out what blood type Mrs Walters was?" He braced himself for bad news.

"Yes she was AB negative. Why?"

The English detective looked at McCall, longing for her to make a connection.

"Yes, so what?" McCall was tired of his games.

He sat down on the workspace by the window. "You don't see? She is a different blood type, the hair is all wrong, our guy prefers blondes. This is a cover-up killing, I bet my badge on it."

McCall thought for a brief second and looked at Tina, who was nodding at her with a sympathetic look on her face.

"OK," McCall mused. "So the husband can't divorce his wife because he'd lose everything, so he kills her."

"Or he gets someone else to do it," Steel said, jumping in.

"So now everyone thinks it's the serial killer's doing, and he is home free." McCall's face lit up with excitement.

They were now facing each other and finishing each other's sentences.

"Oh that just so sweet." They turned to see Tina giving them both a strange dreamy look.

McCall swivelled around towards the door to see Tooms and Tony standing there.

"Hey, are we interrupting something here?" said Tooms, with the same expression as the doc had used.

"No!" said McCall emphatically.

"Yes!" Steel said, almost at the same moment, with a big grin on his face.

"Find Mr. Walters and bring him in." McCall barked as she headed out, leaving the room as angrily as she had entered.

PS Syron-Jones

McCall and Steel watched Mr. Walters pace up and down the interrogation room like a caged animal waiting to be put down. They were sitting on the other side of the one-way mirror, watching him sweat. The Captain entered the small room to join them.

"You had better be right about this," he told the female detective.

McCall just nodded.

"Alright then, break the son of a bitch. But make it fast, as he has probably got a fleet of lawyers on the way."

The two detectives got up and moved towards the interview room, deciding that if they were to do this they had to do it as a team.

"Mr Walters, please sit down," said McCall as they entered the room.

"Do you know why you are here, sir?"

As Walters sat in front of the table he had a confused look on his face, but it masked something, something else: fear.

"Your detectives said something about me killing my wife. But I would never"

"Why didn't you ask us how your wife died?" When Steel spoke, he was standing in the far corner of the room behind Mr Walters.

"What?" the older man's face twisted with anger at the absurdity of the question.

"Answer the question please, sir," McCall jumped in. She was impressed at the way the Englishman had knocked Walters off balance.

"I... err I don't know. I was upset. I had just found out my wife had been murdered."

"You see, the wonderful thing about the human psyche is that people want closure," Steel continued the interrogation.

"They want to know: did their loved one suffer? Was it quick? You know the sort of thing I mean. And the only people who don't want to know are those who already *do* know."

Walters turned to where Steel's voice was coming from and was shocked to find him directly behind him, almost breathing down his neck.

McCall jumped in: "Mr Walters, we know that you have had some gambling problems and how much you owed the wrong people, and so you thought if you could get rid of your wife you could pay your debt and have enough to start over again. How am I doing so far?" She spoke softly as she sat down opposite him and leant forwards over the table.

"No, no, it wasn't like that, you have to believe me! Yes I had a small problem. But I didn't kill my wife." His hands clenched together so tightly that the knuckles were white.

"OK, so who did kill your wife and why?" She leant back in her chair awaiting his next lie.

"Look, the thing is Mr Walters, we've got you. If you tell us who the killer is I can speak to the DA and let him know you cooperated." Her voice had lost its aggressive edge and had become soft and calm.

"I didn't hire anyone, for God's sakes, I loved my wife! Is she dead because of me? Yes! But I didn't kill her!" He was angry and upset. Steel had the feeling that there was more to this story but only Walters could tell it. Sam McCall continued the questioning: "We have a statement from your bank showing a withdrawal of Two-Hundred-and-Fifty thousand dollars two days ago, so don't tell me you didn't hire anyone."

Walters looked up at her. His eyes were tired and burnt with righteous indignation. How could she think such a thing of him?

"It wasn't enough, was it?" Steel chipped in.

"They wanted more, didn't they?" Steel came closer, his voice soft and soothing, like a calming breeze.

Walters nodded, looking down at his open wallet where there was a photo displayed.

"You don't understand, you see I have more family, friends. If I talk they said they would kill them all. And I'm sorry, but I would rather go to jail than talk." Walters had pulled himself together, was now sitting upright in the chair.

"Then don't talk." Steel moved his hand forward over the table and took out a business card from the wallet in Walters's hand. Steel held up the card in front of Walters's face, his scared eyes looked up at the card then he closed them tightly before he nodded.

"See you didn't tell us anything," said Steel, turning to McCall who took the card off him

Oh great, Russians, she thought.

They both came out of the interrogation room leaving a sobbing Mr Walters. Tooms and Tony joined them.

"So what's our next move?" asked Tony, putting on his jacket.

"We go and catch a show." McCall passed the card to the two detectives.

"I'll bring the quarters," said Steel, following McCall to her desk.

"Russians? Are you friggin' kidding me?" barked Tooms. This was all he needed, a stake out at a Russian strip club. *Oh well*, he figured it could be worse. He thought: *I mean, what could go wrong?*

FOURTEEN

THE SURVEILLANCE VAN WAS kitted out with all manner of monitors and listening and recording devices. Tooms and Tony sat in their usual seats while McCall was being fitted out with bugs and cameras.

"OK, you're good to go," said Tony, "Your transmitter is in the purse so don't lose it."

She nodded.

"So where the hell is Super Cop?" Tony enquired. "Was the thought of big bad Russians too much for him?" They all laughed. But if that was the reason, Tooms figured that it probably meant that he was the smart one.

"Ah, who needs they guy, he would just get in the way anyhow," said McCall, checking the rooftops as she got out of the van.

"You need us, we are there, got it?" Tooms's face was full of concern and she knew he had a right to be worried. All of them were wary of this situation.

"OK, wish me luck," she said into her mike, using it as a communications check.

"You are good to go girl, we gotcha," the voice boomed in her ear. She took a small bottle of whisky from a bag and doused her clothes with the cheap booze. She approached the club wearing a slutty outfit with a strange fake animal skin coat that now reeked of booze. As she got to the doormen she put on her 'drunk' act. The two large men who were dressed all in black stopped her.

"Where do you think you are going?" asked the door attendant, holding her arm.

"I'm going for a little party, party yeh party." He held her at arm's length and moved his head away.

"You're not going in you drunken slut," he said shoving her back, revolted by the potent smell of alcohol. She moved in and tried to kiss him.

"If you let me in you can have me later. Later, oohh later!" She stumbled slightly.

"Get the hell away from me," he said, pushing her through the doors.

The other men laughed at him as he wiped the stinking saliva from his lips.

"I see you have a date later tonight, Vladimir," one of them joked. He just spat and gave them the bird.

"OK boys, I'm in. Let's do this." McCall spoke as she headed for the bar, which ran across the right side of the room. In the centre lay a long stage with mirrored sides, where scantily clad girls performed erotic acrobatics on long shiny poles, while others danced in cages, which hung around the dimly lit room. The walls were covered in red patterned wallpaper and the floor covering was of wooden tiles. She arrived at the bar, which also had mirrors on the

Rise of a Phoenix

front of it, as well as brass fittings, which reflected the lights from the stage into her eyes, almost blinding her. McCall sat on a bar stool nearest to a wall which was one end of the bar counter. The seat rocked as she perched on it and she pretended to have lost her balance—the bar keeper quickly grabbed her arm to steady her. She thanked him in a drunken way, and he smiled.

"What can I get you honey?" said the young handsome man in the black silk shirt. He had dark greased-back hair and his bulging muscles tried to push their way through his shirt every time he bent his elbow.

"Get a beer ppllleeease," she slurred.

He backed away quickly.

"Sorry, but I think that you have had too many." He carried on polishing the glasses. "I tell you what. I get you a coffee? Yes coffee," he said, picking up a cup and filling it from the machine behind him.

She thanked him and started to drink the coffee without gagging: one cup of this and you would be sober in no time, she thought. McCall put down the cup and spun round so that the camera could get a view of the room, which was full of businessmen and old army vets. In the corner of the bar sat an old bum who was busy eating peanuts and talking to himself.

"We got anything yet?" she said to him furtively as she pretended to look through her purse.

"No nothing," he replied. "Wait. Guy at the far side of the room, he just came in."

She looked up to see a group of men in suits shaking hands and greeting one another.

"Is that him, is that the owner?" she said softly, but before she could get an answer a man came up to her screaming and yelling.

"Who you talking to lady? Who sent you? My fucking wife?" The short stocky man almost ripped her from her seat. The bartender shot round to try and calm things down.

"You can tell that bitch she can....." Those were the last words the newcomer uttered, just before three bullets pasted through him and also into the bartender, sending him flying back behind the bar.

Chaos ensued as bullets flew and flashes from weapons lit up the dimness. McCall spotted the men disappear from where they came from.

"Suspects moving into a back room, request backup and medical, multiple civilian casualties, I'm in pursuit." She didn't wait for an answer, which she knew would be to stay put wait for the cavalry. But every second she waited, the further away they got.

She made it to the door and, with her weapon ready, she opened it slowly, just enough to see the coast was clear. Sliding slowly through the opening she moved through to the back of the stage. It was dark and silent, the two worst combinations for her, but she pushed on. Her arms ached as every muscle in them was tensed ready for action, and she felt the adrenalin course through her veins. Moving slowly and deliberately, checking corners as she went, until a green light illuminated her, she looked over to the "*Exit.*" sign and smiled.

A black-haired man suddenly burst through the door, his weapon blazing. McCall took cover behind a stack of old crates. Suddenly there was a *click, click, click* which she knew signified an empty magazine. Flying out of the cover, weapon pointing at the goon, she yelled,

"Drop it!" But he just reached for his back up. Putting two rounds into him, he dropped firstly to his knees then his face smashed against the hard floor.

Rise of a Phoenix

Slowly, she inched the door open, keeping as low as possible. Shots rang out and the wood above her head splintered, as automatic fire peppered the door. After returning fire McCall heard someone cry out, then silence. She looked in front of her and saw a stack of heavy looking crates; if she could just get across to them, it would be a start.

McCall got up and opened the door, using a mop. Bullets continued to hail through the alleyway, but now that the door was perched open she had a chance. She sprinted then dived down as bullets followed her movement. But she was safe—for now.

She drew a breath; McCall knew that staying here was not an option. They were getting away or worse, they were setting her up and *where was the backup?* She thought, panicked at the idea of being alone to face this danger.

McCall took three good breaths, then she was ready. She didn't know what for but she was ready. Rolling out, she was expecting a hail of red-hot copper-coated death but there was nothing: the alley was empty. The detective got up slowly and moved keeping in cover, down to where she had just seen a door slowly close. As she passed a dead goon who lay slumped on the ground she realized that some of her shots had hit home and she felt a little easier.

"OK, McCall, you got this," She said to herself. She opened the door slowly and edged her way through. It was dark with only faint shards of light to help her eyes adjust, and as she moved round she could feel some things that seemed to ran upwards and downwards. They felt coarse, as if they could be ropes. Where the hell was she? Moving softly and slowly she came across what felt like fabric, heavy dusty fabric. She found a gap in the material and chanced a look. The sight froze her with fear. She was in an old theatre, and she was probably massively outnumbered. She decided that the best course of action was to retreat and regroup.

As she got to the door she noticed it was now shut and locked.

You have got to be kidding me, she thought.

Her heart sank. The only way out was through the ordinances exit and, due to the large round auditorium it looked to be perfect as a shooting gallery. But she had little choice. McCall moved slowly, avoiding every shard of light that could give away her position. Before her stood a guard. He was of average height and build, and, more importantly, his back was towards her. Creeping up behind him, she held her pistol by the top slide and used the butt of the weapon to knock him out. As he fell she grabbed him so as to avoid a loud crash, which almost certainly would draw attention to her. Dragging him off into the dark, she smiled.

One down, lots to go.

Her purse was gone and she had two ammunition magazines less, leaving only the one in the magazine housing. *Find somewhere to try and get a viewpoint*, she thought, calculating that her best chance was to find these bastards and take them out.

McCall crept along the side of the curtain and found some old props lying around, plus some large prop barrels and crates, trees made from cut-out wooden boarding. There were not many but just enough to provide cover. Sliding behind a load of old barrels and heavy turn-of-the-century chests, she sat for a moment gathering her thoughts, concocting a plan. *Damn it, where the hell is Steel*, she thought? Of all the times he just popped up when he wasn't wanted, why in hell couldn't he arrive when he was needed?

FIFTEEN

IN THE BLACKNESS HE stood alone. Stan was a new boy on the circuit, there was no mistaking that fact, but he had potential and was very keen, that's why they liked him. If they had not, the crew would have kicked him to the curb a long time ago. Sure he didn't really have a Russian background as such, just some long lost grandparent who was later sent to Siberia after the revolt, but that got him in. After all, family is family. He was tall and athletic looking, his physique was more that of a wrestler than anything else, his brown hair was greased back and his new blue tracksuit made an annoying rustling sound but they wore such outfits, so he had to live with it.

He held the MP5 tightly, the feel of the metal and plastic felt good in his hands. He felt the power emanating from it, and he felt invincible. His orders were simple: don't let the cop leave but don't kill her. No, Samuel was going to have that honour and he would make her bleed first. His grin turned sour at the thought of that lady they had brought in days before. Her screams still rang in his ears, he could not believe what they had done to her. But that was the way it was, you had to do such things so people would respect you. His grip tightened and he felt the gun's power once again.

Nothing would get past him. He was invisible, indestructible. He felt cocky as he acted out with the weapon approaching some invisible target.

"Oh, you think you can get past me do you, ay?" He stabbed the air with the machine gun to simulate firing at some imaginary foe. Yes, he was the man.

Behind him a shadow slithered down a rope that had been tied off at the base. The Shadow's movement was slow and easy, taking its time coming down, until finally it was directly behind the gunman Stan, who was now busy fighting off whole hordes of cops. Two outstretched arms came closer and closer until, finally, one cupped his nose and mouth, the other applied pressure onto his neck. Stan fell silent, and with immense control, the Shadow brought him down and dragged his unconscious body away. The victor looked round for a brief moment then his attention went upwards before he disappeared into the darkness.

Ed looked down from the lighting walkway. The large wooden strip was old but still held his weight. He thought of how brilliant he had been to think of going up here, he had a full view of every part of the stage and seating area; nobody would get past him, especially that woman cop. He was a short but stocky man, tattoos covered his arms, and his shaven head reflected the small specs of light that had dared to creep into the hall.

He had tried to join the army but had failed his psychological examination. 'Was too fond of killing, a danger to all around him', was their conclusion. Damn doctors, what did they know, he thought? So he got in with the Russians, since they seemed to like his lust for the job. Even at twenty-five years old, he had done some questionable things for them, but he regarded such actions as thrilling.

Looking down, he saw nothing. Wherever the woman cop was, hiding they would find her eventually. He recalled the phone call from Samuel telling someone from outside to lock the doors so the cop couldn't get out and that he would find her. He smiled at the thought of what he would be able to do to her, he just might film his actions and send the recording to the cops. He chuckled to himself, feeling that this job was too easy. A sound in the far corner got his attention, and he looked off to where the creak of wood had come from, but saw nothing. He stared closer into the darkness, hoping to see something he could shoot at. But this was the last thing he did before he felt a pinch to his neck and the sensation of falling, and then nothing.

Down below 'Boris the Bruiser' walked his patrol, shotgun in hand as he paced the small area at the far end of the backstage. He was a massive hulk of a man who on first appearance seemed to have no neck, just a head balanced on his shoulders. The automatic 12-gauge weapon looked like a child's toy in his grasp but he knew how to use it. The other guys had been placed here and there but his was a great place, he thought. It was right next to the exit, so if someone was to try and come in or out they would have to contend with him. Even for his large size, he moved quietly.

Something in the corner caught his eye. Was someone there? It was not possible, the area was covered top to bottom. He moved in slowly, shotgun at the ready.

Sam McCall hid herself behind the barricade, her back leaning against the cold wood for comfort.

From the right side of her position, she heard a slight noise:

not much of one, but sufficient to attract her attention. Her hands tightened on the pistol grip, her trigger-finger dug into the cold porcelain of the top slide. She felt her heart start to race as the noise came closer still, knowing that she had to be ready and focused.

Boris moved gingerly towards where he had seen something. It may be nothing, he thought, reasoning that this place had not been used in decades. Rats! What if it was rats, he wondered? A shiver ran down his spine at the thought of the beady-eyed rodents, *please don't be rats*, he thought, his weapon now beginning to shake in his hand, as he got closer and closer.

McCall heard another sound to the left of her and she carefully dared to sneak a glance there. Edging round she saw there was nothing. She exhaled, and moved back to her position. As her back rested against the security of her hiding place, she felt someone standing to her right. McCall turned her head slowly; part of her did not want to find out what was there. Her mouth dropped open to find she was faced with a massive bald-headed man. Her breath left her body as he reached down and picked up as though she was a rag doll, pulling her close to his face. He breathed in her fear, and she glimpsed badly fitting teeth as he gave her a wicked grin.

"I'm a police officer and you need to let me go!" She yelled.

He found her mixture of fear and attempt at intimidating him amusing.

"Hello, little fish," he said, in a deep booming voice. "The boss has a surprise for you, do you like surprises?"

She shuddered at the thought of what he meant, but then her eyes widened. He was confused, and she was no longer looking at him but behind him. Was someone there? He turned to look and a wave of fear washed over him.

Rise of a Phoenix

Samuel was the boss. He was a tall well-dressed man, and long white hair rested on his shoulders. He was Russian through and through, and after the Berlin wall came down in the 90s, he knew that it was time for change, so he came to America to exploit the enemy, and business had boomed. He brushed off his blue Italian suit that had cobwebs clinging to it from the stairwell he had come up; he knew he was safe at this vantage point in the presidential booth. *Who knows, maybe this was the booth that Lincoln was killed in, nice touch*, he thought.

From up there he could see everything. A crash from the stage made him grasp his AKM with readiness. Had she given up? Creeping forward to the edge of the stall, he witnessed a massive bulk covered in rats heading for the exit and in its grasp was the woman. In his despair the massive hulk threw McCall to the side as he fought to remove the clinging rats from his back. Crashing into some chairs she rolled and made for cover.

Samuel had little time for games. Somehow this woman detective had taken out all of his men, and the other cops would surely be not too far away by now; no, he decided, he would end her here and then he would disappear. As he raised the weapon to take aim, some sixth sense made McCall looked up and see him. As she stared down the barrel she knew that her gun was at the other side of the gantries—when she was thrown it must have been knocked from her grasp. The question was, who would be the quickest to fire?

Her eyes darted from the Russian to where her pistol was. She had to try, for whatever she decided, he was going to shoot her, and if she could take him down as well, it would be some consolation. Samuel took aim, held his breath and began to squeeze the trigger as he saw McCall dive for the gun. He felt joy, he felt exhilaration. And then he felt something hit him on the back of the head. As he turned, he saw someone come from the shadows, race forward and rugby-tackle him over the balcony. As they fell, John Steel ensured that the Russian man was underneath, and would absorb the impact. A cloud of ancient dust rose up as they crashed onto cardboard boxes full of crockery and props. The English detective rolled off him, out of breath from the impact of the fall, even though Samuel had taken the brunt of the damage.

"Cheers, big fella," Steel said patting the Russian on the head.

"What the hell was that? Did you use me as bait, you sick son-of-a-bitch?" She shouted at him, giving vent to her fear and anger.

"No, no, you don't have to thank me for saving your life, you're welcome, it's fine and I am fine, thanks for asking."

She stared hard at him, not knowing whether to shoot him or kiss him.

Suddenly the exit door exploded and a mass of armed police stormed in. Tooms and Tony almost tripped over the bulk of Boris, who had run into the locked door and knocked himself out. John Steel looked across at the broken body of Samuel.

"Just in time, aye, fellas," he said, still winded from the fall, and then collapsed back on to the floor.

SIXTEEN

IN THE BLACKEST OF nights a figure sat in a small room watching a newsflash. The room's diminutive size made the TV's volume seem loud, and flashes of reflected color painted the dirty brick walls. The room was empty apart from an old armchair and twelve TV sets stacked on top of one another , as if to make one large one. In the chair, the figure swiveled the remote in his long bony fingers as though it was a baton.

The TV report showed the Russians being led away by police and Samuel on a gurney being taken to hospital, and the reporter told of the killing of the millionaire's wife. In addition, the further information that the latest killing had been carried out using the same modus operandi as that of the serial killer who remained at large.

The sound of crunching, breaking plastic echoed through the room as the viewer crushed the remote in one hand and tossed it into a pile of other broken zappers that lay in the corner.

"So, Mr Samuel, you wish to blame me for your sins do you? Naughty, naughty," he cackled, his voice scraping through the air like nails on a chalkboard. "We shall see, we shall see... Oh I think the doctor has a patient to look upon." His laughter was low at first, then as it echoed through the building, it escalated into an eerie nightmarish howl.

Steel made it back to his apartment. The lights were turned off but he preferred it that way, enjoying just the illumination from the city streetlights breaking up the darkness. He hung up his jacket on to the old-style hat and coat stand that stood at the doorway. Then he walked across the large room to be what appeared to be a large oak wall unit and poured himself a whiskey from drinks cabinet part of the unit. He walked up to the window and, raising his left arm as a support, leant upon the glass. Looking down he spied cars and people going on their merry way, happy and contented. Steel smiled and took a sip from the crystal glass in his hand. Next to the window there was a small table with a group of pictures of family members. He reached down and picked up one particular silver-framed photo, which was of a beautiful looking woman in her late twenties; her hair was long and brown, and her blue eyes caught the light and shone like diamonds.

"Good night, my love." He kissed the photo then put it back in its special place; he turned his gaze back to the city through the window and sighed. Moving to a large couch, he lay himself down and fell into a restless sleep. As John Steel slept, his nightmares visited him once more: screaming voices that seemed familiar to him but that he could not place; laughter, deep laughter possibly from a big man, then the sound of six gunshots. The laughter, the screams, and the gunshots all blurred into one cacophonous hell. There was a crash, and he woke with a start. A crash? That was a new addition to his nightmares. And then he looked down and found the glass shattered on the wooden floor.

"Oh great, don't tell me I will need to sleep with plastic glasses from now on," he muttered to himself. He stepped over the glass and headed towards the window, and, looking down, he caught a glimpse of the photo of the woman and smiled gently.

SEVENTEEN

THE MORNING BROUGHT RAIN. Not a heavy downpour, but the slight drizzle that soaked you in seconds. However, the sky was blue with a few patches of the rain-bearing clouds. The English detective walked into the police precinct, and he was greeted with the sort of stares that burnt straight through you.

"Morning," he greeted the desk sergeant but did not expect a response. "Friendly bunch," he said under his breath.

As he left the elevator, the mood was chilling. Everyone stared at Steel as though he had just murdered a cop, not saved one. He made his way to the coffee room, where two female officers stood talking.

"Morning," he said, raising his hand as a greeting wave. But the officers just gave him a dirty look and left by the other door. "OK, I can see is going to be a fun-packed day," he thought to himself. Making McCall and himself a coffee, he brought the cups to her desk, but she was in the Captain's office, obviously giving a de-briefing on last night.

Rise of A Phoenix

The door opened to the Captain's office and McCall, Tooms and Tony came out looking flustered and red-faced. But when they saw Steel, they gave a collective scowl.

"Has Mr Steel decided to grace us with his presence yet?" The Captain looked over to see Steel standing there holding two coffee mugs in his hands and with a surprised look on his face.

"Steel, get your ass in my office now." Steel put down the cups and headed for the Captain's room and its angry looking occupant. On the way Tooms made a point of bumping shoulders with the English guy and staring him in the eye.

John entered the office and shut the door, taking a place in front of the large desk. He stood with his hands behind his back and his feet shoulder-width apart, preparing himself for the ripping of his life.

"Steel, I have no idea what the powers that be see in you," the Captain began.

"I was told that you were this hot-shot detective but so far I haven't seen diddly squat. And now I hear you let one of my detectives enter a building alone without backup with God knows how many dangerous Russian criminals in there."

The Captain leant forward, his knuckles resting on the desktop, his face bursting with rage.

"Son, I don't know who you are and I don't trust you. And believe me, I don't like things I don't know or trust, they make me nervous. So far you have given me no reason to trust you. Now if you so much as fuck up one more time I don't care who you know, you are gone. Do I make myself clear?"

"Crystal, sir." Steel stood motionless.

"Now get the hell out of my office and aim to do some police work without trying to get my people killed."

Steel left the office and made straight for the elevator. On seeing this the Captain shot out of his office.

"And where the hell do you think you are going?" the senior officer demanded.

"To find something that will make you trust me." And with that John Steel departed, leaving the Captain seething with rage, and the rest of the people in the room shaking their heads.

Later that night Captain Alan Brant sat down to a fabulous meal with his wife and kids, and they all laughed and joked. This was a good-hearted family, and the Captain was a good man and a fine cop. With the meal finished and the dishes done, Alan retired to his study to catch up on things. The room was dark but he knew it like the back of his hand. Sitting down at his desk he reached over and pulled the chain switch on his old-style desk lamp. After a click the desk was illuminated. And so was the figure sitting in the chair opposite.

He gasped to find Steel sitting there as though nothing was amiss with the situation; the Captain reached for the revolver in his desk drawer and pointed it at the other man.

"Now, Detective, if you would like to explain what the hell you are doing here before I paint my walls with you, I would grateful." The Captain seemed both furious and somewhat nervous.

"Well, I'm sorry to come here like this, but I didn't want anyone to see me enter and as for shooting, I fear it wouldn't do much good," he said, leaning forwards and putting the bullets from Alan's gun on to the table.

"What do you want, Steel?" Alan put the revolver back into the drawer. Steel produced a bottle of Scottish whisky that had been brewed in 1800s.

Rise of a Phoenix

"I think you may need this," said Steel as Alan accepted the bottle. His eyes opened wide when he saw the date on the label.

"What's the occasion? Are you finally leaving?"

"No, but what you are about to see can't be disclosed to anyone, no matter what. Do I have your word?" Steel was insistent.

"I must have your word on this, Captain."

"Yes, yes, whatever." Alan just wanted him out of his house and out of his precinct.

Steel passed him a folder that was at least two inches thick.

"Goddamn, that's heavy," said the Captain.

"So is my past." The Captain looked up at Steel and for the first time, met his eyes without their usual covering of sunglass lenses. He trembled.

The next morning the entire homicide department were sitting awaiting a briefing from the Captain.

"As you know, for the past week someone has been chopping people up and leaving us with a host of nameless corpses," Alan began.

"Now we have to find this guy before he strikes again." McCall stood up and addressed the audience of cops:

"We know he has a fondness for blondes and he knows their blood group, so we are looking for someone who has studied these women. We know that even though they are found naked there is no sexual abuse; he has a comprehensive knowledge of surgical techniques, so we may be looking for a surgeon. He doesn't choose them at random, he researches them. Unfortunately we have no clue to these women's identities, so we can't make a connection. We need to go through every database and find past crimes that have a similar MO." McCall concluded, sitting down.

"Now we have brought in an expert in psychological profiling, Dr Davidson." The Captain introduced the doctor, asking him to stand. "He is the best in his field, so with his help we are going to catch this guy."

Davidson stood up and gave a slight wave, then quickly sat down.

"OK, people, we got a job to do," the Captain said finally.

"So let's get to it." The crowd dispersed and detectives started phoning and keying into their computers. McCall spotted the doctor and moved over to him, noticing that he looked lost and out of place.

"Doctor, hi, I'm Detective McCall," she introduced herself, noticing how he looked up with a start, as if she'd broken into his thoughts. "Would you like a coffee or anything?"

He shook his head and just looked round him, as if he was a child lost in the school playground.

"Sir, if you would follow me we have set aside a room for you to work in," she explained.

He followed and once inside the room his jaw dropped.

"I hope this is OK, it's all we have at the moment," she apologized, but it seemed as if this was unnecessary. He was in awe of the facilities.

"On the contrary, this is perfect," he said looking round, his face resembling that of a child in a candy store.

There was a large work desk that was packed with files on the case, crime scene photos neatly stacked up next to them, and along a far wall stood a large whiteboard that he could use to construct his own personal murder-board. He walked round the room, eyes wide with excitement.

"So, Doctor, I will leave you to it then. If you need anything Officer Thompson has been assigned to you."

"What? Oh thank you, Detective," Davidson replied, still overwhelmed by everything.

"You know this is a very interesting case," he said, looking at the notes and photos in front of him.

Sam was already on her way out, but she stopped and turned.

"What do you mean?" she asked cautiously.

"Well, most of those we call 'collectors' take a finger or locks of hair. I remember one man kept eyes in a pickle jar" He smiled softly to himself as he remembered the grisly details. The expression on his face made her skin crawl.

"But this man," he continued, standing up and placing pictures of the victims on his board in the order they were found, "He picks certain parts of the body. I find that odd, intriguing, but nevertheless odd."

As McCall left the room, watching him staring at the photos on the board, she shivered.

She made her way towards Tooms, whom she found at his desk; McCall sat on the edge of it and looked around to make sure nobody was watching.

"Did you find anything on Steel?" she asked, making sure not to look down at her seated colleague.

"Well, your boy don't exist," Tooms replied.

"I spoke to just about everyone and information about Steel came up blank. Either he don't want to be found or he's off the reservation and people don't want us knowing him."

This time she looked down at him with a surprised look.

"Oh great, so you're telling me he is a ghost?"

"Don't worry, I'll make some calls, we will find out who he is. But the question is, do we *want* to find out who he is?"

She looked blankly at him.

"What's on your mind?" she asked, worried by his weird remarks.

"I mean, somebody who goes to this much trouble not to be found, I guess they just don't want to be found."

"Well I want to know all about our guy. So make the call." She stood up and walked towards the coffee area: she needed caffeine—badly.

McCall poured the coffee and sat at the table and sipped the hot dark coloured brew. The powerful aroma filled her nostrils as she breathed it in, taking a long drawn out breath, that was like pure heaven to her. Suddenly Tony's head appeared round the corner of the door. He was waving a piece of paper, and his urgency made her sit up and take notice.

"What's up?" she inquired, watching him enter.

"I think we got something on the CCTV footage from the pier."

She got up quickly and they both went to the monitor room.

"OK," she said when they were settled there. "What am I looking at?"

The frame had been paused at 0200hrs.

"Just watch," said Tony as he pressed play. The footage rolled on and at first there was nothing. Then she saw what appeared to be two homeless guys carrying a large object in a shopping cart. They also had what appeared to be some rope, and as they disappeared round the corner she noticed the counter clock had moved forward fifteen minutes, then they returned.

"Stop it there," she told him. "Can you enhance the faces?"

Tony used the mouse to create a digital square round the men's heads and after another click of the mouse, the image was further enhanced.

"OK, make copies," she said. "I want that picture circulated to every shelter, church and hostel, because we have got to find these men."

At last it looked as if they'd got a break. She just hoped that it would lead somewhere.

Once they were back in the main office Tooms's phone burst to life, and reaching over he grabbed the receiver.

"Detective Tooms, homicide, can I help you?" It was the ME's office, telling him that they had something.

"That was the ME's office," he told McCall and Tony as he hung up the phone.

"They got a hit on the last vic: she was a Miss Marie-Ann Talbot from Manhattan."

Walking over to the board, he rubbed out the name Jane Doe and write in its place Marie-Ann Talbot.

"We got an address yet?" McCall asked, as she sat at her desk, pleased that things were starting to come together, even if it was a slow process. Tony was busy checking on his computer for any data on Marie-Ann. With a bleep her picture came up on his screen, along with other information, including her date of birth and address.

"We got her," said Tony, giddy with excitement.

"OK," McCall told him "I will meet you guys downstairs. I'll phone CSU and get them down there to check the place."

They both took off as she had the receiver in her hand ready to dial. McCall made the call, then standing up, she grabbed her coat. McCall headed for the elevator but on the way she knocked on the room allocated to Doctor Davidson, then she stuck her head round the door when he did not reply.

"Hey, Doc, we have an address on the last victim," she said. "I wonder if you wanted to come with us?" Deep down she prayed he would say no.

"What? Oh, I'm sorry no, no, you go ahead I'm just catching up," he said, delving through the photos.

"Sure, I'll leave you to it then." And with that she quietly shut the door and ran before he could change his mind.

EIGHTEEN

SAMUEL LAY IN HIS hospital bed. Almost every part of his body was enclosed in a plaster cast. However, even if he'd been fighting fit he wouldn't have been able to go anywhere anyway: the two large police officers at the door would make sure he stayed put.

The man was conscious but unable to move. The TV in front of him was there merely for background noise, no one was watching it. He heard the door open, then soft footsteps tapped on the floor as somebody came into the room.

"Hey, Doc, is that you?" Samuel cried out, but got no answer.

"Who is there? Answer me!" Still there was no reply. But there was some kind of noise. What was, it he wondered, breathing faster. He strained his ears, trying to make out what the sound reminded him of. That sound, there it was again! Then, there came another noise! Was it music? Yes, it was music, from somewhere in the room. He could just make out a faint chime from a musical box or maybe a pocket watch.

"Please, who is there?" he called out plaintively. Then he felt the presence of someone in the room, and if it had not been for the sedative medication he was on, a shiver would have danced up and down his spine.

"Interesting," said a sickly eerie voice. Samuel was unable to move his neck because of the neck brace.

"Who is there? *Show yourself you bastard!*"

"You do realize that because of you I have to reschedule my plans?" the person said to him. "And that will not do, I'm afraid."

Samuel could feel the man's breath in his ear, as he went on speaking ever so softly and calmly. That was the most disquieting thing: the man was deadly calm.

"Oh goodie." The position of the voice had moved to somewhere above him. He managed to make out a brief silhouette on the ceiling: it was thin and the arms seemed too long, out of proportion to his body somehow, and then the image was gone.

"They have you on morphine," the man said next.

"Well you don't mind if I put up the dosage, do you?"

Samuel seemed puzzled. Why would he increase the dosage?

"What for, Doc?" the petrified Russian asked.

"So that you don't feel any pain and pass out of course, you silly boy."

"Who the fuck are you?"

Now Samuel was really panicking. He attempted to call out for help, but found a sock was being shoved into his mouth. What was this madman going to do? He struggled but in vain as his casts held him tightly immobile. And all the while he could hear this maddening laughter.

Rise of a Phoenix

A blur shot from the dark as the increased dose of morphine was kicking in. His heart froze as a face came into view, but all he could make out were massive blue eyes that held the look of a madman, and large shining white teeth surrounded by a grotesque smiling mouth.

"Oh I hope you stay awake for this," said his tormentor "You wouldn't want you to miss it for the world." Then as Samuel stared up he caught a glimpse of something held in a hand, something that shone in the light reflected from the TV screen. Then, to his horror, he thought he could see a bone saw. And then the madman was gone from view.

A terrifying silence filled his ears. Could it be a joke, he wondered? Maybe it was a trick? Either way he would eventually find this man and makes him pay for what he was doing. He felt a twinge in his shoulder and then a strange dampness on his back. The musical chimes were the last thing he heard before the dark took him.

NINETEEN

THE APARTMENT BELONGING TO Marie-Ann Talbot was quite large, with wooden floor tiles and white walls that seemed to make the rooms seem bigger than they were. The three detectives walked in and found themselves directly in the sitting area, and the view from the large windows was breathtaking. It was obvious that Marie-Ann had a well remunerated job, considering where the apartment's expensive location and her opulent taste in furnishings. They had been let in by the caretaker, who was an elderly gentleman in his late sixties, but seemed still quite active for his age. The team split up, searching room by room, but found nothing relevant to the case. They were searching for any clue as to what sort of person the lady was and what contact she had with others, but there was nothing to help them.

"OK, people keeping things private I can understand," said Tooms, coming out of the bedroom with a disgruntled expression. "But this ain't right. There are no pictures of family, or of friends, there's nothing. I mean she doesn't even have a naughty drawer."

McCall looked up. "So? Your point is?"

Rise of a Phoenix

"Nah, nothing, just blowing off steam I guess, in all the victims' apartments things seem the same. It's more than just being super clean and having no pictures on display. If you ask me, it sure seems weird." He went back into the bedroom to continue his search.

McCall shook her head and smiled. She felt his anguish, they all did, but she had faith something would come up: it had to.

The phone in her pocket buzzed and vibrated, and as she reached in and took it out, the blue screen lit up the words: 'caller withheld'. She looked at it for a moment then pressed the accept button.

"Hi, it's Steel," stated the caller.

She took the cell phone away from her head quickly and looked at it in surprise.

"McCall, are you there?" The voice sounded confused.

"How the hell did you? Never mind, I don't think I want to know. What's up?" she said, adjusting to the shock of hearing from him.

"I got an address and name for vic number two."

"Really?" She sounded surprised that he was capable of doing some actual police work.

"Don't sound too amazed. Anyway the second victim was a Miss Susan Black and she had an apartment in Queens; I just texted you the address."

She tried not to sound too excited about the new lead, not wanting to give him the satisfaction, , but a lead was a lead no matter where it came from. "OK, I will meet you OUTSIDE the block, you hear me! *Outside the block*. No going in by yourself." She was blunt and to the point.

"Yes, mommy," he said and hung up. She scowled to herself at his childishness.

113

TWENTY

SAM MCCALL DROVE UP to the main entrance of the apartment block and parked. On exiting her car she saw Steel leaning against the white plaster of the massive tower block. He wore black jeans, a strange black shirt that had only three or four buttons and what appeared to have a clerical collar, which looked stiff against his neck apart from at the front, where there was a small gap. Over that, he had a long black three-quarter length suit jacket. It looked smart but casual, and his outfit was topped off, as always, by those dammed sunglasses.

"Detective," he greeted her with a smile.

"Detective," she returned the greeting but not the smile.

"Shall we?" he said, opening the door for her. McCall used the other door just out of spite, a trace of a smile on her face, smug in her small victory. He paused for a moment while a very attractive woman went through the door he'd opened for McCall. The woman thanked him and went on her way, leaving him with a smile he would never forget. McCall shot him a disapproving look, but he just raised his hands, palm sides up.

"What?" he said innocently.

As they entered the lobby they noticed a large well-built Hispanic man with short hair at the front desk. They figured that the guy's dark suit and white shirt was part of a uniform denoting that he was part of the building's workforce. Sure enough, as they neared the desk they noticed that the tie he wore bore the name of the tower.

"Good afternoon, can I help you?" he said, his deep voice and with a definite foreign accent, probably Columbian. McCall reached towards the badge clip on her belt and lifted the shiny piece of tin so he could see it.

"Yes, I'm Detective McCall and this is Detective Steel. I believe you have a Miss Susan Black staying here, is that correct?"

"Miss Susan, yes. A very nice lady, she always says hello whenever she sees one of us on duty. Why are you asking? Has something happened to her?" His smile was replaced by a real look of concern.

"Yes," McCall tried to break the news gently.

"I'm sorry to say that she was murdered and we are trying to establish what she was doing in the hours before she died."

"Whatever we can do to help, please ask," he said, the shock of this revelation etched on his face.

"Would it be possible to take a look at her apartment?"

He nodded and called to one of the cleaning girls who was just passing.

"Melanie, can you take these people to 121 please?"

She nodded and asked them to follow her to the elevator. This lady cleaner was all of twenty years old, if that, with short dark hair and a strange light-blue outfit that had short sleeved arms and was buttoned all the way down the front.

"Did you know Miss Black at all, Melanie?" asked Steel softly, noticing her shocked behaviour at the news of the death.

"Not really. We spoke now and then, but just in passing. She was friendly like that. She was a nice person. She didn't deserve to be murdered."

"Nobody does," said McCall, with a strange look in her eyes, that Steel took note of.

The girl let them inside the spacious apartment. Like the other victims, she lived alone, had no photos of family or friends, nothing that could lead them to their human contacts. McCall and Steel searched high and low for something but, just like before, they kept coming up empty. Eventually Steel walked into the living area carrying a pink book with a small padlock on its corner, apparently Susan's diary.

"Look what I found," he said, waving the small book.

"Not really your colour," said McCall sarcastically.

He smiled. "It's her diary and I guess if we want to know something about a person it could be right here…" He was right and she knew it. And boy, how she hated that.

"OK, bag it and we will take it back."

McCall's search of the kitchen found nothing, just the reminder that they needed refreshment, after seeing the contents of Susan's refrigerator. Steel walked back out of the bedroom and looked around, his brow wrinkled with confusion and worry.

"What's up?" McCall asked. Even knowing him for just a short time, she'd picked up on his *'I'm on to something'* expression.

"Did the other victims have computers?" he asked, still looking around the room.

"I think so, why?" Now she was intrigued.

"If you're a successful business woman, you would have

your life planned out. So far, have all the apartments been like this? I don't mean size, just as organized as this place is?"

He had walked into a small room that had probably been designed as a child's room or a guest room. Instead it was arranged as a small office, with piles of business-related papers and a laptop.

"McCall," he called for her, as he looked through a large pile of papers that were on a pine-topped desk. McCall entered and looked round the small office. The walls were painted lilac and many pin boards hung from them, covered with flow charts and diagrams.

"OK, I'll get CSU in here, see if there is anything relevant." She made the call and waited for the crime scene team to take over.

TWENTY-ONE

ON HIS RETURN FROM lunch, the good doctor was busy in his office at the department. Dr Davidson had created his own '*murder board*'; however, this assembly of information was based more on personality analysis than the murder facts. It had pictures of the victims, and lines of writing here and there that aimed to correlate similarities in the women victims, while also trying to analyze what made the killer tick.

And on another board he had put what was known about the killer himself; for Davidson, just the smallest obscure detail that was there, or should have been there, spoke volumes to him. For instance he judged that the way the victims were found, demonstrated a respect or lack of it, for the victims.

The doctor was perched at his desk looking over some medical reports that had come up from downstairs, and he picked up the water glass that was next to him and began to sip as he read.

Rise of a Phoenix

Now that he was banned from the ME's lab (because Tina had thrown out '*the freaky bastard*'), all reports had to be brought to him by Officer Jenny Thompson. This woman was a promising young female officer, so any experience she could gain from being with the homicide department were always welcome.

Thompson knocked on the door but he gave no reply. Again she knocked but heard nothing. One of the detectives noticed her plight and waved to her, indicating that she should go straight in; she nodded and obeyed, and as she entered, she saw Dr Davidson staring at some of the photos from the crime scenes. And she could have sworn that he was actually stroking them.

Shocked by seeing this, she didn't notice the chair in front of her as she collided with it, knocking the table. He looked up at her with maddening red eyes and pupils so dilated they seemed almost black.

She stared, horrified at his gaze, and she found she could not move or scream. It was as if his stare had caught her in some kind of stasis. A long strand of thick saliva slid from his mouth reminding her of a rabid dog. Thompson broke free from his gaze, screamed and ran out of the room crying, attracting a lot of attention. The big detective who had witnessed this scene burst in to confront the doctor, but as soon as the large man caught his gaze he turned white, rushing off to the men's room to throw up. The detective had seen evil before but never felt it, not like that.

TWENTY-TWO

MCCALL AND STEEL STOPPED at a street corner vendor and ordered a couple of hot dogs.

"So, Mr. Steel why don't you tell me something about yourself?" McCall grinned as she shot the question at him.

"Such as what?" Steel smiled. He had been wondering how long it would take for her to ask him something personal.

"Such as *anything*." she said, taking the steaming dog off the man and covering it in ketchup, to Steel's disgust.

"Would you like a hotdog with your ketchup?" John Steel said, still staring at the sauce running off the paper napkin.

She gave him a quick 'mind your own business' stare and bit into it. Steel took his hotdog and paid for the both of them. The air was fresh with a slight breeze, and as they found a bench they both sat down to eat. Steel looked upwards, as if he was trying to gather some of the rays of sunlight from above.

"So what do you want to know?" he asked.

"I don't know where were you born. What you did before you came here? Why did you join the US police and not the British force? You know, little things like why you don't seem to exist!" She gave him a grim look and he just smiled.

"Wow," he said, biting into the hotdog that was mostly bread. "No wonder you put so much ketchup on it."

She could see he was evading the questions.

"Look, I know, Detective, that I seem … How I can put it"

"An asshole?" she butted in with a grin.

"I was going to say secretive but if you prefer that, I guess that works. Thing is, right at this moment I've got a couple of trust issues, but I promise I will tell you everything once I know where I stand, OK?"

It wasn't OK but she could sense there was definitely more to his story. The question was, did she want to know about his life, or be a part of it?

Her cell phone buzzed, and taking it out of her pocket, she pressed the receive button.

"We got a body at 42 and Lex." The voice on the phone was Tooms and he did not seem happy.

"OK, Mystery Boy," McCall told the Englishman after finishing the call. "Let's go, but we will pick this up later, believe me."

"Perhaps over dinner?" Steel said with a hopeful voice.

"Yeh, we just tried that, and believe me that's the only dinner we will be sharing." She gave him a scornful look that made him grin even more.

"See, you're warming to me. Before you would have thrown the food at me, not made me eat it." He looked up as a sudden thought struck him.

McCall picked up on it immediately. "What is it?"

"I was just wondering which would have been worse, eating the hotdog, or wearing it."

She pretended to throw her phone but he just got into the car quickly to evade her anger. She smiled before getting in, but once inside the car her good humour had vanished from her face.

TWENTY-THREE

DR DAVIDSON ROSE FROM his seat after reading the ME's report on the latest victim, took the jacket of his brown thousand-dollar suit off the back of an empty chair and put it on, moving his hands down the arms as if to smooth out the wrinkles. Walking towards the door, he grabbed a black worn-looking briefcase with brass catches on it. As he entered the outer office, he stopped, put down the case and put on some black leather gloves that had lain upon the case earlier on. He looked round, surveyed all the people in the room, and smiled.

When he got to the elevator a voice spat out: "Where you going, Doc?"

"I have work," Davidson replied, without slowing down his pace.

"Thank fuck for that," came another voice from somewhere in the room; this, however, did make him stop for a brief second, and then, as the elevator doors shut behind him, he was gone.

TWENTY-FOUR

MCCALL AND STEEL ARRIVED at the address they'd been given; it was a shabby hotel in the East Side with wallpaper that looked like it had been hung in the 1930s, when the place had been built. It was dark, even though there were wall lights, but their minimal illumination was inadequate.

Outside the victim's room two patrol officers stood either side of the door, making sure nobody entered. McCall flashed her badge and they both nodded. As the detectives entered the room, they donned some blue latex gloves, then walked into the sitting area, where they found a shaven-headed man with tattoos that covered his arms and most of his neck, seated on a chair. They approached from either side, Steel sensing that something was not right. The man was sitting there with his eyes wide open, and he was dressed in blue jeans, white shirt and black army-style boots. His tanned complexion minimized the colours of an array of tattoos, presumably collected in jail, and a beard sprouted from his slim face. He appeared to be dead, however there didn't appear to be any indications of the cause. Steel held his position and started to scan the room. McCall was about to approach the corpse when he yelled for her to stop.

"Stop! Just stop!" he commanded. "In fact, do me a favour and get against that wall." He pointed at the wall behind her, which had no view to or from the only window.

"God, you are so paranoid! Look, the man is dead and we need to find out what killed him and we can't do it from here." She had lost patience with him at this point, maybe a result of the irritations from the past couple of days that had finally gotten to her. McCall didn't know or care why he wanted her to stand still, all she wanted to do was get to the body.

"Don't you find it strange that he is sitting there dead, facing a window with no clear cause of death?" he asked.

"Maybe it was a heart attack, or some other medical explanation. But we won't find it from here," she said.

"Look, I have seen this type of thing before and I just think it's a trap, that's all."

She gave him a weird look and walked forward towards the body. Steel lunged at McCall, knocking her to the floor in a football tackle. Just as he did so the window shattered and there was a popping sound as the dead man's head exploded over the back wall. Blood and head fragments peppered its surface. Catching their breaths, Steel looked at McCall, who lay underneath him.

"You OK?" he asked as they lay there, his legs astride her.

She looked up at him, their eyes met and she felt an attraction that she soon managed to shake off.

"Are you hurt?" he repeated, sounding concerned.

"What? No, but you are squashing me." He realized the position he was in and rolled off her.

"Sorry."

They both looked at the headless corpse.

"I guess you were right, but how did you know?" She gave him a wary look as he got up and hugged the wall.

"I know one thing," Steel muttered, still panting from the adrenaline rush.

"And that is?" she asked, calmly anticipating some hopefully useful information.

"Well, if he wasn't dead before, he sure as hell is now." Steel sarcastically pointed out, as he looked at the pattern of blood and brains on the wall and then give a shrug.

She just gave him a 'Sick bastard' look and called in the incident.

Fifteen minutes later a flurry of police and members of a SWAT unit were swarming all over the building opposite in an attempt to find the shooter or at least some clues. With the area made safe, the CSU teams had split and had two places to canvass. McCall was sitting with a blanket draped around her shoulders getting checked out in the back of an ambulance, when Steel walked up to her with a cup of hot chocolate.

"Here, drink this," he said, passing her the beverage. She saw it and looked puzzled.

"Hot chocolate? Really?" She looked puzzled.

"Yes, the sugar will help compensate for the adrenaline loss so you won't feel faint," he said, sipping his own. "Oh really? And where did you learn that?" she said suspiciously.

"Discovery Channel. It's brilliant—tells you everything."

She knew it was an evasive answer, but under the circumstances, she was going to let it pass. For now. "Thanks." She smiled up at him. "Any time." Steel returned the smile.

McCall was given the all clear by the medics, and prepared to head for the shooter's building, when the

Captain came to join them. "Where the hell do you think you are going, detectives?" He yelled, stopping them both.

"I was…We were just going too." McCall suddenly froze as Brant shot them both an angry look.

"Go home and get some rest, I hope the next sentence was going to be, detective." His look was severe. "Hey, don't look at me Captain, I was just following her," Steel said, innocently sipping his drink."But sir," McCall protested, "we were just shot at from"

"Yes, you two were shot at. So that makes it someone else's case. You're too close to it, so you have to go home. Do it now!"

TWENTY-FIVE

THE EVENING DREW IN and the sun began to disappear into the horizon, leaving behind a sky that looked as if it was on fire, with the dark orange and reds that bled across the heavens. Streaks of dark cloud cut across the view, as if the canvas it had been painted upon had been slashed, hiding the last remnants of the sun. The bar was quiet, but that's how he liked it. It was a place he could come and gather his thoughts. The place was old, dating back to probably before Prohibition; the booths were of heavy oak with dark green leather padding, the tables supported by shining brass pillars, and the floor was tiled. The bar ran the breadth of the room with bar stools lining its counter, ready to house the next happy customer. Tooms loved this place, it was his retreat and that was why he had invited him here. As the detective walked in he was greeted with friendly hellos from the staff, which he returned with equal pleasure. He searched, then he saw a large bulk of a man with short hair, who was sipping a cold one.

Rise of a Phoenix

"Hey, Sergeant Thomas Biggs, you know, you get uglier every day," Tooms said, standing in front of the table, fists clenched, ready for anything.

"Well Tooms, your wife don't seem to mind."

The two men laughed and embraced.

"How long has it been, man?" said Biggs.

"Too long," Tooms replied, happy to see his old friend.

"So what's up, what do you need, man?"

"Information, information on a guy," Tooms answered.

"OK, tell me what you know and I'll try and track him for you."

The two men had served together many years ago in the Marines, but Biggs had ended up in the SEALS and Tooms had become a cop.

"So what's this man's name, anyway?" said Biggs, tucking into the massive burger that had just arrived.

"He's, well, a new guy at the precinct. Problem is he doesn't exist. I can't find any record of the man anywhere." Tooms reached for his phone and pulled up a picture and showed it to him.

"He said his name is—" That was as far as he got.

"Sergeant John fucking Steel!"

Tooms's face dropped. He did not know whether to be happy or afraid.

"You know him then?" Tooms asked, almost feeling embarrassed to enquire when the answer was obvious.

"Know the man? I'd say sure I do. The bastard owes me twenty bucks."

"So how do you know him?" Tooms was intrigued.

"They used to call him The Phoenix, 'cause every time the man went down, the fucker used to get back up again."

Tooms now had a lost look on his face, which his friend couldn't help but notice.

"The man used to be attached to special mission groups," Biggs elaborated. "Now SEAL's are mainly about team work but this guy was special."

"Special? Special how?" Tooms asked, stealing a French fry from the other man's plate.

"You stealing a brother's food?" he laughed. "Nah, this cat could go in and clear a hotspot, they used to send him on hostage retrieval."

Tooms stared at his friend like he was a child listening to a grandfather's stories.

"See, if we were worried about entering a hotspot, they would just send this crazy bastard in. You wouldn't hear a thing unless he wanted you to. I remember one story from Afghanistan in the early days when about fifteen of our brothers were being held for ransom on TV, you know: 'free our brothers-in-arms or we will kill your men'—that sort of thing."

Tooms nodded. He knew that all too well, since a friend had been captured, but the extraction team had gotten them out.

"Anyway, Steel decides to take a walk and gets himself captured. I don't know what happened in the camp and God knows I don't want to, but they said he got them all out and killed all the terrorists, and that's when they made him a 'lone wolf' operative. The man's a ghost."

"So what happened? Why did he leave?"

"Can't really say. But we did one job and it almost went south, he reckoned it was a set-up and he said he had to leave so the teams would be safe. Later I heard agencies were interested in him for recruitment. I don't know." Briggs shrugged. "What I do know is, if you're in the shit, this is the man to have your back."

"And if you're not on his side?"

"Don't bother to run, buddy, just end it there 'cause he will find you."

Tooms swallowed hard, almost choking on the other fry he had taken.

"See? That's what you get for stealing a brother's fries."

They both laughed and went on to catch up on old times.

A shot, laughter, a scream, a smell, caused Steel to wake up suddenly. A smell that was new to his dreams. He stumbled to the bathroom and ran some cool water into the basin, splashing the refreshing water onto his face. What could it mean? He struggled to remember it before he fully woke up and forgot the aroma, then he went to the kitchen and grabbed the juice carton from the fridge and made his way to the sofa where he collapsed. Opening the carton, he filled a glass and then drank, emptying the glass of its contents in no time, but enjoying the cool refreshing drink. The suede leather felt soft on his bare skin as he looked out of the window into the night.

Closing his eyes, he tried to remember where he'd first smelt it, but it was no use, for now he was fully awake. But it didn't matter, if he had dreamt of it once the same thing would happen again, and when it did, he would be ready.

John Steel looked over at the antique clock on the fireplace. The lights of the city allowed him to see that it was half past eight in the evening. *Great*, he thought, he had enough time to shower and change.

The water felt good, the droplets followed the curves of his muscular body. Even though in his clothes he appeared to be of average build, his nakedness told a different story. His muscles was almost like tightened cable that protruded though his skin, his body was firm and tanned, scars from a lifetime of narrow escaped were etched into his body. Each one was a reminder of the path he now followed. As the creamy lather of the soap was washed away by the flow of warm water, his fingers touched the six round exit-wound scars that were on various parts of his body. Each one told of either how lucky he was or of how someone had to pay, and he was tasked to take that payment. He wished he could stay under the water forever, its caress felt somehow therapeutic. However, he had to be somewhere, there was someone he had to meet.

Several hours later a blacked-out limousine pulled up to the entrance of the gala. As the vehicle came to a stop, the valet opened the door and the mayor, who was busy talking to a rather plump gentleman with a balding head and a neatly trimmed beard, suddenly turned round and grinned at the sight of the car. The mayor excused himself and made his way to greet the passenger of the car, the door opened and he leaned forwards.

"It's OK, come on, you will have fun, I promise," he said, laughing to his new guest.

Steel exited the vehicle and straightened his tux, saying: "You know I hate these things, right?"

"Relax. Besides, everyone thinks you are here on behalf of the department. Nobody knows you."

Steel didn't feel reassured but what the hell, he was here now. And besides, who would find out?

TWENTY-SIX

MORNING CAME, BLESSED BY a warm sun and a cool breeze as the city went about its business. Steel sat in the chair next to McCall's desk waiting for her to come in. While Steel sat there, he was transfixed by the sight of a strange tall thin man, who was in one of the briefing rooms that he seemed to have taken over to use as his own personal office.

A young police officer passed by. "Hey, Rachael who's the spooky guy?" John Steel asked her.

She gave him a friendly, but mystified look.

"I'm asking, who's the really strange spooky guy?" He pointed to the room across from where he was sitting.

"That is our local expert, Dr Davidson," Rachael replied. "But I am not sure what he's an expert on—apart from freaking people out!" And with that the hot redhead left him staring at the precinct's new addition.

Sam McCall walked in and sat down. "Morning," she greeted the transfixed Detective Steel.

"Morning. Just who is that guy anyway?" he asked bluntly.

"Well, if you would show up for briefings you would know that Dr Davidson is helping with the murders," she said, sipping the coffee she found on her desk.

"What do we know about him?" he said, watching as the man in the room opposite was leafing desperately through paperwork, obviously searching for something.

"What do we know about anyone?" she replied. Yet he had the feeling that the remark was more directed towards him personally.

"What? Ha, ha, OK, I take your point. But really, something about that guy…"

Steel was unnerved by him, something did not sit right, but he did not know what it was.

"Well, it appears your hunch on the 'date' books being on their computers was right," she said, almost heartbroken that she had to admit it to him. "We are just waiting for a copy so we can run through them together and check for any matches."

As McCall sifted through her emails she saw the doctor; he was looking at the board and ranting to himself, then going back to the paperwork on the desk.

"Do we have anything on Susan Black yet?" asked Steel.

"Not much, just that she worked on Wall Street, one of the top female sellers there and oh yeh, we finally got a photo of her." McCall opened the file and lifted the picture, and Steel's face dropped. Suddenly he snatched the picture from her and rushed to the board.

"Hey, watch it will you!" said McCall in protest. "What's wrong with you?" she asked, looking at the fingers he'd just pulled the photo from.

"It's not what's wrong with me, the real question is, what's wrong with this picture, or should I say these pictures?" As he placed the picture of Susan Black in the blank space under her name, McCall saw something.

"See? They look similar." He turned and looked at her.

"Really similar," she agreed. "I would have said almost identical myself, but that's just me."

Tooms and Tony walked up, notebooks at the ready to spiel off what they had found downtown.

"Hey, is it me or do they look alike?" asked Tony, with a dumb expression on his face.

"Do they? I hadn't noticed," she said with a sarcastic grin. "OK, what did you guys get?"

"Well, we got all three diaries and date planners from CSU and we were just about to run them to see if anything breaks," said Tooms, waving a CD case in his hand.

"OK, let me know if anything comes up," said McCall. She was frustrated because they had too much evidence that led nowhere.

Steel stared at the photos for a moment and then shot up out of his seat.

"May I?" he asked, pointing to the computer on her desk, as she stood with a baffled look on her face.

"What are you thinking?" she asked, leaning on the corner of the desktop as he sat in her place.

"Well, we found no pictures of family," he said, typing something on the PC.

"So, maybe they fell out or something." McCall was up for ideas, sure, but she could not see where this was going.

"Let's say she didn't have any?"

"She's adopted?" asked Tooms.

"No, there would be pictures," Steel replied. "Now what I'm thinking is—"

"—Orphanage!" interrupted McCall, with a 'penny dropped' look upon her face.

The computer spat out some facts on Susan Black, including her old address.

"All Saints' orphanage?" McCall wrote the address down and Tooms snatched it up.

"Come on, road trip." He waved the piece of paper at Tony, who was grabbing his jacket.

"What you thinking, Steel?" She noticed the longing look on the English detective's face.

"If I am right, she won't be the only one who went there." The words slipped into a whisper as he looked up at her with a strange look she had not seen him use before: he looked lost.

TWENTY-SEVEN

DR DAVIDSON WAS FRANTIC. Somebody had been messing with his notes and photos, and this did not sit well with him. He appreciated the fact that the department had called him because they realized his greatness in the field of psychology, but his patience had his limits, and he was horrified to see his board. Someone had written all sorts of garbage on his board!

He sat down and drank some water. His head was killing him—ever since childhood he had suffered from these terrible headaches but nobody knew what caused them. He drank more water and took an aspirin.

As he sat, he looked at the chaos that his system had become. Why had someone done this? Why? For goodness sake, he was here to help! Yes, sure, the publicity would boost his medical practice no end, but did he really need this kind of hassle?

"Must calm down, must calm down," he kept repeating to himself, checking his pulse. Then he noticed the ME's file: it was empty. That was it, he had had enough. As he jumped up the chair slid backwards, pushed by the back of his knees. The wheeled chair careered into the wall behind him."Ladies and gentlemen, I can appreciate that my being here is a problem for most of you, however if we could be a bit more professional about this that would be super. Thank you!" he shouted, as he walked across the main office, only to return seconds later. "And where is Officer Thingamabob who is meant to be working with me? Or did someone get rid of her as well?" He grabbed his blue blazer and stormed off towards the elevator.

"I can't work like this," he growled to himself, and as the elevator doors swung open he entered, leaving everyone leaning forwards over their desks in bewilderment at the goings on. Then the doors closed and he was gone. "Wow, what was all that about?" asked Steel.

"Beats the hell out of me," said McCall, and they went back to their search of the diaries.

Tooms and Tony arrived at the old building. Its white walls, that once shone as a beacon of hope for children, now showed the test of time, but the place still retained a homely feeling. Kids played in the front yard and music could be heard booming through the windows, probably from a home-grown amateur band.

The two detectives walked through the green-colored gate and approached the front door. The sun was high and the reflection glared off the door's glazing. Tooms leaned over and rang the bell. A friendly *ding dong* echoed throughout the building. As they peered through the glass, Tooms and Tony saw kids playing tag in a dining room to their left; to their right was what appeared to be a sitting room of some kind, with a group of children practising on stringed instruments.

Rise of a Phoenix

At that moment a face appeared at the door; it was that of a cheerful woman who appeared to be in her late seventies. She opened the door and they saw the black–and-white of her nun's habit which clung to her ample figure, and the small black-rimmed glasses that sat at the end of her small button nose. Even though she seemed quite elderly, she had the youth and spring in her step of someone half her age.

"Yes, can I help you?" she asked with a beaming smile.

"Yes, ma'am, we hope so. I'm Detective Tooms, and this is Detective Marinelli, and we would like to speak to you if we may about a girl who may have lived here."

She beckoned them into a small office down a long corridor; on the way they passed another nun, who looked to be in her late twenties and quite attractive, Tony thought. The Mother Superior spoke to the younger sister and asked her to bring refreshment to the office. The office was large, with a bay window that let in an amazing ray of light into the middle of the room; old pictures in dark wooden frames adorned the white wallpaper that had gold fleur-de-lys patterns on it. The room was long with a red shag-pile carpet. At its centre there was an almost antique looking coffee table, with four matching chairs placed around it.

She raised a hand to indicate that they should sit down, and as they did so the young sister came in with a silver tray, which held an old crockery tea set. She placed it down and left, promptly closing the door behind her. Tooms noticed a large heavy-looking dark timber desk at the end of the room. Behind it hung a large golden-framed painting of The Last Supper, which almost filled the wall.

"So, detectives, how can I help?" she asked expectantly.

"Did you know a Susan Black?" asked Tooms.

At that, her smile dimmed and her face shone less brightly.

"Yes, poor child."

"What do you mean, ma'am?" Tooms enquired, his curiosity piqued.

"Well gentlemen, she was brought to us in 1972, I think it was. A sad tale," she said, getting up and walking towards a group of black-and-white photographs on the left-hand wall. She stopped and took one of them down and stroked it with affection.

"So what happened?" asked Tony, the abruptness of his question making her shudder slightly, as though someone had walked over her grave.

"She was brought in by a sweet young thing, too young to be a mother you see. Anyway she and her boyfriend gave her up for adoption, hoping the child would get a good home and a better start in life than what they could give, you see."

Tooms and Tony, transfixed by the story, asked her to continue.

"Oh, she was a brilliant, talented young thing, a catch for any parent."

"So why wasn't she ever took on?" asked Tony, surprised.

"Because everyone thought that they were sisters and didn't want to break them apart. She and the other girls were inseparable, you see."

Tony and Tooms looked at each other with a puzzled expression, and then turned their attention back to the Mother Superior.

"What other girls?" asked Tooms.

The nun passed him the photo and there the two detectives' jaws dropped as they saw the girls standing side by side. The three children each wore the same long dark-coloured dress and had the same long blonde hair.

"Good as gold they were, always helping out, and the other kids loved them like big sisters, especially one boy, can't remember his name, though. A real pleasure to have, they were, and then they left for different colleges and universities. But they always sent Christmas cards every year." Her smile widened. "Yes, the other two were called"

"Marie-Ann and Karen," the two detectives said in unison, with a shocked look on their faces.

"Yes, that was their names. Oddly enough they were also brought in at roughly the same time and under the same circumstances."

Then a look of realization dawned on her face. "What has happened to them?" asked the nun, almost collapsing with shock.

The detectives helped her back to the chair next to the table and got some water from the desk for her to drink. She thanked Tony as she took a sip from the glass.

"What has happened to my girls? Please tell me." She began to cry, and, grabbing a handkerchief from her sleeve she patted her eyes, absorbing the cascade of tears that flowed downs her rose-red cheeks.

"I'm sorry ma'am, but they were murdered." Tooms spoke gently, compassion evident in his words.

"Did you kill her?" asked the nun.

Her mood had changed. Now they were seeing another side of the old lady, and it was not pleasant.

"No, ma'am." They both looked shocked at the question.

"Then why are you sorry?" Her eyes seemed to glow red with fury, and the two detectives felt the room close in around them.

"I meant, we are sorry for your loss, ma'am, sorry to bring you the news." What he really meant was that he was sorry they had come here. She seemed to calm down, but there was still a lingering anger in her eyes.

"Do you have any leads as to who may have done this?" she asked, now back to her calm self. However her smile had not returned, nor was it likely to while they were there, they guessed.

"Not yet, ma'am, but we will keep you informed as and when we get something. Do you mind if we borrow this picture?" She nodded and thanked them. The two detectives, badly shaken by the event, said their goodbyes and headed back to the safety of the station.

TWENTY-EIGHT

IT WAS AROUND NINE o'clock in the evening and a light breeze flowed through the maze of tall buildings, the night sky was clear but there was no moon, just the twinkling of millions of stars that sparkled in the heavens. Steel decided to go for a walk just to clear his head, and the streets were not particularly busy, which he found preferable to the daytime waves of pedestrians. As he walked by Grand Central Station he noticed a boy with a shoeshine box. The lad was around twelve years old with black scruffy hair, big blue eyes and an even bigger smile. His face and clothes were dirty, and a pair of grey woollen fingerless gloves covered his hands.

"Want a shine, Mister?" said the lad in a loud positive tone.

As Steel looked at the boy his face reminded him of someone from long ago. A sorrow filled his heart at just the thought of him.

"Hey, Mister, you OK?"

Steel's thoughts returned to the present, his reverie interrupted by the squeak of the boy's voice.

"What? I'm sorry," he said. "Yes of course, why not."

"You from England, Sir?" The question excited the boy. He had shone plenty of shoes, but he could not remember meeting an English person before.

"Yes, but I haven't been home for quite a while." His tone was friendly, and he was smiling at the boy.

"Wow, have you seen London? What it is like? I've heard it's great there. Lots of castles and stuff, must be so cool." The boy was full of enthusiasm, and his innocent exuberance made him good company for the English detective. They sat and talked for a while about England and the kid spoke of his dreams of going places, travelling and exploring the world. Steel smiled as the boy's eyes widened as he talked about his hopes and dreams, but at the same time, Steel wondered how the boy could achieve his dreams by doing such a badly paid job.

Steel stood up and looked at his boots: they shone like new. He smiled at the kid.

"What's your name, kid?" asked Steel.

"Luke, sir, Luke Johnson," he said proudly.

"Well, Luke Johnson, it's a pleasure to meet you, I'm John Steel. So what do I owe you, young Sir?" he said, reaching into his pocket.

"That's two dollars please, sir." The boy stood up and whipped his buffing rag over his shoulder.

"Well that's a shame, I only have a fifty. Tell you what, you keep the change, and get yourself some new clothes, OK?"

The boy looked shocked at the offer.

"Sorry, sir I can't take that, just two dollars." The smile had gone from his little face and Steel sensed something was amiss.

"OK, tell you what," John said, putting the money back in his pocket. "Here is your two dollars plus another twenty as a tip."

The boy looked unsure until he saw the detective's badge clipped on to his belt. On seeing that, the smile returned.

"Thank you, sir, hope to see you again soon," said the lad.

Steel ruffled the boy's hair and walked on, a big smile on his face as his memories returned.

The next morning there was a cold wind, even though the sun was up and the skies were cloudless. Steel walked out into the bustle of the early morning chaos, and, hoping that the crowd would act as a windbreak, he ventured out towards the precinct.

As he reached the corner where the boy had been last night, he saw him again, and noticed something different about him. He was holding his right ribcage as if he was in pain. Steel moved closer and called out to him.

"Morning Luke." Steel called out. But his face dropped as the boy turned round and Steel saw that his left eye was almost completely closed by an angry looking bruise.

"Morning, Sir." The boy tried to talk but his words ended as he winced in pain.

Steel bent down and put a gentle hand on his shoulder but the boy winced again. Steel's blood began to boil.

"What happened?" Steel asked him, his fists clenched ready to take action if only the boy would give him the information he needed.

"Fell down the stairs, Sir, that's all."

Steel was angry that he was lying, but he knew in his heart that unless the boy said something nothing would change. Clearly the boy was scared, he could see that, but not of him. No, there was something else he was scared of, *someone* else.

"You need to go to hospital, young man," said Steel, standing up.

The boy grabbed his trouser leg and gave him a pleading look. "No Sir, please do nothing, everything is fine, really."

The Englishman knew that the boy was lying but what could he do, call child services? If the boy left, that would not get rid of his problem. There was no alternative, he had to respect the boy's wishes, no matter what his personal feelings were.

"Here is your usual fee." Steel gave the boy the same amount as yesterday but the boy gave him back the twenty.

"It's really too much, Sir."

Steel could see that the boy had been beaten, probably for having too much money.

"See you tomorrow then, kid." Steel braved a smile as he stood in front of the suffering boy.

"Sure, see you tomorrow, Sir," replied the boy, trying to break a smile.

"Steel, call me Steel."

The boy nodded.

As Steel walked off his guts moved. He had a bad feeling about the boy, and he had to do something fast.

TWENTY-NINE

AT THE STATION, STEEL left the elevator and headed for McCall's desk where he found her checking her emails from the previous day.

"Morning," she greeted him, but her words fell flat when she saw the expression on his face.

"Morning," he replied, the thought of the bruised boy still uppermost in his thoughts.

"What's up?" she said, appearing to be actually concerned.

"Yesterday I got my shoes shined by this brilliant young lad—we spoke for ages about this and that. He had so much life, it was refreshing."

McCall was now waiting for the punch line.

"This morning he looked like he had gone twelve rounds with Tyson."

"Did he say anything about it?" she asked, now feeling actual concern.

"No, he said he fell down the stairs, but it's so frustrating when I know he's covering up for someone." Steel looked as he could hardly contain his anger.

McCall tried to reason with him: "You know, unless he, or someone else, says something we can't do anything."

He knew she was right, but what could he do?

"Look, do you want me to call child services?" she asked, picking up her phone.

He gave her a puppy-dog look and put his hand on top of hers, and she put down the receiver.

"I get the feeling that if we did that, things would get worse."

She knew he felt the situation was bigger than either of them could know, and she felt he was powerless to stop the inevitable, whatever it was.

"Coffee?" he asked, grabbing her cup.

"Yes, please." She was surprised at this sudden change in mood.

The English detective walked over to the coffee room to make a couple of cups of the foul-smelling brew. On his return, he placed the cup of steaming coffee down on the desk. She thanked him and smiled. This was a new type of behavior that she had not expected from him, and she had to admit it fitted him admirably.

Steel sipped the coffee, trying not to inhale the fumes that arose from the cup. Taking a sip, his face screwed up as the vile-tasting liquid pierced the back of his throat and the taste of burnt coffee filled his mouth.

"Really, you actually drink this?" he said in incredulity. "Or is this interrogation coffee?"

She smiled and took a big sip of the brew, looking him straight in the eye as if it was some macho test. All the while, she was concealing the need to vomit because of the horrible taste.

Rise of a Phoenix

A shiver ran down Steel's spine at the thought of the ghastly flavour.

"What's wrong, Steel?" she giggled. "Can't take your coffee?"

The two of them spent the next few hours looking though the diaries and date planners, not coming up with anything of interest. McCall leant back in her chair, her arms stretching wide; this had the effect of her tight-fitting V-neck jumper being pushed close up against her ample breasts. A young male officer who was passing by saw this and, as he stared, he bumped straight into the Captain.

"What are you doing, boy, were you bottle-fed or something?" the senior officer bellowed at the frightened young cop. "Now it was goddamn lucky one of us wasn't carrying a cup of that puke we call coffee!"

The young cop looked like he didn't know which way to run. He spotted the opening elevator and made for it, leaving the Captain chuckling to himself.

Then he turned to McCall. "And as for you McCall, watch what you're doing with those things will you? Someone could get hurt."

They both laughed.

"Sorry, Captain. What's more we don't want Mr Steel here getting a heart attack, do we?"

Steel looked up at the mention of his name. "Those are things that I can handle." He hurried on, not wanting to encourage any bawdy comments. "The coffee, however, No!"

He stood up and made for the elevator.

"Where the hell are you going?" asked the Captain, still chuckling to himself.

"To get a bit of heaven," he replied, "To get a bit of heaven."

THIRTY

DR DAVIDSON HAD RETURNED to his room at the precinct and was busy with the new data on the victims. As he sat there at the desk which was now brimming over with paperwork, he made notes from this page and that; "*fascinating*," he kept saying to himself, going through the transcripts with equal fascination. He was a man possessed by what he had found; this killer was, for him, the ultimate psychopath.

As McCall and Steel entered the room she knocked loudly, but he was busy and didn't seem to hear. She looked at Steel with a *can you believe him* look, then she tried coughing, but still he didn't answer.

"Morning, Doc." She said loudly. This certainly had an effect. The doctor glared at her and she stared right back at him. He seemed discomfited by her actions. After all, he was usually the one in charge but she had somehow turned the tables. It was a new, fascinating experience for him.

"Can I help you, Detective?" he said slowly, his voice grating, ranging in pitch from high to low.

"Well, yes, I thought that was the point of you being here?"

Steel tried to hide the smile as she took the doc down a couple of pegs.

"Forgive me," Dr Davidson apologized.

"You see I'm used to working alone you see and, er…"

Then he looked at Steel in surprise. "Who is he?" He pointed to the other detective, who was looking at the doctor's information board.

"That is Detective Steel, don't mind him, he's British."

Steel turned round and adjusted his sunglasses with his middle finger.

"Pleased to meet you, Sir." Steel walked towards the strange doctor and extended a hand so they could shake, but the doctor ignored it and looked straight through him.

"So what have you got so far?" Sam McCall asked, laughing to herself at the Englishman's rebuff.

"Well, your man is calculated, brilliant, methodical, and cunning, which makes him the most dangerous character you may have ever tracked."

They all moved forwards towards the information boards. There were pictures of the victims and their particular characteristics written down under their names.

"He is a master with the scalpel and other medical tools; he is well-versed in surgical methods," added the arrogant medical man.

"And you know this how?" asked Steel, somewhat uncomfortable with the way Davidson appeared to be practically in awe of the killer.

"Well let's look at the fact. All the cuts are precise—we know this because most people when they cut someone up, there are saw marks all over the bone." He pointed to a close-up picture of the severed stump where an arm had been removed.

"As you can see, it's a straight cut, no jagged cuts, which means he took his time and he knew what to use."

Steel looked closer at the photos and shook his head.

"What's wrong, Detective, not got the stomach for this?" The doctor laughed. "Doesn't surprise me, though." He was clearly on a mission to undermine the Englishman.

"Really?" Steel replied, keeping his cool. "Please do tell me why you're not surprised?" Steel stepped back from the board to face the doctor, who had a very strange grin on his face.

"Well now, let us see. You feel that you are a man of action but something tells me the only fighting you have seen is on television. You wish to feel as if you are intimidating to others so that's why you wear those sunglasses. And I bet you wear them all the time, don't you?"

McCall stood there and, as she listened, what he was saying started to make sense.

"Anything else?" Steel asked in a cool and calm voice, his arms behind his back.

"Well, if you insist."

By now a crowd had formed outside the room with Tooms and the Captain in the front, ready to jump onto the man who was being insulted, just in case he decided to rip the doctor apart.

"I imagine your mother and the rest of your family lived in a slum residence and your father took off when you were just a child. And that's why you seem to be in awe of people with money, yet you try to dress like someone who has the funds, because you want to be one of them."

Steel stood there, arms still behind his back, unflinching

as the doctor made a fool of him, ripped apart his reputation and his family. By this time everyone could see the expression of blood-lust on the doctor's face as he proceeded with his assault.

"You are a nobody, Detective," said the doctor with a vicious grin, "and by the way, how did an Englishman become part of NYPD?"

This question suddenly touched a nerve with everyone in the room. Steel saw the crowd in the adjacent main office suddenly start to talk amongst themselves. *The doc was right*, they all thought: Steel could see that sentiment on their faces.

"I must say, Doctor, what you said was most entertaining, for a piece of fiction. Unfortunately as I have been reminded several times by the finest cop I have ever had the good fortune of knowing, we work on facts, not hunches or feelings. I mean if we did work that way, I would say that you are a man that likes to put down people that you consider a threat, using any means necessary. You reached the top of your field, and now you probably spend all your days treating old women who have lost their pets, or are depressed for some other reason." This time the smug face of the doctor had turned sour and his teeth began to show.

John Steel wasn't finished with him. "You tried to malign my family, so I would have to say you were an orphan. Probably were never were picked by adoptive parents. No, I would say that you were so odious that you scared people, for which reason they never put you in the limelight to be picked. I would also say you that have a problem with women, that's why you avoid talking to the pretty ones."

Davidson's face soured.

"Added to that, you have a strange fascination with death, *too much of a fascination* perhaps. Cops have to live with the ghastly aspects of death, but someone with your qualifications?"

Davidson's face was almost purple at this point, but McCall noticed that throughout the confrontation Steel was calm, maybe too calm. Steel was just about to slam another nail in the man's coffin when they were all disturbed by the *ding* of the elevator, and an officer from downstairs brought in the small shoe-shine boy, Luke. Steel turned to see the boy and he forgot all about the idiot doctor, to the relief of the Captain and Tooms.

"It's OK, Colin, he's with me." The officer nodded and his hands left the boy's shoulders.

"So did you get it?" Steel asked his young friend.

The boy nodded and handed over a large duffel bag to Steel, who unzipped the bag, looked inside and sniffed.

"Oh yeh, that's the stuff," he said.

Everyone one looked puzzled.

"You see?" piped up the doctor, who had found a new weapon to use against Steel, after witnessing what had just happened. "He has brought drugs into the precinct. And he has used a small boy as his courier."

Davidson stood pointing at the boy and Steel. The other man turned towards him and smiled.

"Wow, OK, Doc, you got me. The bag is stacked with bricks of drugs. How much would you say?"

Steel turned to the boy, who was sharp enough to know when the doc was being played.

"I couldn't say, Sir, but I know you owe me a tip," the boy said with a grin.

The detective cracked a smile and tossed a hundred dollars to the kid, who quickly pushed it into his pocket.

"Now you get back to your shoe stand, oh and the same again every two weeks." He looked round the room. "Tell you what, I'll let you know if there are any changes."

Rise of a Phoenix

The boy shot off, using the side stairs.

"Steel, what the hell is in the bag?" Sam McCall asked.

Steel grinned and headed for the coffee room, followed by the detectives who'd been watching the incident, leaving the doctor standing alone, unwilling to move, trying to prove a point. Getting to the refreshment area, Steel took the jugs from the machines and emptied its nasty contents; he prepared the three machines then reached into the bag and took out a small black-and-blue vacuum-wrapped packet.

"Steel, what the hell is?" asked the Captain. "Is that what I think it is? Now don't you mess with me."

Steel just stood there and slowly nodded as he raised the brick up.

"Ladies and gentlemen," he said, tipping away the old coffee and replenishing the water in the machines. He opened the package and topped up the machines with the dark powder, then, after pressing the 'on' button he waited. Before saying another word he listened for the distinctive *burrrr* as the hot water was being passed through the coffee powder.

"I give you a little taste of heaven." The machines stopped and the detectives poured into the room like some a zombie horde. Steel sought refuge beside the doctor who, as Steel approached, scowled at him.

"And what do you want now, detective?"

Steel bit his lip at the doctor's unfriendly tone.

"Look, Doctor, we are both professionals and we are here to do a job. I'm here because I have to be, you are here because you need to be, so let's just forget out differences and be professional." And with that he produced two cups of coffee from behind his back, and giving one to the Doc he raised his as a sign they should clink them together in agreement.

The doctor paused, shrugged, and tapped his cup against

Steel's. McCall stood watching the display between the two rivals and shook her head. Every time she thought she had gotten a read on Steel he threw in a curve ball. She sipped her coffee for the first time; *oh it is good*, she thought as her eyes rolled back.

THIRTY-ONE

THE HOUR WAS LATE and Steel said his goodnights. The sun had sunk below the horizon and washes of colour painted the skyline with purples, reds, and oranges. He decided that he would go and check on the boy. As he approached the spot where the boy's shoe-shine box normally stood, there was just a blank space, and a sickening feeling crawled over him like a heavy blanket. He kept walking, hoping to see a sign of Luke but he saw nothing. The streets were silent as he ventured home and he hoped and prayed the boy was OK.

As his key slid into the door and Steel entered the apartment, he hung up his jacket, then moved to the drinks cabinet and picked up the bottle of Glendronach whisky, poured the golden colored liquid into a crystal glass, and took a hit. Putting down the glass, he poured another, and, the glass now half full, he moved to the window, and sat at the chaise longue that faced the window. He looked out across the expanse of the city and feared for the boy's safety.

As the dawn came, everything appeared to be covered with a blue-grey tint. The air was fresh and moist, and a figure in a black hooded tracksuit pounded his way towards Battery Park. The streets were almost empty, with only the noise from the garbage trucks' hydraulics echoing through the maze of buildings, cop cars raising here and there, sirens tooting now and then.

Detective John Steel liked to jog at this time of day; the coolness of the air cleared his airways from the filth of the previous day's traffic. He stopped by the railings that overlooked the bay, the brown-coloured water lapped up the sides of posts that were sunk down into the murky depths.

Taking a bottle of water from the pouch on his belt, he popped the stopper top and took a mouthful of the cold liquid and swilled it in his mouth, then swallowed. Finding a bench, he sat and looked out across the bay and saw the blood red of the sun rise. He reflected that in ancient times a blood-red sky meant blood had been spent the night before. He hoped to God that was not the case, thinking back to the boy, Luke. Jumping up, he set off once more.

Sundays held a special place in McCall's week. It was the one time she could go and see her mom in Boston. She would go every weekend if work allowed. Her mother had a small place in the quiet part of the city; it was a small residential area with white picket fences and kids playing in the street. The sun shone brightly, a breeze rustled through the trees, and as she stood at the front porch of her mom's house she closed her eyes and listened to the nothingness, and it was great.

Reaching forwards she pressed the bell. A loud *ding dong* echoed through the house, and moments later a cheerful voice called from somewhere near the back of the house.

"I'll be there in a minute," was what she heard, then she

Rise of a Phoenix

saw through the small slits of glass embedded in the door a figure moving quickly towards her. Her mom opened up the door, a small elderly lady in a long white dress that had flowery patterns on it, reminiscent of the 1970s. Her hair was dyed brown and showed signs of a recent perm.

The two women embraced at the sight of one another.

"I don't understand why you never use the key I gave to you," her mother said, a big grin on her round face.

"You know why, Mom? It's because I love the look on your face when you open the door. It's great to be here." Her mother dragged her inside.

"Leave your case there and come into the kitchen," her mother told the detective. "I made some coffee and an apple pie."

McCall didn't need to be asked twice; as she entered the large kitchen a waft of freshly percolated coffee and cinnamon filled her nostrils and tickled her taste buds, causing her to stop and to inhale the rich smell of home. She sat down one of the wooden chairs in the middle of the room. The kitchen was quite large with old-style fittings, and Sam had always loved it here. The house was fitted with a lot of stained wood and brass doors and cosy furniture.

McCall's mother passed over some cups, saucers and side plates, and Sam helped set the table . Her mother brought over a large bone-china pot filled with fresh coffee and a large pie on a plate that matched the tea set. The younger woman poured the coffee and her mother cut slices of the hot steaming pie and put them on plates. Placing mounds of fresh cream onto the side of her plate, Sam dug into the pie with a small fork, the hard-topped pastry cracking down upon the apple filling, causing chunks of apple and filling to ooze from the sides before the top broke with a mouth-watering crunch.

The two women talked about this and that, who was going out with who, and all the normal local gossip, which Sam so enjoyed to hear. Sometimes McCall thought, why didn't she just quit and have a normal life like this? And then she remembered the reason she became a cop in the first place. Remembering something difficult, Sam's face straightened and her mother held her hand, sensing that her daughter needed comfort. McCall snapped back to reality at her touch.

"It's OK to remember him, dear, don't let his death drive you along the wrong path," The older lady said.

McCall looked puzzled for a second. "What? Oh no Mom, it's not that I'm thinking about, it's something else."

Her mother had one rule: don't bring your work home with you, and McCall liked it like that.

Steel made his way through the park. He had already run for miles but he found it was that he needed to get the past week out of his system. The path stretched on through the landscape, the leaves on the trees glistened with morning sunlight. He had caught the metro north to run in Central Park: the open space and the endless green gave him time to think things through without being under pressure.

As he ran down the dusty path he went under an overpass. The small red brick bridge echoed with the clip clop of horses working hard to carry tourists up and down the park. Reaching the other side, he noticed a man slumped over. Steel stopped for a moment, and looked round, finding that he was alone apart from this person. As he approached he saw that the guy wore a tracksuit, its red colour reflected off the bright green paintwork of the bench. He approached the man cautiously. Using just two fingers he pressed against his neck, checking for a pulse. But before he could react, some material was flung over his head—it felt like a bag of some kind. He fought hard, but he felt a sharp pain in his neck. Then, just before he blacked out, he heard a voice that was deep and gravely:

"Nighty, night, princess."

Then John Steel slipped into darkness.

McCall and her mother sat in the garden of her Aunt Peg's house, attending a family barbeque. Sue McCall had moved to the area, closer to her sister Pegg, after the death of Sam's father, because the old family home was too big and had too many memories. Pegg was on 'salad duty' and Martin, her husband, was on the 'grill duty'. Sam watched as the tall grey-haired man stood in front of a large black grill that had been built into what appeared to be the old chimneystack of a house. The garden was in full bloom with an array of colours, and people were mingling, laughing and joking.

It was a glorious day; the sun was high and not a cloud spoilt the blue sky. The McCall girls stood talking with another group of people who were waiting for the food.

"So Beth tells me you're a police officer, wow, that's brilliant. Say have you got anything to do with those grisly murders?" said a tall balding man.

McCall looked him up and down.

"You're a reporter, right?" she shot back.

The man seemed shocked at first, and then it came to him where he had seen her before. "Hey, are you *the* Detective McCall? Wow, I must say this is brilliant."

She looked puzzled.

"Well, having you in the family," he enthused, "well that could really be good for business, I can tell you."

McCall was just about to put him on his ass when her aunt stepped in.

"Henry Pollack, you should be ashamed," she told him. "Plus you know the house rules, no work talk in this house."

She gave him a saver look, he apologized and moved on.

"Mother, who is that," Sam asked her mom "Do you know him?" she said quietly, unobtrusively pointing in the tall man's direction.

"That, my dear, is your cousin Beth's new man, Henry Pollack."

McCall searched her mind for the name and came up blank.

"Never heard of him," Sam shook her head.

"No, nobody has. Apparently he's new in the game and is aiming to make it big, as fast as he can, so I would watch it, kiddo." Her mother tapped the side of her nose.

THIRTY-TWO

JOHN STEEL WAS WOKEN by a blast of cold water in his face, some of which went in his mouth. He tried to spit out but his lips were blocked by something, it felt like some kind of cloth. That's when he remembered the bag pushed over his head before the pain and the blackout. He knew he'd been abducted, but something else felt really strange about his predicament too. The bag was ripped from his head and then he realized why he had this weird feeling of disorientation. He was hanging upside down, his hands bound by what felt like handcuffs.

In front of him stood three large men, each wearing a blue shiny tracksuit. Another man, who was obviously the boss, was sitting on a bar stool. He was bald headed, stocky and had the beginnings of a straggly beard, and wore a black pinstriped suit.

"Good morning, Mr Steel, oh forgive me, it's Detective now isn't it? My name is Sal De Torre." The seated man's voice was as heavy as his build.

Steel felt a massive blow to the back of his head, but had no idea where it came from. As the momentum forced his body to turn, he noticed several others dressed in the same type of tracksuit, each of them as ugly as the next. The central man of the trio was obviously the hitter. Steel noticed that one of the others, who looked to be in his early twenties, , was dancing on the tips of his toes.

The detective took a moment to assess the situation, straining to see as much as he could:

A: he was upside down, tied in position by a rope that was attached to a large hook. The hook was on a chain that ran down from a movable crane device.

B: he was handcuffed.

C: there were around five goons guarding him.

He made a note of their weapons, the exits and more importantly, the best way he could get down. He had been stripped of his hooded top, and just his t-shirt remained covering his upper body; as he gently circled round, dangling as he was, he could see that the men were not heavily armed, which was always a good thing in this kind of situation.

"So it's still morning is it?" he asked.

Again, he felt a blow, but this time it was to his back. He winced but didn't show any pain in his face, just anger. He looked around to see the youngest of them with a large grin on his face. He looked like a kid, a bruiser trying to make his mark with the big boys.

"Indeed it is morning," answered Sal de Torre. "I don't believe in wasting time, do you?"

"Well now that you—"

Smack.

He felt another punch. This time the kid laughed aloud.

Rise of a Phoenix

"Why am I here may I ask?"

Smack.

His ears rang after taking a kick to the head. He shook off the pain.

"We ask the questions here, got that?" The young man spat out the words, while the boss raised a hand to calm him down.

"Now, now, that's no way to treat our guest. Detective Steel has a right to know why we have brought him here."

"Thank you."

This time he felt a kick to his lower back. The boy was skipping at the excitement of it all. As he swivelled on his chain, the attacker saw Steel's eyes for the first time and felt the full intensity of a stare that nearly made him pee his pants.

"So, Mr Steel, it is true what they say about you?" De Torres laughed. "Please return Mr Steel's glasses to him before young Stan loses his breakfast, will you?" A man walked forward and slid his sunglasses back into place.

"Now to business," The large man went on. He was now playing with a pearl-handled stiletto blade, picking bits out of the chair beneath him. From his name, Steel assumed him to be Italian. "Why are you looking for Santini and why did you put several of my colleges in the hospital?" .

"For a start—"

He took a hit direct in the small of his back. Steel was now getting bored with this and just wished they would cooperate before he killed them all.

"Look if dick head is going to keep hitting me every time I open my mouth this may take some time," he growled. "So you may need to order refreshments."

There was another blow, this time to the back of his legs.

"Yes, you are absolutely right, Mr Steel. Stan can you lay off? Just until we are finished? Then you can have some fun, OK?" He looked at the kid, who was all ready to deliver another blow.

Young Stan reached above Steel's handcuffs, and was relieved to find that the man's watch had not been removed. Feeling behind the main body, he found the handcuff key.

"Your colleagues started hitting him," Stan replied. "I just defended myself and my business with Mr. Santini. I wish to take it up with Mr. Santini." The kid lost his frustration and kicked Steel in the back, but the detective had anticipated the move and had tensed his muscles. Instead of absorbing the blow, Steel was therefore pushed forward. As he swung backwards fast, he managed to use his body's momentum to come crashing straight into the face of the kid. The air was filled with blood and bone as the boy's face exploded from the impact. Steel used the momentum once more to try to swing across to the other side and even the odds a bit, but as the goon in front of him stood ready for Steel's crashing body, all he felt was something thrown at his face.

He looked down to see a pair of handcuffs laying in the dirt. By the time the goon looked up at Steel he was ripped off his feet and thrown into the path of two others who were racing forwards to get the Englishman. All three men disappeared behind some old crates. There was a loud crash.

Steel was now swinging about like a clock's pendulum gone wrong. Bullets flew all over as one man raced through with an automatic machine pistol. Sparks flew everywhere, and people started to dive for cover. Two men raced towards Steel brandishing baseball bats, planning ready to play piñata with his head; unfortunately for them, as he swung in their direction a stray bullet cut him free from his foot shackles. Maintaining his momentum and direction he clothes-lined the goons, then rolled to safety.

Steel found himself behind a group of bashed-up old lockers, which had been laid flat. He lay there hiding from the erratic gunfire from the man who had inadvertently shot him free. Hollow loud thuds filled the air as the bullets impacted against his shelter. Steel dared to risk glancing out, to see De Torre standing at the far end near a door, shouting for the others to kill Steel. He was suddenly pulled back as a hail of bullets impacted near his head.

"Nearly got you that time, you son-of-a-bitch!" yelled the man holding the machine gun. Steel heard a click then the sound of metal hitting the floor followed by another click: the man had reloaded the automatic weapon.

Steel knew he had to do something, but what?

The hail of bullets rained against the lockers again, but the firing sound from the weapon was getting louder, which meant he was getting closer.

Steel scanned the area in front of him and found a container, which was full of what appeared to be old metal fence rods; he saw the sharp points sticking out and judged that they might have been old church railings or something similar.

"Come out, Mr Steel," called the man with the gun. "I will make it quick. OK, all you have to do is stand up and it will all be over."

John's enemy had the weapon held out in front of him, the butt of the gun dug into his hip for stability.

"You got that right!" Steel yelled.

The gunman was shocked at the sight of Steel suddenly standing up and throwing something. Before he realized what was happening, the point of the rail impacted into his left shoulder, making him turn as he fired. The spray of bullets swept up the room towards the boss.

De Torres's large face dropped as he realized the oncoming hail of hot brass was heading his way. He made for the door but was too late, as one of the projectiles found its mark and blew a hole in his leg. The pain shot though his body but he grabbed on to the door frame to stabilize himself and, with a trail of fresh blood marking his way, he managed to escape.

Steel smirked to himself as he watched the large man limp away. *That should slow him down*, he thought.

Then, apparently from nowhere, a hook attached to a long steel cable came crashing down in front of the detective, making him leap backwards. The man who'd thrown it was large and muscular, and covered with tattoos, his shaven head blue with regret. He was grinning like a maniac.

As Steel observed the psycho with the hook and cable, he couldn't help notice his oversized stubble-covered jaw.

The hook impacted again, this time to the side of the detective. Steel rolled out of the way. The man swung the steel cable above his head, picking his target. Steel stood up and the cable and hook flew towards him. As Steel ducked the man saw with horror the blades of the giant cooling fans behind them spinning fast. There was a load clank as the hook and metal rope was caught up in the fast-spinning wheel. As Steel's attacker looked on, the trail of cable quickly snaked its way towards the turbine only for him to then remember he had tied it around his ankle.

He was ripped forward, screaming as he went, trying to unravel the knot he had made to secure the weapon to him. The man slid closer and closer to his fate, when suddenly a mass of metal and wood came crashing down, as the stacked-up cargo crates to his front were tipped over.

Rise of a Phoenix

To his relief, the crates were blocking his way to certain doom. As he took a breath, a figure leapt upon him, knocking him out.

John Steel had to find a way out and fast. His quarry was getting away and he had questions he wanted to ask. He ran for the door De Torre had escaped through, running across the body-ridden floor. But he suddenly stopped and started to back off as a massive hulk of a man stood in his path. The hulk was bald-headed

With some sort of tribal tattoo covering one side of his face, he was a mix of flab and muscle and stood around six-foot nine inches tall. But Steel was more concerned in the fire axe he held.

The Englishman stood in the middle of the room semi-crouched, ready for anything, except for the speed with which the monster came at him, swinging the red fire axe. Steel managed to roll out of the way just in time to avoid a blow that could have split him straight down the middle; sparks flew from the concrete as the axe impacted.

I thought this was too easy, Steel thought to himself. The huge man turned and came forwards once more. Steel ran to the side, where there was plenty of cover, but he didn't have time for this skirmish. Quickly he looked round and found a staircase leading upwards to a gantry next to the dirty windows. The swoosh of metal slicing air was followed by the clang of metal against metal. Steel dropped to the ground, narrowly evading another killer blow. The beast looked down to see Steel's boot kicking him full force into his groin area, but he just smiled at Steel and swung the axe downwards. There were more sparks as Steel made a backward roll, again narrowly being missed by the razor-sharp axe blade.

He made his way to the other side of the room, throwing

bits of heavy metal at his pursuer, but the only effect this had was to show Steel that hand-to-hand combat was definitely out of the question.

The detective stood with his back against a wooden pillar; he was sucking in air, his hands on his knees. The man came up slowly, savoring the seconds before he put him down, a large grin across his massive face. Grasping the axe's handle in both hands he swung with all of his might, always keeping Steel in view. A massive crash filled the room as the axe splintered and smashed the wooden beam, which acted as one of the supports holding some sheet metal on which stood around fifteen steel barrels. The man screamed and covered his face as he was suddenly buried under a mass of metal and wood.

"Smashing," Steel said to himself with a grin.

Picking himself up, Steel headed for the stairwell, and the old metal gave a tinny sound as he ran up towards one of the dirty windows. The building estate was large and mostly disused: rows and rows of hangars and warehouses stood lined up, only broken by the odd path for vehicle access. A large man limped his way towards a warehouse with a faded green door. He was panting heavily, and then stopped to get his breath. Sal De Torre had heard the crash, and reasoned that maybe his large henchman had disposed of Steel, yes, and that was the nose. He savored the image of Steel being broken apart, then split in two. He smiled to himself. However, his joy did not last as he witnessed one of the upper level windows being smashed, allowing Steel to get out.

"Shit, shit!" he said, panicking as he limped towards his goal. Reaching the door he swung it open. The metal door creaked and scraped on the concrete floor, and slamming it shut behind him he looked for old desks and lockers, anything to make a barricade. Inside the room he'd found it was dimly lit, and the only source of light came from the filthy skylight above him. It was a perfect hiding place, filled with shadows and large empty storage crates. He would be safe for now.

As Steel broke free from the building, he stepped out in time to see his quarry disappear into a building across from where he stood. Stopping for a moment to get his bearings, Steel made a plan of action, taking note of possible dangers and ambush points, and, as he surveyed the ground, he saw something that made him smile.

Making his way to the roof by means of some old stacked-up crates he found a quick way down. A telephone cable ran from the tower behind him to the building across the way, and, jumping down again, he found some chain. *That will do nicely*, he thought with a grin. Going back to the cable, he threw the chain over, then slid down. A trail of orange sparks followed him until he dropped down and rolled behind the wall.

He stole a look at the building that Sal had gone into. There were no guards outside, and none on the roof. This was too easy. Moving from cover to cover he made his way down past the building to set things in motion.

It seemed like hours that Sal had been waiting in the safety of the building, and he began to feel anxious.

"He is playing with me, he thinks I will come out first but I have news for him," he thought, laughing to himself.

However, he knew he couldn't last long in there: something would have to happen soon.

BANG! BANG! BANG!

The sound echoed through the small storage room in

which Sal De Torre was hiding. Had Steel found him, he wondered? Sal found an old shovel and grasped the handle and held it as if he was playing baseball.

BANG! BANG! BANG!

Again, the door shook with every impact,

"OK, you bastard, I'm ready for you," he said under his breath, panicking as sweat poured from his forehead. He had just seen Detective Steel take a team of his men apart while handcuffed. He didn't dare to think what he might do free-handed.

"Boss, boss you in there?"

Sal's heart skipped a beat at the sound of the man's voice.

"Tony, is that you?"

"Yeh, I got Kenny here as well."

The boss smiled. Good, he thought with relief. They could finally get the hell out of there.

He threw the barricade out of the way and ripped open the door. Before him his two men stood there, battered and bruised, but alive.

"Come on, let's get the hell out of here before that psycho cop comes back," said Sal, ignoring the arguments from his boys. They saw their black saloon waiting for them, and it was the best sight Sal had seen for a long time, and leaping into the driver's seat, Tony turned the key to start the engine, but nothing happened.

"What's wrong?" asked Sal, looking round for any sign of Steel.

"Damn thing won't start," said Tony in a panic. Both men looked at each other, then they noticed Kenny on the floor, pointing out of the side window. As they turned to look what the fuss was about the side windows exploded inwards and the whole car was pushed sideways.

Rise of A Phoenix

"What the f—" Tony nearly finished the sentence before realizing that the car was being lifted.

Steel sat in the cab of the large forklift and had a satisfied grin on his face. To his amusement he could see the men being thrown about inside the car. One of the guys was trying to get out of the other door.

"Now, now we are just getting started," Steel said loudly and then swerving, he rammed the car into the corner of a building. , now completely sealed in he made his way forward.

Sal and the others were battered and scratched, glass and bits of masonry filled the car.

"Where the fuck are we going, boss?" screamed Tony over the din of the forklift's engine.

"I don't know but it can't be good, the guy is fucking nuts."

With a crash, the car was being tipped onto its roof. They came to a stop, and the sudden silence cut through the air.

"OK, boys let's get out of here before that whack job comes back," said Sal, but he spoke too soon, as a shadow fell across the tarmac in front of them.

"Sal DeTorre, good morning." Steel said, sounding amused.

"Screw you!" said Sal spitting the words.

Steel came and knelt down in front of them.

"OK, so where were we? Oh yes, where is Santini?"

"I don't know, plus I wouldn't tell anyway. So go on, cop, lock me up!"

"See, that's a very tempting idea, but not really effective." Steel answered.

Sal was now getting scared. This was no ordinary cop, he was something else. He felt it, and it didn't feel good. Steel got up and walked away. The men let out the breath of anticipation they had been holding.

"What the hell is that noise?" asked Kenny, as the faint sound of an engine, possibly from a rig, was getting closer. Then the car shook with impact as Steel, who was sat in a semi, ploughed into the engine side of the car and was pushing it in to another. There were two semis nose-to-nose with the saloon car in between them, on its roof. The men screamed for their lives at the sound of metal and plastic being compressed. Then there was silence.

"OK, as I was saying, where is Santini?" Steel had lost his smile and his patience.

"I don't know, I swear, nobody does." Sal was begging, his hands clenched together so tightly his knuckles were white.

"How does he contact you?"

"Different ways, note under doors, under windshield wipers always, but never by phone."

Steel smiled slightly, *smart boy*, he thought.

"You don't find him, see," Sal said, the colour returning to his face.

"He finds you."

"Not if I find him first."

And with that, John Steel was gone.

Sal and the others scrambled to get out before the wailing sirens of the cop cars got there.

"What a fucking day," Sal thought as they made it out of the car.

THIRTY-THREE

MONDAY MORNING BROUGHT IN a new sunrise to a new day and Detective Sam McCall was hoping for a fresh lead on the killer. McCall sat her desk reading some reports when Steel walked in. Even she had to admit he looked good in the black suit, with its strange three-quarter length jacket that almost hid the shiny black silk shirt, that had the top few buttons undone.

She tried to pretend she hadn't seen him and hoped she had not had her mouth open in surprise. From behind him came a wolf whistle and he just raised his hand to thank his unknown admirer.

"Morning," she said, still burying her head in the paperwork,

"Good morning. And how was your weekend?" he asked, clearly happy with himself.

"It was good thanks, I went to see my mom," she replied, somewhat surprised at his interest."And yours? Did you do anything for fun or were you just chasing bad guys?" she giggled at her joke.

"No, but it was very positive. I tracked down some old friends, got tied up with them all morning but then they had to go—I guess they had a pressing engagement," he smiled, at the thought of what had really happened.

McCall flashed him a concerned look, not really wanting to know what he was talking about, but she had the feeling that either way it could not be good.

Tony and Tooms came in, their expressions spoke volumes, suggesting that their weekends had not been successful.

"Hi guys, what's up?" she asked, not really wanting to hear of any problems until at least midday.

"While you were off for the weekend we got a nasty one." Tooms's face screwed up at the thought. He held the file close to his chest as McCall reached for it, a puzzled look crossing her face,

"Why didn't anybody say we got a case?" she asked.

"Cause we got assigned the case. Sorry, the boss said you two would be too close to this one."

Now she really was puzzled and annoyed. "What do you mean, close to it?" she asked, clearly put out.

"It was your boy from the theatre that Tarzan here decided to put into hospital after using him for a crash mat."

"Yes, what about him?" asked McCall, a terrible feeling creeping over her as she looked at Steel.

"Someone went to pay him a visit," Tony said, sounding angry,

"Cool. So who was it and did we get a name on them?" asked Steel, looking excited.

"No, not really. Whoever it was crept in like a ghost and

Rise of a Phoenix

cut him up pretty good." Tony said, looking as if the memory made him nauseous.

"OK, not cool. But how did it happen? There were cops on the door, right?" Steel said in surprise.

"Like a ghost, you said?" McCall commented. "So what did you do this weekend, Steel?" Her eyes were burning with suspicion.

"Come on," Steel replied, resenting the implication. "You can't be serious! You don't think I went in and stabbed the silly bastard, do you?"

"Look, Friday I was playing poker with some friends." Steel said at last.

"I bet you're good at that, because you don't give anything away, do you?" She taunted him. Her voice was cold and hard. Ever since the theatre incident she'd begun to get good vibes about him but now, well, she had no idea what to think.

McCall grabbed her cup and made for the coffee room, and Tooms and Tony followed, leaving John Steel behind.

"So what did you find out about him?" She asked Tooms as he sat on the edge of the table while the others gathered round.

"Well, I spoke to my buddy from the SEALs and he said that our boy there was attached to whatever team was going out. They classed him as a '*lone wolf*', and he was real good at making their job easier. He mainly specialized in hostage rescue. He would go in before a building was going to be stormed, and even the odds or get intelligence. They used to call him 'The phoenix', 'cause nothing could put him down." The room went quiet as they absorbed the revelation.

"OK, so he was in the military," McCall sounded almost disappointed he had a past.

"Nice, now we have a lead. What else did he say?" Tooms looked round making sure they were not been heard.

"If he is on your side you can walk away from pretty much anything."

"And if you're on the other side?" asked Tony.

Tooms just gave him a '*Don't go there*' look.

"And before that?" she asked confidently.

"Nothing. Officially the man didn't exist till he got to the TEAMS, then after an incident he fell off the world again until now." They watched Steel looking at the information board and flicking through notes.

"Oh yeh, you know who he is really friendly with?" Tooms said, getting some pictures out.

McCall shrugged. "No, who?"

He passed the photos across and McCall and Tony looked. "The mayor, Steel's buddy is the mayor."

"OK, we keep this to ourselves but if it becomes a problem we see the Captain," She told them. They all nodded in agreement. Tooms then pulled out a bit of paper and waved it around. McCall looked at him warily, unprepared for any more surprises.

"What's this now?" she asked, the strain of recent days starting to show in her voice.

"It's an address," said Tooms, with a smug smile.

"Is it a witness?" McCall asked.

Tooms shook his head.

"So whose address is it? Steel's?" Tony seemed almost excited at the prospect of knowing where this man lived. Tony had many images in his head of where John Steel lived, but he was also starting to feel a bit treacherous to be investigating another cop, even one as strange as Steel.

Rise of a Phoenix

"We I guess we all have somewhere to live, but most of us don't have an apartment on Central Park West."

The other two detectives' mouths dropped open.

"He lives on Central Park West?" repeated McCall.

Tooms nodded.

"How the hell can he afford a place there?" Now she was mad, McCall could feel the anger begin to swell within her. Was he a hit man or something? All sorts of weird ideas began to fill her head.

She turned to look towards the information board, where Steel had been moments earlier, but he'd gone. Had he caught on to the fact they were investigating his life, she wondered? She moved quickly out of the room just in time to catch Officer Brenda Grant walking past.

"Where is Detective Steel?" McCall asked urgently, surprising the female officer.

"Don't really know, he got a call from downstairs and shot off. He seemed quite upset." Officer Grant shrugged and headed towards the filing room.

McCall waved the others to follow and ran to the ground floor using the stairs. "Had somewhere to go, did he?" She said to herself. She had the address, which was in Harlem, so taking both cars they raced there to confront Steel about what the hell was going on.

As they approached, they saw police cars, ambulances, and two coroner's trucks. They pulled up and parked, got out of the cars and rushed forward. Then Sam saw Tina finishing some paperwork off. She had never seen Tina looking so sad before now.

Then she saw him. Steel was sitting on a step looking at his blood-soaked hands as though they did not belong to him.

McCall ran towards him, passing Tina as she went, unaware that her friend was trying to stop her. She was furious. Suddenly all those days of John Steel wearing down her defenses had made her angry enough to tell him how she felt.

"What's the matter?" she yelled at Detective Steel. "Did some gang member piss you off? Is that it? God, you come here thinking you can stop every little crime, well you can't!...This time you have gone too far, Mr. Steel!"

He looked at her and stood up slowly, his clothes sodden with blood. What the hell had he done, she thought?

"You're right, Detective, I can't," he answered. "Maybe I should stop trying." And with that he walked off, leaving her still boiling.

"We are not done yet, Steel," she shouted after him, but he just raised a hand as if to wave her away.

She made her way to Tina, who had just processed the last body and closed the body bag.

"So what has Dirty Harry done this time?" she asked, hoping to share the joke with her friend, but instead Tina just gave her a look of anger and disappointment.

"What?" Sam asked in surprise. "Why are you looking at me like that?"

Tina opened the bags, saying, "Look."

As Detective McCall peered inside she saw what appeared to the mortal remains of a boy. The other body bag contained the corpse of a woman, presumably his mother judging by her age and appearance, with similar injuries to her body. She noticed that the boy's jacket was the same type worn by the lad, Luke, who had brought the coffee into the precinct that day.

A lump filled her throat and tears rolled down her face. She was not just weeping for the boy and his mother, but for what she had done to Steel and what she had become.

Rise of a Phoenix

Detective McCall was told to go home and Steel had disappeared, so Tooms and Tony had to pick up the slack. The murderous Steve Johnson was now the DA's problem, and his lawyers would have a hell of a case due to the fact that when the cops burst in he was in the process of putting a hammer through his wife's skull. Plus, when asked why he did it he said that she would not give him money for booze and she just got in the way, after which he laughed. The lawyers would probably go for the insanity plea but the bastard deserved the chair, but that was not their call. "Thank God," Tooms thought.

McCall did not go home. Instead she went to the station gym and rode a million miles on the bike, followed by several rounds with the punch bag. Her black all-in-one gym suit clung to her sweaty body, enhancing her every curve; she could feel the hungry eyes of the men nearby on her, and she used the angry feeling of resentment at their uninvited attention to kick the hell out of the black worn bag. It swung with every hit as she gave it everything she had. Sam McCall showered, changed, and bought two coffees from the coffee shop round the corner. As she approached the morgue, she hoped to find Tina in a forgiving mood.

When McCall entered the morgue she was greeted by an angry ME, her eyes still red with rage. Sam McCall gingerly moved forward, coffee cup held in an outstretched hand, almost as a peace offering. Tina took the cup, almost snatching it from her friend's hand, while still giving her the evil eye.

"Look, I'm sorry I lost my temper back there and"

"Uh uh, girl, you do not apologies to me." Tina raised a hand to stop her. "You know who you have to say sorry to."

THIRTY-FOUR

FATHER GABRIEL O'DONNELL was always cheerful and good-spirited. He had no reason to be otherwise, for he had originally been a military chaplain and now he had a decent parish in New York, so all in all, life was good and less complicated than before. He had dark hair and his superficial appearance was that of a thin man, but in fact, under his garments his muscles and physique were those of an athlete.

Entering the church, he moved to the middle of the red-carpeted gantry and knelt, prayed for a few seconds, then crossed himself before the cross that stood at the end of the building. Standing up, he then made his way to the door in the far corner that led to the back rooms and his office. On the way he noticed that the confessional box was occupied. He entered his side of the cubicle and sat down, and slid the small shutter that separated the two cells. He crossed himself and kissed the rosary in his hand.

"Forgive me, Father, but I could not sin," said a shallow voice.

The priest shot up and opened the communicating door to find Detective John Steel sitting there covered in blood. The priest, shocked at seeing him, looked round and carried him to the back of the church and into his private office. Father O'Donnell was relieved and concerned that none of the blood was Steel's, but he had questions. He walked over to a large wooden globe that stood in a dark corner of the room and lifted the lid; inside sat several bottles of whisky, brandies, and scotches. Taking two glasses, he poured them both a drink from a well-aged whisky. Passing Steel the glass, O'Donnell brought his chair forward slightly and sat facing the confused-looking detective.

"Do you want to talk about it?" asked the priest, leaning back in the creaking leather chair. Steel stared into his glass, swirling the contents round, watching the liquid rise near the top and fall again to the bottom.

"A couple of days ago I was walking down past Grand Central when this kid pops up out of nowhere; 'can I shine your shoes Mr?' he said." Steel took a sip as the priest leant forward slightly.

"I swear when I saw him I thought it was Thomas, you know, the kid was the spitting image of him." Steel smiled slightly but was lost in his thoughts again.

"OK, so what happened, Jonny?" asked the priest, not really knowing if he actually wanted to know or not.

"Anyway, this kid and I got chatting and it turns out that he is earning the money to go to school, trying to make something of himself, but his dad is a drunk and a bully so I figured that the guy was swiping the boy's money."

The priest looked confused for a moment. "How do you know about the father? Did you follow the boy?"

"No, but I could tell. Every time I saw him he had fresh bruises, and there was this scared look on his face when I mentioned family."

The priest nodded. He too had seen what Steel had described, far too often.

Steel washed back the contents of the glass and the priest just swopped their glasses. He felt that if he got up to get a fresh one the moment would be lost.

"At the station today my work colleagues were having a private chat and I can only imagine what that was about." Steel took a swig from the glass.

"That's when I got the call from the uniforms downstairs, a disturbance at the kid's address."

The priest got up. He needed a drink, as he could only imagine what was coming next. Walking to the cabinet, he just grabbed the bottle and returned to his seat.

"We got to the address and there were other uniforms there waiting to go in." Steel looked up at his friend, but his pained expression was lost behind his glasses. "We burst in to see the guy with a hammer beating in the heads of the kid and his mother. There was blood everywhere." He downed the contents of his glass and the priest refilled it, his hands shaking, something that Steel noticed.

"Are you OK, Gabriel?" asked Steel, now concerned about his friend. The priest nodded and begged him to continue.

"As we get in Officer Pike, just a young kid but a good cop from what I have seen, well he goes in to disarm this scumbag and gets himself slammed against the wall. The guy has Pike pinned there and has a hammer raised, ready to smash the cop's head in." Steel shook his head and looked up at his friend, who was now pre-empting everything he was about to say in his head.

"So what did you do?" Knowing the answer before he said it, the priest asked anyway.

"The guy has this big blood-dripping hammer over his head and he stops and looks at the cop for a second then at me, then he smiles and raises the weapon further back to get a better swing."

"Did you shoot him?" Knowing Steel for so long, the question seemed redundant, but he asked it anyway.

"No!"

O'Donnell's face froze with surprise; Father Gabriel O'Donnell used to be in the TEAMs and knew Steel well. John Steel was a man who scared most of the toughest SEALs, not just because when he exploded he was nothing short of an animal, but because the man could move like a ghost: one member of the team called him 'unnatural' and another, who was of tribal Indian descent, called him a 'wraith'. But what he had just described went against the nature of the beast. Steel saw the look on his friend's face and smiled.

"Don't get me wrong, Gabriel, I wanted to blow this guy away so badly, but in a split second I had to make a choice."

"Between what exactly?" The priest was getting more and more surprised, and excited at the progress Steel had made.

"Between going back to what I was and losing everything I had worked for, or being a cop and not letting down the people I work with, and letting down you, my old friend."

The priest smiled and put a reassuring hand on Steel's knee.

"But one thing hasn't changed, my friend," Gabriel said, still grinning.

"What's that?" Steel looked worried.

"You're still full of crap, buddy."

They both laughed.

"Anyway, go on, now you have my attention," said the priest, sliding back in the seat and getting more comfortable.

"So this guy is smiling at me, the other cops have their pistols raised, and what do I do? I rugby tackle the bastard and while he is on the floor, *that's* when I drew my piece. I put it on his temple and looked him in the eyes." Steel took another hit from the glass.

"At first this guy taunted me to kill him—dared me to do it. But I knew that death was too quick for him and too much paperwork for me. No, this bastard was going to jail, where every depraved nut job with family waiting would want a piece of him."

At that point, the priest knew that the old Steel was still there, it was just that now he used thought instead of force to get things done. The problem was, which was deadlier?

"I had him. I could feel the anger swelling up inside of him, but then I told him he was going to live and that I would visit him every day if I had to remind him of what he had done, and that put the fear of God into him."

"Did you enjoy it?" asked O'Donnell, now getting worried.

"At first yes, but then I calmed down and cuffed him. Helped the cop who'd been attacked to his feet and the uniforms booked him."

"So are you OK, Jonny?"

"Yes, fine and that's the problem, after everything that happened. Well you know?"

The priest nodded.

"I'll get you a coffee," Gabriel said, taking the glass. Steel smiled and nodded.

THIRTY-FIVE

MCCALL WAS BACK AT her desk; after having a bit of a bawling out from the Captain, she returned to work. She sat at her work station and flicked through the many files on the three murders, forensic reports, and ME reports but she still drew a blank. Slamming the file she was reading shut, she stood up and moved to the set of information boards set up in front of her desk. One of these was a map of the city, which was covered by a plastic sheet so it could be written on repeatedly.

Standing back, she looked at the pins that had been placed there denoting which victim was found where. She sat on the back edge of her desk and looked closely at each pin, each line, and each name of every street. What was she missing, she wondered? Tony and Tooms walked up to her and both smiled at her. She had had a rough couple of weeks, there was no mistaking that, and she probably did deserve a ticking off, but what had happened was really bad timing.

"What are you thinking?" asked Tooms, as he sat next to her and sipped his coffee.

"Don't know yet," she said slowly, as though some idea was stirring at the back of her mind.

"Did you get anything?" she asked.

Tony shook his head as he polished off the rest of the hot dog.

"Homeless guys struck out, these guys are either in the wind or dead." Tony remarked.

She had to agree, but she wasn't about to give up yet. She stood up and took different coloured markers.

"What are you up to?" asked Tooms, who was looking puzzled. Taking another pin, she placed it on the map, then McCall drew lines from one victim to the other. Wherever they crossed, she put a pin.

"You are working on the basis that all serial killers have a comfort zone?" said a voice from behind them. They all turned to look at the doctor, who was standing there.

"What if this guy doesn't have a comfort zone?" asked Tony.

The others looked at each other, hoping someone would say something to shatter that horrifying thought.

"Well, Doc?"

Doctor Davidson scanned the map for a moment. "You said he used homeless people to move the body?" he asked, still looking at the board.

"Yes, why do you ask?" asked McCall. If the doc was a genius, now was the time to prove it.

"Well, this could mean he felt he was close to the victims and couldn't see them in their end state, as it would shatter the illusion he had built of them."

All three detectives looked at one another, mouths open in surprise.

"What do you mean? That this killer feels he has a relationship with the victims and so cuts them up, keeps parts but can't get rid of the rest of their bodies?" Tooms spoke, completely confused by what he had heard.

"This man you are after," the doctor continued, "from what I can tell he does not identify with the entire victim, just the parts he likes about the person, in the same way that a man with a foot fetish cares little about the appearance of the person, he's just interested in their feet."

"Ok, Doc," Tooms replied. "Given this information, where do we start looking?"

The strange medical man turned to them. McCall could sense that an idea was blooming inside that thin skull of his.

"Check men who work at beauty salons and anywhere that guys might have had contact with our victims, especially situations where he could see them partially dressed." The doc moved closer to the board, and a strange look crossed his pale face that was almost sadness, or perhaps it was remorse.

"You're looking for someone who has been fixated by the victims for a long time, even years maybe. Look at co-workers who may have played sports with them on occasions. Anyone who has seen them in the flesh. Judging by our victims' lifestyles that list should be quite short."

Tony raised a hand once he had jotted the information down. "What about the kid the sister was talking about?"

The doctor's eyes still stared at the photos of the women as they had been in life.

"It may be a lead, OK, go for it," McCall instructed him, then turned to the Davidson. "Nice job, Doc," she said with a smile, the first proper smile she had given him. He returned the smile, but she wished he had not.

It sent a shiver shooting through her spine.

The midday sun burnt brightly, but in the homeless shelter it was cooler. The empty old school building was now was home to the lost, the destitute or those who just didn't-want-to-be-found. Raggedy people scuffled here and there just to find a hot meal, a bed for the night or both.

The queue for food was long and the seating places in the dining hall were getting shorter, but still, for them even a place on a clean floor could be considered a relief.

Eric and George were buddies, they had seen many cold winters and blazing summers together, and in this world they lived in, a friend to watch your back was never a bad thing. The pair had endured much but still managed to keep cheerful.

"So, have we got another job coming up, Eric?" asked the stockily-built George, as he moved along the queue. George was smaller than Eric was but his build was more that of steel worker: his many years in the navy had given him some bulk. He had seen many wondrous places in far off lands; however, after his life in the services he'd fallen on hard times, and now he roamed the open road with his pal.

"No. It's kinda strange we haven't heard from him, don't you think?" replied Eric. He spoke and carried himself well. In his former life he'd been a distinguished surgeon, but he had succumbed to the urges of drug addiction and lost everything: his job, his wife and kids, everything. Eric was a tall skinny man with brushed back, receding hair; his long thin face was noticeable for its long Roman nose and large mouth, whose broad smile could crack his face apart.

"Shame, we sure could have used the money, oh well," Eric said, straightening his filthy red tie. Even though he was down-and-out he still insisted on wearing a suit. George found this strange, but Eric had never done him wrong and now he hardly noticed his friend's eccentricity.

Rise of a Phoenix

"Work, did I hear you say?" They both turned to find a bearded hunchback next to them, asking a question.

"What of it?" Eric addressed the stranger. "And it is most impolite to eavesdrop, sir, now be gone with you." Eric turned back to his friend, and the bulky hunchback, who was almost the same height as George, moved a little closer, cupping his hands together, as if he was asking for forgiveness.

"Please, sir, I meant no disrespect to you or your friend, it's just the thought of work excited me so much, apologies," The newcomer said.

Eric turned and gazed upon the man who had spoken so politely. His speech had touched something within him.

"You spy upon me, Sir," continued the man, "as though you wonder what a man of such disposition can possible do for work, but I assure you sir I am as strong as an ox."

Eric considered things for a moment, patting his bottom lip with a raised index finger. "If we want you to help us, where can we locate you?"

"Under the Williamsburg Bridge, it's nice and dry there."

The queue moved forwards.

"Again, I'm sorry," said the hunchback offering a hand to shake. "I am Pat."

Eric shook his hand, noting the firmness of his grip.

"This is my work colleague and friend, George, and I am Eric," he said. The thinner man gave Pat a large smile that chilled him to the bone. They had reached the food serving area at last and held out their trays, awaiting whatever delights were on offer.

"OK Pat, welcome aboard," announced Eric. This time his grin held something different, something sinister.

THIRTY-SIX

MCCALL'S PHONE STARTED TO ring. Still looking at the monitor she picked up the receiver and hooked it between her head and right shoulder.

"McCall, Homicide, can I help you?" She spoke as she typed something into the database about one of the vics.

"McCall, it's Steel."

The phone almost dropped from her grip at the sound of his voice.

"Steel! Where the....?"

"Look, I got a tip," he interrupted her. "Something is going down under the Williamsburg Bridge tonight to do with the killings. So I would suggest you come heavy and silent." And with that he was gone, leaving her looking down at the receiver.

Her heart was racing. Was she falling for this guy, she wondered? "No," she thought to herself. "Don't even think it."

She waved to her two colleagues to follow her and they went in to see the Captain. Captain Brant waved them in as

Rise of a Phoenix

McCall knocked on the door. As they entered they waited for him to finish his phone call.

"What's up, Detective?" he asked, putting down the receiver.

"Steel just contacted me and said he had a tip something was going down under the Williamsburg Bridge tonight. Something connected with the killings," she said, shifting her posture.

"So do you think he has something?" the Captain asked, leaning back in his chair.

"I hate to admit it, Sir, but he has come up with some useful information at times, so yes I think there may be something to it."

Captain Brant nodded to himself, realizing that she had made the right call.

"One more thing, Sir," she said, as she was just about to leave.

"Yes Detective?"

"He suggested we go in heavy and silent." The Captain looked worried.

"Do what you got to, McCall." He frowned. Knowing about Steel's past as he did, his words probably meant that the shit really was about to hit the fan.

THIRTY-SEVEN

THE NIGHT AIR WAS still and cloudless, and the sky was a dark blanket of twinkling beauty. Under the vast metal construction of the bridge sat a hunchbacked man in front of a small fire. As he sang to himself, he poked the fire, causing the flames to rise, and embers to spew up and be carried on the slight breeze like fireflies.

McCall and the SWAT team moved in, and Tooms and Tony followed in behind her. Suddenly the team leader went down on one knee and raised his left fist. The others went to ground, disappearing into cover.

"What's wrong?" asked McCall softly. The point man indicated a package on the small wall next to him.

"Bring it," said the team leader. The lead scout picked it up and tossed it. Catching the package, the sergeant looked at it and passed it to McCall.

"It's addressed to you, Merry Christmas," he said jokingly. As she opened the package, they noticed there were

Rise of A Phoenix

four earpieces and a recorder which was connected, possibly by Bluetooth. She passed the pieces of equipment to Tooms, Tony and the team leader.

"I guess someone wants to be heard," the sergeant joked. They all put in the earpieces and the sergeant gave the signal to proceed forward. Creeping past smashed-up vehicles and the bridge's large supporting metal struts, the cops reached a safe haven where they could observe what went on. Hearing a voice they all took cover. The sergeant asked for a situation report (known as a sit rep) from the lead scout.

"Just some homeless guy, all clear ...wait." He saw several men approach the homeless man, all dressed in some sort of black tactical gear.

"Hey, old man, have you seen a cop round here?" The new arrival was tall and broad shouldered, and his blond hair was cut short.

"Na, sorry son, just me, what you want him for anyway?" asked the hunchback.

McCall had a bad feeling about the situation.

"We were sent to clear up a loose end, our employer don't like loose ends, you see." As the man spoke another man, behind them, was screwing a silencer onto a pistol. The hunchbacked guy saw this and ran towards the river. McCall watched as the shooter let him think he was home free, then put three rounds into his back. Pat was thrown forward from the impact of the rounds, straight into the swirling waves.

"STOP! POLICE! Put down your weapons and put your hands up," cried McCall, her weapon trailing the obvious leader of the team.

"Sorry, officer, no can do."

And with that, a blaze of automatic gunfire rang through the night air. Both sides opened up as bullets shattered brickwork and caused sparks to fly off the steel bridge. She dived for cover as a stream of brass and lead flew her way. The SWAT team took down two of the assailants but lost one of their own.

"Damn it, Steel, where the hell are you?" swore McCall, making pot shots as she and Tooms tried to get round the side of their opponents. As they edged round into the open her earpiece activated.

"McCall! Above you!" Instantly she leapt for cover, and at that moment the ground exploded where she had been standing. Tooms and Tony trailed their weapons up and took down the sniper. He fell from his hiding place just under the bridge. The support harness stopped him from falling all the way, but they knew he was dead. The firelight came to an end as most of gang lay injured or dead on the ground.

"OK, you two, get up with your hands on your heads," screamed McCall to the two who lay on the ground spread-eagled. All the cops stepped forward, weapons trained on the crew.

"McCall, get the hell out of there," a voice screamed as one of the uninjured men got up. There was a CLINK as the distinct noise of a grenade safety was released, and seconds later the noise of gunfire as the SWAT team took the man down just before he was able to throw it. A loud explosion echoed through the metal beams and the ground shook as the grenade activated, sending deadly shards of metal in every direction.

"Is everyone OK?" asked the voice in their earpieces.

"Yeh, we are fine, thanks," replied McCall. There was a pause.

"Uhm, can you give me a thumbs up because this thing is only one way? Sorry."

Rise of a Phoenix

"Asshole," she said, raising a fist with the middle finger standing out straight.

"Yeh that will do," said the voice with a chuckle.

The area had been sealed up tight and CSU were having a field day marking all the bullet strikes and collecting evidence. The SWAT sergeant, McCall, Tooms, and Tony were debriefing the Captain on the events that had taken place.

"Steel never showed up but led us into a war zone instead," said McCall, angry that she had trusted him.

"Well, your boy was right, something was going down, plus who's the cop they were after? You?" asked the SWAT leader, looking at McCall.

"What cop?" asked the Captain. He looked concerned, wondering if Steel had lied to everyone.

"One of the guys asked the homeless guy 'where the cop was', I don't know any more than that." McCall was tired and annoyed.

"Could Steel have led us into a trap?" asked Tooms. "I mean, the boy's not here, is he?"

"Couldn't be him, he was telling us where the sniper was, and he alerted us to the guy with the grenade," interjected the sergeant. "No, he saved your butts. All of our butts actually."

"I want to know where Steel is, Captain." Detective McCall was really mad. "I mean, he led us here but where is he? He's just a voice. So, no, I don't buy it." The thought of John Steel being dirty was ripping her up, after the way he had been leading her on.

There was a rustle of undergrowth and then they saw a hunchback moving slowly towards them, his arm outstretched, making a silent cry for help, just before he collapsed. Tony and Tooms rushed forward, the medical teams not far behind them. Tony put two fingers on the man's neck: there was no pulse.

"He's gone," said Tony, standing up. "Why did they have to kill the guy? He was no harm to anyone." Tony kicked an empty can that lay on the floor, sending it sailing across the open area.

"I will get him back and see if he's got any evidence on him," said Tina with a sympathetic smile.

THIRTY-EIGHT

NORMALLY TINA WOULD HAVE music playing while she worked but today felt different, something sad was in the air, but she didn't know what to ascribe it to. McCall had followed the transport and was now sitting on the swivel chair waiting for the body of the homeless guy to be brought in.

"So what happened out there?" asked Tina as she stirred her coffee.

"Don't really know," Sam replied. "We got a call from Steel, who said that something was going down, next thing we know we are at the OK Corral."

"So where was Steel in all this?" asked the puzzled ME.

McCall shook her head, "Don't know, but he was talking to us. God, it was weird, it was as if he set us up but couldn't go through with it."

Tina frowned. "I can't believe he set you up."

"I know, you're right after everything that has happened."

"No, I mean I CAN'T believe he set you up, there has to

be more to it." Tina hadn't spent that much time with the mysterious detective but she was good at reading people. And what she read in him was goodness. He was a little messed up maybe, but nevertheless a good man.

The doors of the morgue flew open and two orderlies arrived with Pat's body on a gurney and transferred it on to the wash table.

"Thanks, guys," Tina said. She took a deep breath and put her gloves on, ready to search for fibres or anything that may have been transferred to him from the killers. She looked at his large round face and, even in death, he held what appeared to be a smile.

The door burst open in the other room and footsteps could be heard. Tina and McCall looked at each other and headed through. There stood the Captain, Tooms, and Tony, all with cell phones in their hands.

"So what's the matter, Doc?" asked the Captain, shocked that he had been summoned

Tina looked at McCall and shrugged in surprise

"We didn't send for you—for any of you," said Tina, just as confused as the others.

"No, I did," a muffled voice came from behind them, and then from the shadows came the figure of the homeless man, Pat, who they'd last seen in the gurney. Tina and McCall shot to the other side of the room, where their colleagues stood open-mouthed. Pat walked up to where Tina had been standing and reached for his left ear and pulled. They all looked away in disgust as he screamed. Eventually, the screams turned into laughter.

Daring to take a peek, McCall saw Steel standing there with pieces of latex still stuck to his face. "You asshole!" she screamed, slapping him on his padded shoulder.

"But I checked your pulse," said Tony, completely baffled by the experience. "You were dead."

"Don't be hard on yourself, Tony. It's special latex, real, feel it if you like," said Steel still grinning. Tooms grabbed his hand and as he shook it brought him close and hugged him,

"Cool move, Bro," he said.

The Captain, however, was not in a brother-hugging mood. "Steel, do you want to explain what the hell is going on?"

Steel's smile vanished. "Sir, if I may get changed, then I'll meet everyone in the briefing room."

The Captain nodded. "You got ten minutes."

As Steel entered the briefing room everyone was sitting around the large table, and he felt a touch of déjà vu, remembering the previous such meeting.

"OK, Steel, what the hell is going on?" asked the Captain. "You disappear and then you get people in a fire fight, I mean just what the hell are you up to, boy?"

Steel looked lost for a moment, as if a thought had just occurred to him.

"Well?" reiterated the Captain, who was by now at breaking point.

"They asked for a cop." said Steel, with a long staring look above everyone's heads, apparently at nothing as he sat down.

"At the bridge, they asked where was the cop. At first I thought he meant me but of course"

"You were in disguise." McCall finished his sentence, sharing a conspiratorial look with him.

"Steel, what the hell are you talking about?" asked the Captain.

Steel pushed the thought away and started from the beginning. "I'm not sure. It's still puzzling me, who they were and how they are mixed up in the case, unless this is now two completely separate affairs, but my gut says they are tied together somehow." His expression was distracted, as if he wasn't concentrating on what he was telling them.

However, with a shudder he finally came back to earth. "Yesterday I got to thinking about the homeless guys we have been looking for." He took a sip from the coffee, and his eyes rolled back with pleasure at the excellent taste.

"I was thinking that the occasion when they moved Marie-Ann move was not the only time these guys were used." Steel put his cup down for a second. "We have been thinking about routes for vehicles, and how long it takes to drive from here and there. Well what if we were looking for, say, a shopping cart or something similar?"

McCall's face came alive as his words started to make some sort of sense. "Of course! Everyone would remember a van or a car, but they wouldn't think twice about seeing a homeless guy moving something," she added.

"Anyway," Detective Steel continued. "I got to thinking that the only way to find them is to become one of them."

"And did you find them?" asked the Captain

"It took some time but I got them. They were talking about doing another job for 'the man'. My idea was to stir up their interest and, well, get noticed." Steel nodded as he took another sip of coffee.

"So what went wrong?" Tony asked, leaning forwards with interest.

"At the most I thought 'the man' would pay me a visit, not some goons from The Expendables. I was just trying to get a reaction."

"Well you got that, my man, big time." Tooms laughed

"Yeh well I was expecting hordes of homeless guys on a pay

check, not mercenaries with a death wish." This struck a chord with everyone in the room, and the mood changed.

"What makes you think they were mercenaries?" asked Tooms, a strange look on his face.

"Tooms, man, you were in the forces, you would recognize a private soldier, right?"

Tooms nodded in agreement.

"They did appear to me to be professional solders, bought and paid for."

"Well, for a start these were not some last minute buy types, they were organized and kitted out." Tooms added, nodding in agreement with what Steel had said.

"So what are you thinking, Detective?" asked Dr Davidson, who had been sitting through all of the previous revelations watching not the room but Steel: his gaze was focused on Steel alone.

"Actually I'm wondering how a group of highly trained soldiers, a couple of homeless guys and a psycho killer come together in the mix."

The Captain stood up and put his hands on his hips. "So, how do they?" he asked Steel, but deep inside he knew he didn't want to know the answer.

"They don't," said Steel, taking a sip from the cooling coffee.

"What do you mean they don't?" yelled Tooms.

"Let's go over it again. The mercenaries asked for a *cop*, not a bum, a *cop*."

McCall's suddenly looked scared, and then she glanced up at Steel, who must have read her mind because he nodded in confirmation; he had also had the same thought.

"The hotel room," she said, her mood one of mixed emotions. "Did we get the sniper rifle from the guy you lads so brilliantly found under the bridge?"

Tony and Tooms looked at each other and both simultaneously began to make for the door.

"Ballistics should match the hotel room," said Tony, as they left.

"You know, it's so cute the way they do that, are they a couple?" Steel asked, making the Captain and McCall smile.

Steel saw Dr Davidson out of the corner of his eye, and felt himself being carefully observed. He shuddered with revulsion.

"So what now, Steel?" Sam McCall asked.

The Captain was sitting on the other side of the table and crossed his arms.

"We carry on," John Steel replied. "We carry on as though last night never happened. If we go chasing mercenaries we lose sight of what we are really after." Steel sunk back into the chair and finished the now-cold coffee.

"And what about the mercenaries?" the Captain asked.

Steel thought for a moment. "We have no idea who sent them or why." He paused. "But we do know that someone knew that either I was going to be there or Sam McCall was. Bottom line, you got a snitch in the department."

The Captain looked round the room and shook his head in disbelief.

"Our best bet is to forget about them, carry on, and solve this investigation." Steel stood up.

"And if they try again?" asked McCall with a lump in her throat.

"Then we make sure we catch one alive. Either way our plan should be if we don't bother them they don't bother us." Steel shrugged.

They left the briefing area, and Steel headed for the coffee room. He badly needed a refill. Hours of drinking bad coffee and bad booze had numbed his taste buds.

THIRTY-NINE

AS THE AFTERNOON GREW late the workforce had cross-checked known whereabouts for the two homeless guys, possible sightings, indeed anything to find a pattern. Earlier McCall had told everyone to focus on the two drop-off guys, as they were the link. Find them, she explained, and they were one step closer.

Steel walked in to the office with a large box which looked and felt quiet heavy.

"Hey, man, what's with the box?" asked Tooms, as he peered over the top of his monitor screen. "Is dinner on the way?"

The team dropped everything to see what the English detective had brought.

"Wow, Chinese," said McCall, helping to lay out the boxes on desks.

McCall walked up to Steel who had half a red-hot spring roll in his mouth. She smiled as he tried fanning cool air into his open mouth to cool it down.

"Can I have a word with you, please?" she asked standing over him, stretching out an arm towards the coffee room.

"Yeh, sure, after you," he said, dabbing his mouth with the logoed napkin. They walked into the room and she shut the doors.

"What's up?" he asked, his voice calm and soothing.

"Look, about the other night," she began to explain. "I never gave you a chance to explain that it was your friend who got killed. I'm sorry." She looked into his sunglasses and hoped he was staring back at her with the kind of emotion she was feeling.

"It's fine," he reassured her. "It's my fault for being so—well—secretive. I'm the one who should be sorry. Like I said before, I have some trust issues and after the bridge I think I was right to" She gave him a sharp look of anger and disappointment, which he picked up on straight away.

"I didn't mean you guys," he assured her. "It's someone else, here. I trust you guys with my life."

He held out a hand in friendship. "Friends?" he asked.

She looked at him and smiled. As she took his hand he pulled her close and hugged her. "I'm so happy," he said jokingly.

She pushed him off quickly. "You are such an ass," she said. But as he walked off, she felt her knees go weak at the lingering sweet smell he had left behind: a mixture of male pheromones and sweet-smelling deodorant and aftershave. She looked round and straightened herself up as though nothing had happened.

McCall and Steel returned to the group and delved into what was left of the meal once the guys had stopped feeding.

Rise of a Phoenix

"OK, people it's getting late, we have all had an excitable day so let's get home, shake out and come in fresh tomorrow," the Captain said as he stood in the doorway with his coat over one arm. And with that the police staff gathered there started to thin out once they had shut down their computers and tidied their desks.

Steel was sitting in the chair next to McCall's and shouted after the Captain: "Hey, Captain, when do I get a desk?"

The Captain smiled as he stepped into the elevator, saying, "You find one, it's yours!" And with that the door shut

Alan Brant blew a sigh of relief at the thought of another day gone. But in truth he knew that once this case was done Steel was gone. It wasn't that he didn't want him there, but that was the nature of the man.

Steel stood up and put on his long coat "Did you want to get a drink or something?" he asked Sam McCall. "It's not a date or anything, just two people getting a drink," he tripped over his words.

She looked up at him and smiled. "Sorry I have plans, but you go ahead."

He returned the smile.

"Hey, guys, want to get a drink or something?" he shouted to the other two.

"Cool," said Tooms, putting on his jacket.

"Where we going?" asked Tony, logging off on his computer.

"Oh, I don't know there is a little place I know."

And all three detectives walked off towards the elevator. McCall watched them leave and shook her head with a large smile on her face.

FORTY

THE DIMLY LIT BATHROOM was aglow with the tiny flames of a dozen candles and the steam from the running shower caused a haze that hung in the room. A fog of condensation blanketed the mirror over the sink, and the screen around the shower unit was full of mist that billowed from its open top.

Sam McCall took a sip from the large glass; the red wine appeared almost black in the dimly lit room. Placing it down on a small side cupboard she moved to the shower and slipped off her robe, the silk of the gown caressing her firm body as it fell to the floor. She placed the toes of her left foot gently under the running water to test the warmth; *just right*, she thought, and then entered the small glass compartment.

The cascade of water ran down the contours of her athletic body, washing away the troubles of the day. She lathered up a sponge with sweet-smelling soap then with care she massaged the soapy foam into her skin. Soft music played in the background and the strong smell of candles and soap filled the air.

Rise of a Phoenix

Placing both, hands against the tiled wall of the booth she stood under the shower head and let the water pour over her. McCall was lost in the moment, when suddenly she felt a pair of strong hands start to run their way from her shoulders to her hips. She shuddered as she felt small kisses caress her back, moving slowly downwards. Her nails pressed against the wall, making scratching motions as her body tingled with excitement.

Then the hands moved back up towards her firm breasts and pulled her back, as he began to bite her neck and ears.

She reached back and felt his firm hard body as he pressed against hers. Slowly she leant forwards and her hands steadied herself against the wall as the couple slowly became one in a passionate embrace. Feeling his hard body grind against her she began to groan with pleasure, her hands moving backwards, digging her nails into his muscular thigh as the speed of his movements began to increase. Water splashed against the glass, and bottles of soap and conditioner cast aside in all directions as they began to reach the ultimate.

Her knees began to buckle as she felt him move against her, her arm reached back and grasped at his hair as he began to bite hard into the side of her neck, his hands ran up and down the front of her body, gently feeling the shape of her breasts. She began to gasp as she felt every hard muscular inch of him, her moans of pleasure drowned out by her hands banging against the safety glass.

Then together they climaxed with an earth-moving crescendo. She turned, her eyes unable to focus. Then they kissed, and she fell back against the hard tiled wall, her arms bracing herself against the walls of the shower until as her legs felt weak, and what felt like small electrical shocks buzzed through her body. Her eyes opened to see Steel's firm naked body. She looked at his firm chest muscles and saw what appeared to be a tattoo of a strange bird.

With a start, she sat up and looked around in a panic. Where the hell was she? She leant over and found the light switch. She blew out a sigh of relief. She was in bed—alone. She looked around the room then her head fell down onto the pillows.

What the hell was that, she thought to herself? She grabbed a pillow from the other side of the bed and put it over her head to hide her shame.

FORTY-ONE

THE NEXT MORNING MCCALL sat in the ME's office with Tina and described the recent goings on over a cup of coffee bought from the store round the corner. McCall often came down before the day had started to play catch up if they had chance, before somebody died early and ruined the whole 'ease into the day' thing. The two girls had known each other a long time and been through a lot together, so it seemed only right every morning or sometime after work, that they got together and just talked. About nothing in particular, just anything that wasn't work. This was girls' hour and they both needed it.

But this time they did talk about work. Tina wanted to know the ins and outs of what she had heard about the other day; she found that the drawback with being closeted down in the ME's office was that she missed all the chatter and gossip.

"God, Steel really pisses me off sometimes," Sam growled as she spoke his name. "I mean he shows up out of nowhere and messes up crime scenes."

"Saved your ass two or three times," Tina butted in, then

hid behind her coffee cup as McCall shot her a disapproving look.

"Comes and goes like he owns the place, sits at my desk and bothers me," Sam went on, trying to fake her anger. "I can't believe I actually had a dream about the son-of-a-bitch the other night."

Tina spat out her coffee and stared at her friend with a 'do tell' look on her face. McCall then realized her mistake and looked away trying to look innocent.

"What sort of dream?" asked Tina in a slow meaningful tone.

"Um, nothing, forget it—it's not important." McCall blushed, cursing herself for letting slip the fact that she'd had an erotic dream about the man.

"Come on, what sort of dream?" Tina pressed her until she looked at McCall's expression and the penny dropped.

"Oh my God! You had that sort of dream about him? Okay, I want details." So saying, Tina made herself comfortable and prepared to hear the rest.

McCall then felt obliged to reveal the explicit details of the dream, making her friend's mouth drop open in surprise.

"What does it mean?" asked McCall, hoping to get some deep insight into the meaning of this kind of dream.

"I know what I think it means, but what do *you* think it means?"

McCall shot her a look of reproach. "Well maybe it was the excitement of the shoot-out. Or, I mean we have been through a lot together, so maybe…" she fumbled her words, trying to find some other explanation for the experience.

"Really? So you're going for PTSD." Tina gave her another long stare.

McCall paused for a moment before replying, as the thought ran through her head. "Yeh, that sounds good to me."

Sam smiled while Tina laughed at the idea and drank her coffee.

FORTY-TWO

STEEL HAD GOT IN to work early. The night before had been a good one, probably one of the best he had had in a long time. He put the coffee machines on in anticipation of a couple of sore heads, and after making himself a coffee he moved to the white board and looked over the evidence. As he perched himself on the edge of McCall's desk and sipped the fresh coffee, his gaze was redirected to the map board. The loud DING from the elevator disturbed his concentration; he smiled as Tooms and Tony crawled in, looking a bit worse for wear.

"Morning," he shouted, making them flinch slightly at the loud noise in their hangover-sensitive ears.

"The coffee is ready." They replied by raising their hands, and made their way to get some refreshment. After topping up their cups they joined him at McCall's desk.

"You guys okay?" he asked, amused, whilst sipping his coffee.

"Us? Never better, man, and you?" replied Tooms, shifting his sunglasses around to screen out as much light as possible.

"Fine, fine," Steel said as he stared at the two boards.

"What you looking at?" asked Tooms as he took a sip from the coffee, his glasses steaming up as he did so. Steel smiled as he took notice of the hangover condition of his colleagues.

"Something's bugging me but I cannot put my finger on it," replied Steel, with a look of intense concentration as he stared. "I'm thinking that the homeless guys may have moved all of the bodies, but…"

Tony scratched his head as he tried to follow John Steel's train of thought, finding it hard to concentrate.

"Wow," Tony said at last, "so you think the homeless guys may have moved more than one body. Pushing those trolleys must have been a right bitch."

Detective Steel suddenly stood up bolt upright and kissed Tony on the forehead. He then looked at the map board, taking note of the pins that showed the locations of the bodies. Using his two index fingers he appeared to measure something on the map, then turning suddenly, he raced up to Tony, saying: "You little dancer," as he made for the elevator, leaving Tony to wipe his forehead, and try to make sense of it all.

FORTY-THREE

TINA AND MCCALL WERE laughing and joking, and Sam felt more at ease with her friend, now she had told her about her secret erotic dream. She didn't have to be back upstairs for a while, and if somebody had been unable to find her, she could just say she was checking something out. The door swung open and in rushed Steel.

"Well, speak of the devil," said Tina with a large grin on her face. Steel stood for second, confused by the welcome.

"Well, Mr Steel, do you have a special mark on your right shoulder?" Tina asked, still smiling. His face registered surprise and McCall also detected something new in his expression: a look of being emotionally hurt. .

"You know, a tattoo?" Tina quickly worked in, noticing his distracted expression.

"Um, what? No. I have no tattoos, sorry. Why do you ask?"

McCall gave Tina a slap on the arm and shot her a nasty look.

"Never mind. Okay, Steel, you found me, what do you want?" McCall asked.

"Well actually I was after the good doctor." He smiled at Tina, who could feel her cheeks turning to a nice shade of red.

"Oh, right," Sam said, feeling hurt and embarrassed.

"Okay honey, what's on your mind" Tina asked, and then continued sipping her coffee.

"You remember Miss Talbot? I want to know how much she weighed."

Tina and McCall gave him a curious look. Tina searched through her notes.

"She was around fifty-four kilos. Why?" Both women moved in closer, intrigued by the question.

"Oh, just a little experiment I had in mind." And after saying that he went straight out of the door.

The ME and the detective looked at each other for a moment, and then took off after him.

McCall and Tina burst out of the elevator and onto the homicide office floor. Tooms and Tony looked up from their desks to see the two women racing in like a couple of kids at Christmas, heading for the tree.

"Have any of you seen Steel?" asked McCall, who was slightly out of breath from the run.

"He was here earlier," replied Tooms. "He just looked at the board and took off after Tony here mentioned something about shopping carts.

McCall and Tina rushed to the boards. As they studied the murder board, suddenly Tina yelped in excitement. McCall looked over as Tina pointed to a post-it that had been left on the map under the pin which pointed the location of where Marie-Ann's body was located.

It was a simple note saying: *meet me here and bring Tina. J. S.* Sam and Tina looked at each other and said in unison "road trip," and rushed off, leaving Tooms and Tony confused and upset.

"Never again, man, never again," said Tooms, sipping his coffee and rubbing his forehead to try and ease his hangover headache.

FORTY-FOUR

THE SUN WAS HIGH in the cloudless sky, flocks of birds darted acrobatically over the water in formation, and boats of all shapes and sizes cruised aimlessly up and down. Tina and McCall sat on a bench and enjoyed the coolness of their ice creams, pondering at how nice it was to be outside in the fresh air and not cooped up in an office, or staring at a corpse.

"Okay, where the hell is he?" asked Tina. She was enjoying herself but she did have other things to do. She looked at her watch for what seemed to be the tenth time.

"I don't know, he's probably sitting up on top of the building watching us."

They laughed. McCall looked across the bay and breathed in the air as the fresh breeze blew from across the water. As they sat there a homeless man came and sat down next to Tina. She stared at him for a moment whilst edging away. He smiled but she did not. She studied him closely and suddenly her body shot backwards. Casting an angry glare towards him she yelled: "And where the hell have you been, you know you are late, right?" Her voice was bitter. The man looked shocked and surprised, and he looked behind him on the off chance someone else was there. There was no one.

"Come on then, where have you been? Look it was you who invited us down here."

The homeless guy now looked at her as if she was some sort of crazy person.

"Well, sorry I'm late, not that I remember stating a time, but sorry again."

They looked round to see Steel with a shopping cart full of heavy-looking items. Tina's jaw dropped and McCall tried to hide her laughter.

Tina and Sam got up and joined Steel, and the homeless guy lay down on the bench enjoying the warmth of the sun.

"So, detective, what's the big experiment?" McCall asked, laughing. "Push the cart till we are tired?"

"Sort of, but he will be pushing it." He pointed to the bench where they were greeted by an up-stretched arm and a dirty hand waving to them.

"I take it you have met, Jerry." He smiled broadly as Tina wiped herself down as if she had something dirty on her clothes. They looked at the bulging cart he'd brought along. It was covered with flies and other insects swarming around.

"So what have you got there?" asked McCall. She frowned in distaste as if she didn't really want to know but couldn't resist asking.

"Oh this? I just killed someone and wrapped them up for this experiment. I mean if you're going to do it you have to do it right." He smiled, watching their faces.

Rise of a Phoenix

"Yeh, really." Tina was still brushing herself down as she spoke.

"Yes, really," he replied, trying to sound serious, amused that for a split second maybe they actually believed what he'd said.

"Seriously, you thought I had actually done that? Please!" he said, pretending to sound disappointed in them.

"You're a real bastard, you know that?" said Tina, smacking him on the shoulder. He bowed slightly as if to thank her for her comment.

Steel had found the homeless guy, Jerry, in an alleyway while he going through the garbage hoping to score some 'disposable items' as he put it. And now Jerry was about to help break the case, or so Steel thought.

"So, why him?" As Tina studied the man, he leant forward from his resting place and shot her an evil look.

"Now, I didn't mean it like that," she responded, returning the look, waiting for Jerry to lie down again. "What I meant was, why go for the small guy and not the thin one that you mentioned?"

Steel shook his head. He had already rehearsed the scenario carefully in his head, and after the brief encounter with the men he knew who to match with each role.

"No, George was the muscle, Eric was the brains," Steel explained. On the mention of his friends' names, Jerry sat up bolt upright.

"What do you want with George and Eric?" He sounded confused but McCall was quite sure there was an element of fear in his words.

"You know them?" asked Steel, surprised at his luck. The man nodded as he saw Steel return from the small coffee stall with a fresh doughnut. His eyes were transfixed by the pastry Steel held.

"Jerry, how do you know these men?" Steel waved the doughnut, and then clicked his fingers to snap the man from his trance.

"What? Oh, we did some moving jobs together." Jerry smiled and edged closer to Steel, eyes fixed on the doughnut. Steel looked down at the pastry and realized that this was the key to getting him to talk.

"Moving what?" asked McCall, sliding closer to the man, making him feel a little edgy.

"Oh, I don't know. Packages. Big ones, long ones—all sorts." Steel had passed him the sticky prize which he bit into slowly, savouring every morsel of the doughnut.

"Did you pick up from the same place each time?" Steel's interest was growing. He couldn't believe his luck in finding this guy, and in the back of his head alarm bells were ringing. Yes, very lucky find, wasn't it, he thought. Jerry had devoured the pastry and was dabbing his lips as though he was royalty.

"Sure. We would pick up from this old warehouse in the meatpacking district, a real spooky place, lots of dark rooms, but we got our stuff from the big store room at the back," Jerry recounted as Steel passed him another doughnut, which he ripped from the detective's hand.

"Jerry, can you take us there?" McCall's words were soft and calming to his ears. He nodded, and attempted to get as much of the doughnut into his mouth as possible. Steel watched Jerry turn a nice colour as breathing became an issue, but finally Jerry swallowed hard and his large mouth was free to take in air.

"Jerry, take us to the place and I promise to buy you as many doughnuts as you like," He promised.

The man nodded hard, just the thought of them making his mouth water. Tina decided that as no dramatic experiment was about to happen, she would head back to the desk full of paperwork she had got to attend to.

FORTY-FIVE

TODAY WAS A SPECIAL day for Jenny Thompson. She had worked along the homicide detectives for many years hoping to join their ranks, and now her dream had come true—Her beaming smile said it all. As Jenny approached Tooms and Tony they just sat in their chairs as though nothing had changed.

"Well?" She stood next to their desks, hands clenched together and bouncing on her heels, just waiting for some recognition from them.

"Well what?" asked Tooms, trying hard not to laugh.

"I made Detective." She showed off her badge like a six-year-old that just came in first at a school race.

"Cool," replied Tooms, lifting his cup to her. "You can get the coffees then, rookie."

She scowled at them as the two men burst out laughing. Then they got up and shook her hand and hugged her, offering congratulations. The Captain walked out of his office and headed for her.

"Thompson? Your desk is a mess—sort it out."

She looked puzzled until she looked in the far corner and saw a desk with a name plaque on it that said 'Detective J. Thompson.' The words were etched in white with a shiny black background. She picked it up and felt the lump in her throat grow larger.

"Thanks, Captain." She felt like she wanted to hug him.

"Oh, don't thank me, you're still working with The Doc."

Her face fell.

"Is there a problem, Detective?"

She stiffened up and put down the plaque.

"No sir, no problem." She faked a smile and walked off; the Captain grinned.

"Where are McCall and Steel?" Alan looked at the fresh scribbles on the white board and the pins on the map.

"They went up town to check out an old warehouse in the meatpacking district, but they had to pick up some doughnuts or something first," replied Tony, shrugging. The Captain nodded in response, and Tony and Tooms got up and joined him at the boards.

"Steel had a theory that homeless people were used to move the bodies to locations in shopping carts," continued Tony.

The Captain turned to them. "Makes sense, after all, who would notice a homeless person? Everyone would remember a van or car, but a homeless guy, nah." Steel's theory held ground, but to prove it was another matter.

There was a loud ringing sound coming from the Captain's office and he headed off to answer the phone. Tony watched as the Captain answered it and proceeded to bawl someone out.

"I don't get it, Tooms" Tony picked up the files and flicked through them as if he was looking for something.

"You don't get what?" Tooms watched his partner getting agitated.

"These women. Apart from growing up together, they have nothing in common; hell, after they left to go to college I don't think they even had contact with one another. I bet they didn't even know they were all living in the same city."

Tooms sat on the edge of his desk as he pondered the question. "So what's on your mind, man?" Tony slammed down the files and leant back, putting his hand over his face in frustration. "There has to be something that ties our three vics together other than sharing their early upbringing. I mean who waits thirty years to kill someone?" Tooms had to agree, he had nothing else to offer.

FORTY-SIX

NORMALLY THERE WOULD HAVE been witnesses, people of interest, someone stewing in the interrogation by now, but this was different and Tooms felt it. He looked at the board nearest where he was sitting and he felt sad for the victims, not so much because they had been murdered, but more because they all seemed to lack a personal life.

Tooms stared at the framed set of photos on his desk. The silver frame held snapshots of a group picture of him and his family. He picked it up and smiled, then he looked up at the pictures of the women victims, and his sadness returned. Tony saw the look on his partner's face and walked up to him.

"What's up, man?" Tony could see the obvious signs of Tooms's displeasure on his face.

"What do you figure would make these very attractive women give up having a personal life and just live for work?"

Tony studied the photos on the boards. "Don't know, man, but some people do and they are happy."

Tooms's computer made a DING noise to signal the arrival of an email, and Tony walked back to his desk, reminded that he needed to check his own inbox.

Detective Tooms sifted through the many items of junk mail waiting for him, noticing that one stood out. He looked around, making sure nobody saw him before he opened it. The address was from a friend of his in financials and it read:

HI JOSHUA.
GOT YOUR E-MAIL.
REF: JOHN STEEL.
NATIONAL BANK……$ 56,457.99.
OFF SHORE ACCOUNT DIFFERENT NAME:
$443, 867, 897.95
WATCH YOUR BACK BUDDY.

Tooms's jaw dropped. Who was this guy and how was it he had so much cash in an offshore account?

For him there were too many questions about Detective John Steel and not enough answers.

Quickly, he printed off the email and headed for the Captain's office. He needed to know the truth regardless of the ticking off he would get for delving into another cop's private affairs, but he had felt it to be necessary.

As he got to the closed door he stopped for a moment and looked at the piece of paper, wondering if he was he doing the right thing? Before he could turn round, the door opened and before him stood the Captain.

FORTY-SEVEN

AFTER DRIVING AROUND FOR what was literally hours, McCall and Steel arrived at a large disused building. On first appearance it looked like an old delivery or storage place. Its red brick walls showed their years and the wooden framed windows held thick glass in place that appeared to be encrusted with the dust and dirt of forty years.

McCall pulled up and parked some distance from the building, just in case someone was watching: the last thing they needed was a welcoming committee.

"You're sure this is the place, Jerry?" she asked, staring at the homeless man in the car's back seat through the rear view mirror.

"Are you really sure, Jerry? Because this is the fifth place you have brought us to," Steel added, turning round in his seat to look at him.

Jerry could feel Steel's eyes burning into his own, even through the sunglasses.

"Yes, that's the place. Can we go now?" Steel and McCall had now both turned around to face the nervous man.

"What's your rush, Jerry? We only just got here." Steel had a bad feeling, the *you've just been set up* feeling, and that was one experience he didn't need. All three of them vacated the car and moved towards the building.

An eerie silence filled the air, and as they ventured closer Steel couldn't help but notice Jerry was lagging behind.

"What's the matter, Jerry? You've gone a little pale." McCall suddenly had the same feeling as Steel and drew her weapon. Clutching the pistol grip tightly with both hands she let her arm hand downwards by her side, keeping alert and ready for whatever was to come.

"OK, Jerry, when we get inside I want you to show me where you got the parcels, OK?" Sam told him.

Jerry's expression suddenly turned to one of fear, the sort of fear you would expect to see from someone facing a savage lion. Or someone who knew exactly what was inside the building.

"No!" Jerry yelled suddenly. "You can't make me go in there! I won't go in there. Fuck you, lady!" Jerry turned to make an escape, but McCall grabbed him by the arm.

"What about your free meal we promised you, Jerry?" Her appeal wasn't working.

"Fuck your meal! Fuck them! Fuck you all!" he screamed.

Steel grabbed him and dragged him to the nearest dumpster. "You don't want to go in, fine, but you are not leaving either," and with that he picked the man up and threw him into the rubbish container. A large THUNG echoed through the empty steel box as Jerry hit the bottom, and, whipping out his handcuffs he secured the handles that closed the container, effectively locking him inside.

"Shall we?" Steel raised an open palm in a *ladies first* gesture. They both proceeded cautiously, keeping close to the walls, McCall in the lead. As they neared the doorway she turned and looked at Steel's empty hands. Shooting him a disappointed look, she grabbed her back-up Glock pistol and passed it to him.

"I can't believe you don't carry a gun, Jesus."

He shrugged and cocked the weapon.

As they entered a long corridor the musty smell of a decaying building filled their nostrils, and they quickly covering their nose and mouths until they adjusted to the stagnant air. Moving along they covered each other's backs, weapons held firm in their outstretched arms, as they came to the first set of rooms which were on opposite sides of each other along the long wall. They stopped, backs against the brickwork and counted together.

"Three, Two, One, Now!"

Swinging round, weapons ready, they charged through the door, but they found nothing but an empty room. Edging down the corridor they did the same for the next four rooms until they arrived at the blue door at the end of the long hallway.

"How do you want to do this?" Steel asked. Sam was surprised he was consulting her.

"We go in on three, keep low, find cover and we check it out,"

He nodded. "Did you call for back up or something before we came in?"

She smiled at him with a cocky sort of grin. "Why? Don't you think that we can handle it?"

He noticed the smirk and realised she was teasing him. He grasped the handle and turned it slowly. McCall was crouched in front of the door, ready to move in as soon as the door opened.

"Okay," he said. "Three, Two, One!" He shoved the door open and she rolled in, while Steel just looked into the room, still holding the handle.

"Houston, we have a problem." His words were more for himself than for McCall, but she stood up and turned towards her colleague.

"New plan?" she asked, shrugging.

The room was vast, and its high glass roof had been painted or boarded over, allowing only a few shards of light to creep in. Around the room there was a vast number of stacked large wooden container boxes around six-foot square, arranged so as to form some kind of maze.

The labyrinth was too high to be clambered over, meaning that the only way to investigate was to move in amongst them. Slowly they crept in, towards the first corner, that led straight for a couple of feet. Creeping along slowly, then they stopped. Before them a junction.

"Left or right?" Steel asked. She looked, finding that both directions looked exactly alike, and equally dangerous.

"Right, we go right," She decided.

The maze of passageways they found themselves in were evenly spaced and the only light seemed to be from the chinks of daylight coming from the ceiling. As they approached one of the beams of light, Steel noticed that the illumination was large enough to cover the space between the two opposing walls. He raised a hand and stopped her.

"Do you like movies?" His question puzzled her: now was hardly the time to invite her for a date, plus she would never agree to one.

"Steel, this is not the time or place," she snapped.

He turned to her, crouched as he was with his back against one of the containers. One side of his face was in a pool of light, and she could see he was smiling.

"One of my favourite films was Raiders of the Lost Ark," he told her.

Now she was smiling: McCall understood where he was going with this.

"Stay out of the light," he said, scraping up some dust from the floor and throwing it into the ray of light.

"Stay out of the light," he repeated. As the dust fell they saw tiny red beams that crossed the gap before them.

Steel turned to McCall. His expression said it all.

"We have to leave, NOW!"

FORTY-EIGHT

TOOMS WALKED INTO THE Captain's office. The decision to talk to his boss about John Steel had been made for him, but it didn't make him feel any better. The Captain closed the door behind them and he manoeuvred himself round to his desk and sat, leaving Tooms standing in front of him.

"So what's on your mind, Detective?" Brant sat back in his chair, causing it to lean back against the hinge mechanism.

"I got some information back from financials and came up with something disturbing," Tooms admitted, passing the copy of the email to the Captain. Brant leant forwards, leaning on his desk. After reading it he looked up at Tooms, his face filled with disappointment and also a trace of anger, which didn't however seem to be directed towards the junior officer.

"What's this, Tooms? Are we are checking up on our own guys now?" His voice tried to mask his disappointment.

"Sir, something felt off about the guy, so I" Tooms didn't know which way to look.

"Had him checked out," completed the Captain. "Well the thing is I probably would have done the same in your position."

Tooms's face lit up for a second.

"However, you need to stop any more investigations on Steel, is that understood?"

Tooms's stomach turned.

"OK, Tooms, if that's all, I believe we still have a killer to find." He ushered Tooms out of the room.

"Um, yes sir." The detective was filled with confusion and dismay at the implications of what he'd just heard. Was the Captain in on something bad, he wondered? Tooms went back to his desk and sat down.

As he watched, the Captain he picked up his phone and dialled quickly, waited for a moment, then began to talk. As he spoke he saw Tooms looking at him and turned in his chair, as if to conceal the conversation.

Tony walked up to his partner and saw his hardened expression. "What's up, man?" he asked his stony-faced partner.

"What's up is we have a problem, man, and I think the Captain is part of it." He showed Tony the piece of paper. Tony read the words, his eyes widening in astonishment.

"What does it mean?" he asked, passing it back to Tooms.

"I don't know, man, but what I *do* know is things have turned pretty bad since this guy showed up. Worst of all he is out there alone with McCall." Now they both had a bad feeling.

Suddenly Tooms's phone rang. He grabbed the receiver quickly as though expecting the worst, and as he listened he scribbled something down. It was an address in the meat-packing district.

"Yeh, OK, we'll get there quick as we can, see you later." He put down the receiver and ripped off the piece of paper from the pad he'd been writing on.

"Trouble?" Tony asked, grabbing his coat and following his partner to the Captain's office.

"Not sure yet but we got to go." Tooms knocked on the Captain's door and put his head inside the room, and the Captain waved him in.

"What's up, Tooms?" he asked, putting down his phone's receiver into its cradle.

"McCall and Steel need back-up, the special weapons type."

The Captain stood up and grabbed the slip of paper from him.

"OK, you two, get down there and I'll meet you at this address with the teams. And no heroics from anyone."

Tooms smiled and left.

Brant picked up the phone and dialled the extension for SWAT and the bomb squad. He couldn't help but think, *"what the hell have they gotten into over there?"*

FORTY-NINE

IN LESS THAN AN hour the building was surrounded, streets blocked off and helicopter units hovered above. The Captain pulled up, with Tooms and Tony arriving soon afterwards.

"So you two, what sort of hell have you for me today?" As the three of them stood outside their vehicles, the Captain looked pissed but his anger clearly wasn't directed at them. A banging sound emanated from a dumpster container next to Tooms.

"What the?" yelled Tooms, as he and Tony both drew their weapons. Steel rushed forwards and darted between them and the dumpster.

"As much as I would love you to shoot the bastard, he may be a witness." Steel removed his handcuffs from the container's handles and dragged the man out, tossing him towards his fellow officers.

"This guy may have some answers." McCall said, giving Jerry a swift look of contempt.

"Get him out of here." yelled Brant, and two officers grabbed the man and took him away.

The group gathered next to a patrol car. Standing around the vehicle stood two sergeants; one was from the bomb squad, the other was a SWAT commander.

"Captain. I'm Sergeant Matt Carter of E.O.D and this is Sergeant Jack North of SWAT," Said the bomb squad man. The Captain shook their hands.

"Gentlemen, I'm Alan Brant of Homicide and these unlucky pair of sons-of-bitches are detectives McCall and Steel." After doing the usual courtesy handshakes, they moved to the car where laid out on the hood was a blueprint of the building.

"OK, what we got?" asked the tall ageing Sergeant Carter. Carter had been in the force a long time but he knew everything there was to know about explosives. The tall African-American man was bald and had a small beard. He was tall and had the build of a prize fighter rather than that of a technical type. The other man, Jack North, was much younger and had an arrogant presence about him: McCall noticed his body language towards Steel, almost as if he found Detective Steel to be some kind of threat. He was shorter than the others and his large-jawed head terminated in a blond flat top hairstyle. The man was keen and looked as if he might have a complex where authority was concerned.

Detective Sam McCall stepped forwards and scanned the plan. Using her finger she explained about their entry into the building and what they had found in all of the rooms up until she reached one particular door marked on the plan.

"This room here was the problem." She looked round at her captive audience, and scowled as she noticed that Steel had found a squad car to lie upon while she gave the briefing.

Rise of A Phoenix

"Inside we observed that the place had been set up into some kind of maze."

The two sergeants looked up, suddenly curious.

"A maze?" Sergeant North stepped back and crossed his arms, as if to show his disbelief.

"Yes, a maze. Large cargo boxes stacked up around, I don't know, seven feet or more."

Sergeant Carter beckoned for her to continue.

"That wasn't the problem however. As we continued further in we noticed pools of light created by holes in the ceiling. Steel threw some dust at the pools and that's when we saw the lasers."

This got everyone's attention; Steel smirked to himself as he felt the mood change.

"What sort of lasers?" asked Sergeant North, his arms falling to the sides of his body.

"Strings of light, pretty much like on a laser sight," she shrugged. *These were the experts*, she thought.

"Any ideas, Jack?" asked Sergeant Carter. The two men faced each other almost as if they were in a private conference.

"Well, it could be some kind of alarm system," replied the SWAT commander.

"Claymores," shouted Steel from his rest place, making everyone turn to look at him.

"Excuse me?" Sergeant North looked at Steel with an air of contempt. "And what makes you think claymore?"

Sergeant North turned away from the recumbent Steel, as if dismissing the idea.

"New type claymores have laser trip wires, not conventional cord ones," Steel added still lying down, getting some sun. Sergeant Carter nodded to concur, studying the floor plan once again.

"So what are you thinking, Mr Steel?" Carter asked.

Rolling off his comfortable perch, Steel walked forwards and looked at the floor plan. "Our best bet is to take a bird's-eye view, see what's down there, and then plug the holes." He stood back slightly and let them figure it out.

"OK, you lost me." said Sergeant Carter.

"The glass roof," McCall spoke up, her face suddenly animated. "The building has a glass roof, that's where the pools of light are coming from. We can look through the roof then plug the holes."

The Captain smiled as he noticed how his pair of detectives sparked ideas off each other.

"To what end?" Carter asked, then went on, "Ah, I get you, Ok, I got it, good idea. Plug the holes, then we have a better chance of seeing the lasers."

"But just in case, when we send the teams in they will have infra-red attached." added North.

"So what do you think?" Steel said, turning to Tooms.

The detective was caught off guard. *Why was he asking me?* Tooms thought to himself. His guilty mind was working overtime. Had the Captain been on the phone with Steel after their talk?

"Why you asking me?" Tooms asked nervously, crossing his arms in front of his chest to try and show some sort of defiance.

"Joshua, you were Special Forces, weren't you?" Steel asked.

Tooms suddenly found himself muddling his words. "Yes, why?" there was a defensive tone in his response.

"Hey, look man, I just want your opinion." McCall gave Tooms a strange look; she had never seen him behaving like this.

"Oh, OK." Tooms answered. "Well, the thing about those mothers is knowing which is the business end. It's not like the cable ones where you can just snip it in the middle, no, these are a real bastard." He looked at Steel, who shot him a friendly smile.

"Plus the other problem," announced Steel. Until y now McCall hadn't realised how bad the situation was. With Steel's next words she learnt the worst.

"The other problem being secondary devices. If they are mad enough to put claymores out they are sick enough to do that. That's the bad news."

Everyone gave him a look of surprise.

"And the good news is?" asked Tony, whose head was still spinning from hearing about the possible devices inside the building.

"My guess is there is something inside worth getting rid of, don't you think?"

The Captain had to agree: there had to be something really important inside, that was worth booby trapping the building, and blowing it up rather than letting it be found.

"Sir, how long could a laser light last for?" McCall asked Sergeant North.

The sergeant looked puzzled. "Couldn't say really. Why?" He leant forwards onto the hood of the car and looked at the plan, trying to look busy.

"Well how long would it last, unless it was plugged into the mains, which I doubt very much. The fact they're still working suggests to me that someone had to have recently turned them on." The Captain now had a bad feeling where this was going.

"And your point, Detective?" North didn't have time for games.

"It means we were set up. Again." McCall's words were bitter. Steel had always maintained his fear of revealing too much on the off-chance of a mole within the department. Now his uneasiness was hers, she hated the thought that someone in the station could set them up like this.

FIFTY

NOT WANTING TO RISK anyone seeing them through the weathered skylight, they sent a tactical helicopter. The small but nimble craft was propelled by quad rotors and had a built-in camera that could transmit data back so that the room could be mapped out. Before anything else was done, the holes in the roof had to be plugged to ensure complete darkness: one lucky volunteer made his way onto the roof and sprayed over the unpainted parts.

"OK, Sir, roof secure. Teams Alpha and Bravo report ready," reported the radio op to Sergeant North.

"OK, move them in but first sign of trouble move them out." North replied.

The man nodded and relayed the instructions.

The two teams moved in slowly. While their pistols were drawn, the men's Heckler and Koch UMP machine guns were slung on their backs and ready to go. Creeping in, they reached the large room. Both point men stopped and looked at the mass in front them. Through their night vision goggles the scene looked immense and somewhat terrifying.

"Fuck me," said Alpha's point man.

"Report teams, what do you see?" asked the HQ party. Inside a blacked out large van was the operations room for the SWAT team. Monitors flickered and voices came over the loudspeaker.

"Sir, put it like this: what we see don't look good," the reply squawked over the speaker.

Moving in further the units split apart, taking both sides of the junction; suddenly the two teams stopped and went to ground.

"Sir we have a big problem." The two point men switched on a small camera so that HQ could see what was happening.

"What in the name of everything holy is that?" Sergeant Carter eased forwards to get a better look. On the small monitor they saw a long corridor of boxes and down the centre they saw the lasers, what seemed like hundreds of thin beams of light: some going from top to bottom, others travelling from left to right. It was almost a nest of beams.

"Get your teams out now!" yelled the Captain, but North didn't require the prompting, he was already nudging the radio operator to retrieve the teams.

All teams came over the net to confirm they were at a safe distance and returning as ordered., Sergeant North grabbed the comms set from his head and threw it down on to the makeshift operations desk.

"What now?" asked Brant. He could see the frustration on North's face and he felt the same.

"We blow the building, make it safe." Carter stepped forward, he was calm and knew that this was the only option.

"We can't do that, there could be evidence inside," yelled McCall.

"Yes, there could be, but we don't know that for sure, do

we?" North was still mad, his face was red and beads of sweat rolled down his tanned skin.

"We have to check first." McCall lined up beside Sergeant North.

"Oh, really and who is going in? You?" he replied sternly.

"What about the copter?" asked Steel. Everyone turned to look at him. Steel was still lying on top of the squad car grabbing some rays of sun.

"What about it?" Carter stepped towards Steel, looking at this strange man and wondering who he was and where he came from.

"Well you fly the copter in, have a snoop round and if there is something we can get to we just drop in from above." Steel didn't move, he just casually lay there looking up and admiring the beauty of the day.

"From above?" North looked puzzled.

"The roof has a skylight, remember?" McCall added, smiling at his plan, knowing this would infuriate Sergeant North if it worked.

"Sounds good to me," announced the Captain confidently.

"But didn't the copter map out the grounds before?" asked Tony.

"No, we had to bring it in when everything went south," announced North with a regretful look. They talked at length about the possibilities and equipment required. SWAT had pulleys and lifting gear available, so a team was assigned to go up on the ageing roof to assemble the cross beam construction ready for use.

"OK then, so who is the lucky bastard who is going in the harness?" Sergeant Carter asked, rubbing his hands together. The group turned and Steel could feel all their eyes burning into him.

"It was his idea." North pointed at him with a wide grin.

"Thought so." Steel got up and moved to McCall's car and popped open the trunk; removing a large black canvas bag, Steel headed for one of the other disused buildings.

"Where the hell are you going?" asked Sergeant North, thinking Steel was making off.

Steel turned and smiled. "Just slipping into something more comfortable," and so saying he headed into the building.

"Captain Brant?" Sergeant Carter asked the officer, as he watched Steel disappear into the building.

"Yes?" Alan Brant was watching the others as they saw their colleague go to get ready for this dumb-ass mission.

"Captain, where the hell did you find this guy?"

The two men looked at each other, and eventually Brant smiled. "He found us, man, he found us."

The Captain turned and headed back to check on the copter operator.

FIFTY-ONE

IT HAD TAKEN SOME time for the metal construction to be put together, and now it resembled the skeletal structure of a medium sized marquee tent or the roof frame to a house. This framework would be put over the skylight and would support Steel as he went down into the room below. The detective walked out of the building and headed towards the command centre. Everyone there stared at Steel's outfit, which was black and, as far as McCall could see, fitted snugly. The all-in-one outfit resembled a driver's wetsuit apart from having carbon woven patches on the knees, elbows and shoulders. The gloves and boots were attached to the strange-looking suit so it was entirely one unit, with only John Steel's head remaining uncovered.

McCall ran up to the English detective. "You don't have to do this, you know," she said, urgently.

He just smiled. "Are you are volunteering then?"

"Sorry, not my style, but it's a nice outfit."

He shrugged and smiled at her, as she stared into the strange new glasses he had on. "Look, someone has to go in, I know he has left something, it's part of his game."

Sam McCall knew that he was right but on the other hand he had grown on her. She turned and saw the small helicopter take off and make its way to the entrance. All doors had been locked open, thus facilitating easy access for the helicopter.

"He's right," said a sickly sweet voice from behind them. As soon as she heard his voice she knew that it was the creepy Doctor Davidson. McCall and Steel looked over to see a quite perturbed doctor. McCall concluded that it was most likely the dirt that was bothering him, McCall thought, as she studied the way he kept brushing his trousers. He didn't want to be here, and frankly most of them would have preferred him to stay away.

"Any thoughts, Doc?" Steel didn't really need any psychobabble pontifications to know that this was one big trap, but on the other hand he felt kind of sorry for the guy.

"It's clear that the person we are looking for has a flair for the dramatic, he is meticulous and brutal," Davidson responded in his usual heart-warming manner, but still seemed more concerned about the dirt on his suit.

"In other words! Watch your ass." Tooms added. He didn't like the idea of the coming operation either, but like Steel said, someone had to do it. Steel continued his way to the command centre, where the chiefs were waiting for him.

"Steel, what the hell are you wearing, Son?" The Captain's face showed an element of surprise and laughter as he studded the tactical suit.

"You know it's not under water, right?"

Steel shot him a patient smile. "This suit blocks any heat signatures given off normally, so if there are any sort of sensor traps it should block them."

The Captain looked puzzled as he studded the suit more closely.

"I don't know, I find it kind of fetching," announced Tina as she walked up to the party, her eyes trained on John Steel.

"The doctor is here on the off chance that there could be casualties." The Captain said it quickly, then changed the subject.

The man at the flight controls yelled for the others as his copter had moved to the middle of the room.

"Hey guys, I think we have something here," he said. The camera showed the centre of the maze and in the middle sat a man in a chair. Steel stood up and looked puzzled. McCall turned to him, concerned at his sudden movement.

"What's the matter?" she asked.

"Is it just me or does this guy have a really bad thing about putting people in chairs in the middle of really bad situations?"

McCall had not thought of it like that, but she had to agree.

"OK, so we have one male in the centre of a room, any theories?" The Captain asked, standing up after leaning in on the monitor. He looked searchingly at the others.

"We go with the plan," Steel said firmly and shrugged as if to say *no other options*.

"OK, you go in from the roof and then get the hell out of there, understood?" the Captain told him. Steel had no other plan in mind. He didn't like the thought of going in anyway but staying in there was worse.

Steel broke off from the group and headed for the warehouse, and then McCall grabbed him.

"You know this has TRAP written all over it?" she said to him urgently. "So why are you going?"

"We need this evidence—you need this evidence. Besides it's a piece of cake: I go in, he comes out they get me out, we go home. Simple."

But she knew it sounded too simple, and wished that she could see into his eyes to know what he was really feeling.

"You better get your ass back here." She hoped that a display of anger would mask her concern.

A man ran up to Steel and tapped him on the shoulder. "Sir, we have to go," he said. Steel nodded and ran off with the other man.

"He is too much of a pain in the ass to die," Captain Brant said to her quietly. "Hell wouldn't have him I bet, too much trouble and you know he ain't ever going upstairs."

She smiled and looked up at Captain Brant who had approached her as Steel had left. Brant had noticed the tears building up in the corners of her eyes and put a massive hand on her shoulder.

"It's like Dad all over again." She had lost the smile.

Brant shook his head. "This is nothing like your father's murder, nothing. Now Steel will get in and out of there, you hear me, Detective?"

She nodded and turned back to watch as Steel was being lowered into the building. A bad feeling came over the two of them.

"We have to go." She dried her eyes and turned, and as she looked up at her Captain she could see the worry on his face, and his concern made her feel a little better.

The roof had been made secure and a hole had been cut above the target. Steel stood open-armed as the team put the harness on, finally latching the cable onto him via the clip; the man tugged on it to check that it was securely attached.

"OK, central we are good to go here." The team's leader gave a thumbs up to Steel, who stepped off into the open frame of the window. As he fell into the open air the gears of the mechanical pulley locked in, leaving him hanging in mid air a few feet from the roof's entrance.

FIFTY-TWO

BACK AT THE COMMAND centre they watched a second monitor, which held live feed from Steel's head cam. They saw the rocky motion as he was been lowered into the depths. Suddenly, with only a few feet to go, Steel yelled for them to stop.

"What's up? You changed your mind?" North spoke into the head set.

"How did you check this part of the room?" Steel asked.

North look somewhat confused at the question. "What do you mean? We used every sort of sensor and view that the bot has, you're safe to proceed." North shook his head as though to comment how unbelievable this man was. "Did you use x-ray?"

North's back stiffened. "And why would we use x-ray? So far he has used every gadget we know."

"Because, this guy is smart and at the moment I'm looking down to a large area that could have anything in it.

Rise of a Phoenix

Listen, if I know this guy he will start with technology and revert back to old school just to throw us off."

North looked at Doc Davidson who gave him a nod that signified that Steel was right.

"Listen Sergeant North, all your scans, can they pick up old fashioned trip wires?"

Then North's face changed, and he ran over to the techs. Steel knew from the silence that that answer was no.

"OK, bring back the bot and set it up for x-ray, even though I know it will be a waste of time." North was mad. He felt as if he had just been shown up as incompetent, and he didn't like that.After some readjustment and new equipment the copter was good to go. Flying through the gap in the ceiling it did a sweep and found all to be clear, and they also found the man to be alive. Using the x-ray they scanned the man for any sign of movement, which was slight but definitely discernible.

As they watched through Steel's cam, the Captain and the rest saw Steel untie the man and bring him forwards towards the cable. Locking him off onto the winch the man then disappeared into the haze of light above Steel. Everyone cheered as the man was retrieved through the skylight.

Alarms sounded inside the complex and a loudspeaker activated. McCall and the others listened in fear as they made out a countdown being hailed from within:

"30, 29, 28, 27…" the voice continued.

North ordered his men off the roof. As he did so McCall turned to him and screamed abuse, telling him how he couldn't leave Steel in there on his own. Then everyone fell silent as they heard: "5, 4, 3, 2, 1."

Steel listened intently, as the next thing to come over the speakers was Sinatra singing *My Way*. "Nice touch," he thought, looking for cover. He spied the perfect spot: a metal plate, like a manhole cover, stuck slightly out of the ground, and he dived for it.

Using all his strength he ripped up the metal cover and climbed in. A clang of metal echoed in the small crawl space as the cover crashed down behind him.

"Well, this is going to hurt," thought Steel out loud, crouching in his hiding spot and covering his ears. McCall ran forwards from the HQ with two SWAT members chasing after her.

A blinding white flash came from within the building, then the area where the extraction team had stood moments before was blown apart as the roof structure was swallowed up by a blinding flash. Four simultaneous explosions could be heard, followed by the building being consumed by a fireball. Then a loud explosion ripped the construction apart, throwing Detective McCall and the two SWAT team members across the ground, where smoldering bricks and timber rained down on them.

North and Carter stumbled forward, their faces registering the shock of what they had just witnessed, while McCall crawled to her knees and screamed Steel's name in the hope that this phantom of a man would rise up, desperate that this annoying partner of hers would be perched on a building somewhere, laughing at them for being so foolish as to think he was gone. But there was only fire, smoke and death in front of them.

McCall tried to throw off the two SWAT guys who had to restrain her from running into the inferno.

"Ma'am, there's nothing you can do, sorry about your guy but he's gone," one of them said.

Her eyes were blazing, as if she was snarling at the two men, who let her go, raised their arms and backed off.

"They are right, McCall, as much as I hate to agree," the Captain told her. "Steel gave his life for this sorry son-of-a-bitch. I just hope it was worth it." Brant could see how upset everyone was, and he ordered them all off the scene, even if 'off scene' was just around the corner.

Brant knew that CSU would be there soon too set up a canvass, and because the area was large they would have to move quickly providing the weather held. The press had wasted no time in setting up their crews, and cameras and vultures with microphones circled the scene, hoping for something to broadcast. The response crew stared at the press and shook their heads.

"Look at them, building burns down, couple of press guys arrive, said Tooms. "Put a cop in it, whole fucking precision." There was nothing that the homicide department could do, not here. They had two people to question; unfortunately one of them had to go to hospital, but the other was all theirs.

FIFTY-THREE

THE NEXT MORNING THE press was giving maximum coverage to the story about a cop in a booby-trapped building. It was reported that he had gone in to get a homeless guy out of danger. McCall smiled softly to herself, grateful that at least the press made a hero out of him. She had gotten in early, not wanting to waste any time. They had someone to talk to and she thought that he had better have the answers, for all their sakes.

As she sat at her desk McCall sipped her coffee and her gaze was transfixed on the empty chair next to her desk. She felt the presence of someone standing behind her and she turned quickly, hoping to find Detective Steel there wearing his black suit. Her face fell when she saw that it was the Captain.

"Thought it was him?" Brant smiled, reading her mind. "Yeh, the bastard really knew how to get into your head." He sat on the edge of her desk as she looked up at him.

"Why, Captain?"

"What do you mean why? Why did he pick here? Why did he choose you as a partner? Or why did he go into that building?" He shrugged. "Thing is, Sam, I really don't know. But I do know he cared about this team, and he cared about you."

She looked puzzled.

"What, you think he needed to sit here?" he said, pointing to the empty chair beside her. "The man had an office of his own." He stood up and laid a caring hand on her shoulder. "All we can do is to catch the bastard who did all this."

She looked up at him, and then her smile turned to a scowl. At that moment Brant pitied whoever was responsible for his murder.

Tony was on the phone to the CSU department. He was speaking to Cindy Childs, a one-time girlfriend from his college days, now a professional colleague. They talked for a while about this and that but mostly she was sympathizing with his loss of a fellow officer. She had spent some time down at the scene and her heart went out to the people in the department.

"Hey, are you guys OK?" Cindy went on. "I mean I saw the scene and everything and well, all I can say is I'm sorry."

Tony was touched at her words. "Yeh, well to lose someone like that is just—well you understand how I feel." She quickly changed the subject to the reason she called in the first place. "Mike from ballistics came up trumps for you."

He looked puzzled for a moment.

"You know that sniper rifle you sent down from the shooting at the bridge?"

He sipped his well-needed coffee. "Yeh, don't tell me it was used at the hotel shooting as well." He dismissed the idea as ludicrous.

"It's not that. There was another shooting." She explained some details of the weapon's history, which came as a shock to Tony. The detective, having gone pale at the news, thanked her and slowly put down the receiver.

McCall was with the rest of the team in the briefing room. The Captain was giving a breakdown on the events as they had happened, to try and elucidate some clues from the other people involved. Tony knocked and slowly walked in, and the Captain stopped talking and looked at him.

"What's up, Detective?" he asked, reading trouble in Tony's pensive expression.

"Uhm, I got the report back from ballistics." He fumbled with a piece of paper which he was grasping tightly.

"And what did they come up with?" asked the Captain, unable to figure out what was wrong.

Tony ignored him and looked across at McCall. "McCall, can I speak with you alone please?" he said.

The female detective wasn't in the mood for messing around. "Tony, if you have something, spill it right now, will you?" She leant back in her chair and rubbed her eyes, feeling as if she hadn't slept for a month.

"Okay. The weapon that was used in several of the shootings. One time it was used in the hotel room and the other was around eight years ago."

Sam's eyes lit up. At last they had a lead.

"Who was the target?" she asked excitedly.

"Detective Samuel Robson." His heart sank as he watched her stagger slightly as if she had been shot herself. She looked across at him, feeling as if her legs wouldn't support her.

"Are they sure?"

He nodded.

She took off, making for the ladies room. Meanwhile, Doctor Davidson and Thompson looked puzzled.

"Who the hell was he?" the doctor asked.

Captain Brant sat down and composed himself before he spoke: "About ten years ago I got partnered with this hothead; he wanted to save the world—a good guy, a good cop."

His audience listened attentively.

"We kicked some serious ass back in the day, bustin up all sorts of shit. Anyway one day on a big raid we busted big: weapons, cash, and oh I mean serious stuff. Now one detective made it his mission to find who was shipping the stuff and he shut them down."

Pausing only to take a sip from his coffee mug the Captain continued. "Around eight years ago he tells me he is close, he needs one final piece of the puzzle and he has everything. But he warned me it was bigger than we thought." He coughed and loosened his tie. "We were called to a hotel room somewhere in the Bronx, disturbance and possible use of weapons, so we go in nice and quiet, not wanting to spook them so they can run, you know? Anyway we get to the room, the door is open, Samuel goes in to check his vitals."

The Captain stood up and walked round, finding his admission of past events difficult.

"So what happened, Captain?" asked Doctor Davidson. He could see the pain in Brant's face and sympathized with him.

"A bullet from God knows where landed in my partner's chest, sending him across the room. I tried to do CPR but that was useless, he was gone." He wiped his eyes, weeping at the memory .

"So who was he?" asked Thompson, still confused.

The room went silent as McCall re-entered the room. "He was my father," she told them.

FIFTY-FOUR

JERRY, THE HOMELESS MAN who'd led them to the building, sat in Interrogation Room One. On the table in front of him sat a large plate of hamburger and fries. For a moment Detective McCall watched the man through the other side of the two-way mirror. She felt loathing for the man who sat calmly eating, while her partner had been vaporized by the blast. The Captain, who was standing next to her smiled.

"You okay going in there?" Alan Brant's words were a comfort, but she knew she had to do it. As she stood outside the door of the interrogation room she blew out a lungful of air, readying herself for the ordeal.

As McCall entered, Jerry looked up at her, looking beyond where she was standing, expecting to see Detective Steel.

"Where's the big guy?" he asked.

She sat down slowly, not saying a word, not even looking at him. She sorted out some paperwork in front of him then she looked up and gave him a smile.

"Hello, Jerry, how is the food?"

Rise of a Phoenix

He began to chew slowly, sensing that something was wrong.

"It's real good. Thanks." He suddenly became more nervous, looking at the door and hoping that Steel would enter. Then, when the realization hit him, the man began to tremble with fear.

"Where is the other detective?" he asked.

She shot him a look that was so evil he almost wet himself.

"Don't you even speak his name, you do not have the right to ever speak his name, you piece of" A bang on the glass behind her shocked her back to reality.

After a lengthy period of questioning, all McCall could get out of Jerry was he didn't know anything about the bombs or the fact that his friend George had been tied to a chair in the middle of it all. George was in hospital, guarded by four men; the Captain was not prepared to risk losing another witness.

"So, Jerry, tell me again about the deliveries?" The man she was questioning was tired and just wanted to sleep, but she figured that put her at an advantage.

"We would pick up the parcels and take them to wherever we were told to go." He drank the coffee she had put in front of him. "We would get word through Eric where to be and we would just deliver the goods."

"What sort of goods?" She leant back in the chair so it rocked backwards.

"I don't know. Some big, some small—just parcels," he said, taking another sip of coffee.

"Where to?" She could see he was breaking. *Just a little further*, she thought.

"All over the place. We would bring them to parks, disused places—all sorts." He was so tired that his hands were shaking. His eyes widened as she opened the file and laid out the crime scene photos of the women. Tears ran down his face as he realized the locations.

"I had nothing to do with this," he declared forcefully. "Really, this is wrong. As God is my witness, I didn't know what was in the parcels." He began to cry. "I was just told to bring the parcels there and leave them. That's all. Please, you have to believe me." He collapsed forwards on the table, the horrific images on the pictures burnt into his brain.

"Okay, Jerry, I believe you," she said, putting the photos away. "So these parcels. How long has it been going on for?"

He looked up at her, surprised at the question.

"Months? Years? I really don't know." He had stopped sobbing and took another sip of his coffee.

McCall got up and went to the door and spoke with another officer outside the room. She sat back down and regarded Jerry. She had so many mixed emotions about this poor soul. Because he had led them into a trap, she would have liked to put a bullet into his brain. But on the other hand, this poor bastard was just being used.

Moments later there was a knock on the door and a hand appeared with a map and some pens. McCall got up and took them, returning to her chair.

"Jerry, can you show me on this map where you delivered to?" she asked, placing the map on the table in front of him.

Jerry looked round nervously, then nodded. "But, see, if I help you, I have to disappear."

McCall leant back in her chair, and her cell phone buzzed. Taking it off the table she saw a text from the Captain, saying: *get the locations I will speak to witness protection.* She nodded to herself and put the phone back on the table.

Rise of A Phoenix

"Okay Jerry, you show us and then you disappear. It's being arranged as we speak."

He looked back at her suspiciously. She picked up her cell phone and showed him the screen displaying the text from the Captain. She saw the beginnings of a smile of relief touch the corners of his lips. A moment later there was a knock on the window and she knew the deal was done. His head shot up, looking round desperately.

"Are you expecting someone, Jerry?" She noticed his fingers rasping on the table, beads of sweat pouring down his dirty brow. He grabbed the pens and started to mark spots on the map. She instructed him to put a red dot to signify where he'd delivered a large package and a blue mark for a small one.

"You never know, he could be here, couldn't he?" Jerry's nervous scribblings on the map continued frantically.

"Who could be here?" Sam asked, intrigued. Who was it who was terrorizing him?

"THE MAN, of course! That's who! He is everywhere and everyone." As he picked up his coffee mug she noticed that his hands were shaking violently.

"Who is he? Have you ever met this THE MAN?"

He shook his head still looking around anxiously.

"Listen Jerry," she tried to reassure him. "You know you are safe here. Nobody can get to you here."

He looked up at her, his eyes full of fear and remorse, before looking back at the map.

"No," Jerry replied at last. "I have never met him. Nobody has. All we know is Eric gets a call and we go to wherever and move whatever." He shrugged, and as he sipped his coffee McCall could see he had calmed slightly.

McCall looked at the map he was busy filling out, then she stood up and reached for it. "I think that should be more than enough, thank you, Jerry." She headed for the door and knocked to be let out. The door clicked open slightly until the officer was satisfied that it was her and not the prisoner, then he let her through.

"Well, did we get anything?" asked the Captain.

"Sure," she said, holding up the map.

"Wow, we are going to need more people," said Tooms.

The map was almost full with red and blue dots, which all seemed to be located around particular areas.

"What about Jerry?" She sounded concerned about his welfare, which surprised her colleagues.

"Witness protection will be here in the morning," the Captain assured her. "Until then he will be kept in a cell, with a guard."

"Good." She nodded.

"So what now?" asked Tony.

McCall headed for the computer room. "Now we try to narrow our search down."

Once inside the IT centre, she met the computer tech, who was a man in his late twenties with spiky black hair and large black-rimmed glasses. His clothes were more street wear than NYPD but he was there for his brains not for his street cred.

"Hi, Louis, how are you today?" she greeted him with a smile.

He looked up at her from his monitor and returned the greeting. "How are you doing, Detective?"

She shrugged. "Guess I can't complain."

"So what have you got for me?"

She put the map down in front of him. "I need to know about all of these marked areas. Are there any warehouses or disused property nearby?"

Rise of A Phoenix

He looked at the groups of multi-colored dots, and smiled a confident smile, which reassured her a little. "Sure I can help, but it may take some time," he said, and got up and put the map onto a board so that he could get a better view.

McCall re-entered the interview room where Jerry sat nervously. She had brought him another coffee, which she placed in front of him as she sat down.

"Jerry," she began. "My Captain has spoken with some people and by tomorrow you will have a new life and a new identity."

He looked up and she could see the relief in his eyes. "So, Jerry, let's talk more about THE MAN. How do you know he exists at all?"

He leant forwards and she moved forwards to hear him, as he was now talking in whispers.

"I have seen Eric on the phone with someone and he always called the guy 'Sir', then he would turn to the other man and say: 'the man said we are still go'."

McCall looked puzzled for a moment.

"This other man, what did he look like?"

"I don't know. Tall, blond. Had some sort of black uniform on."

McCall shot a look backwards towards the mirror. Pieces were falling into place.

Sam excused herself and left the room where the others were waiting for her. "The asshole at the bridge that got away," said Tooms. She nodded but her thoughts were elsewhere.

The Captain looked through the two-way mirror at Jerry. "What the hell is going on here?" He was as puzzled as ever. He turned and faced the others. "OK, there's nothing more we can do here till tomorrow." He looked at his watch, realizing that the hours had just melted away. It was now nine o'clock in the evening and he needed to go home to his family. "Go home, get some rest and hopefully we'll have some doors to kick in tomorrow. All of you go home."

McCall watched as Jerry was taken to a quiet cell for the night and she smiled with relief. They had got through the day and no one else died. That was something to be grateful for.

FIFTY-FIVE

A WIND BLEW ACROSS the remnants of the warehouse, taking with it pieces of small debris, while its scorched walls lay broken and scattered. Loose timbers where windows once stood now smoldered and released ash into the air on the wind. Metal beams lay bent and deformed where the blast had twisted them into angry-looking shapes. What had once been the large storage room that held the maze was now a scene of devastation, its appearance more like a scene from a war movie than a crime scene. Burnt shattered fragments lay strewn across the blackened floor. The wind howled through the carnage like a wounded beast that brought a chill to the bones of the two officers sent to watch over the crime scene.

Rats scurried across the pieces of broken timber and brick, hoping to score a meal, but the officers knew that if anything edible had been inside it would have been turned into ash instantly.

The beams of the officers' flashlights cut through the night causing long haunting shadows as they swept past the gnarly looking ruins. The two men walked slowly through the areas they had been told to patrol.

"This place gives me the creeps," announced Officer Timmins, who was a young man of around twenty five, the last five of which he had been working with his current partner. Timmins was tall and thin with mousy coloured hair.

"Yeh, I hear ya man," replied Officer Doyle. "But still, it beats the hell out of that alleyway we had to guard." Memories still lingered about the ghostly figure they had seen, and Doyle shuddered at the thought of the place.

Doyle was a good cop but while he was not the brightest officer on the force, he was good at his job and he kept everyone happy; he was shorter than his partner, but stocky and well built, with a bushy moustache that compensated for his baldness.

Their route was specific, because much of the scene was covered by large plastic sheeting to conserve whatever evidence there was for CSU. As they walked they noticed a strange mist starting to cover the scene. Though it was low on the ground, it still blanketed the floor, giving the place an even eerier feel.

"Oh boy, you have got to be kidding me." Doyle said as he watched the foggy build up. He did not want to be here and this extra unpleasantness did not help. The mustachioed officer stopped and turned his head slightly. Timmins stared at him as though something was wrong.

"What's wrong?" Timmins asked, only to have Doyle put a large hand over his partner's mouth.

"Do you hear that?" the shorter man asked, forgetting to remove his hand. He looked up as Timmins made a muffled sound, withdrawing his palm.

Rise of a Phoenix

"Tell me, did you hear that?" Timmins listened carefully, and then he heard it. The noise was more of a scraping sound, distant, but definitely a scraping noise. Rushing forwards towards the sound they came to the entrance of the large storage area. Beams of light scanned the space like the searchlights from a war. They froze. There it was again! It sounded as though something underground was clawing its way to the surface. The two men drew their weapons and held flashlights aloft, ready to lock on to whatever it was.

Moving slowly towards the sound they noticed the mist was getting thicker as they got closer, and a great white blanket of fog clung to the ground, covering it completely.

As they watched from one corner a figure broke out of the cover of the fog and stood up slowly. The two police officers watched as this phantom straightened itself out.

"Uh—Hey you! You're not supposed to be in here!" yelled Doyle nervously.

The figure just stood motionless for a second, its left side towards them. Doyle nudged his partner saying, "You go ahead I'll cover you."

Timmins stepped backwards. "Fuck that! You go, I got your back."

Both men were sweating buckets, their quivering hands ready for anything.

The figure turned and faced them. It reached down and picked something up from the mist that resembled a blanket or was it a long coat? Doyle and Timmins looked on in horror as the figure put on the long coat and suddenly they realized that they had seen this phantom before.

Hesitantly the two cops moved to shine their flashlights on him when a loud crash made them spin round. A startled rat scurried away after knocking over a mangled ceiling light that had been balanced on top of a ruined piece of wall. The two turned back seconds later, only to find that the figure had disappeared into the fog.

With shaking hands the two terrified officers re-holstered their weapons; they slowly began walking backwards as if afraid to be snuck upon, and made their way back to the entrance of the crime scene. Doyle mumbled quietly but loud enough for Timmins to hear: "You know what, this is the last time we guard a goddamn crime scene." Timmins nodded in agreement, still unable to speak, Then as they broke out of view of the large room the two men ran all the way back to the main entrance.

FIFTY-SIX

THE HOUR WAS LATE and Eric and the blond mercenary sat in a large dimly lit room. The furnishings were a mixture of modern and antique. Their chairs faced a large dark wood desk that displayed curious carvings on its panels. The chairs on which they sat had tall backs with red velvet cushioning, and the ornately carved wood was decorated with gold leaf. The room itself was large but had very little in the way of furnishings from what they could see apart from the chairs and desk. The only light that partly filled the room was emitted from the large monitor screen on top of the desk.

"So, gentlemen, what news?" The voice was soft and somewhat gravely, but had a note of authority. Eric was mesmerized by the swirling patterns that swept across the screen of the monitor. Each time the voice sounded the smoke-like images moved with the strength of each note of the voice's tone.

"The one called Steel is no more, sir." Eric was sitting bolt upright in the chair as he spoke. Something about this whole faceless charade made him uneasy, but on the other hand the money was good. His words came out as a squeak, making the mercenary next to him squirm with unease."And the operation is safe, we can proceed as planned." Eric concluded, nudging the mercenary beside him to speak.

"Well, sir, everything is in place, and the police are still chasing their tails." The blond man said, speaking with a hint of a German accent, his tone hard and confident.

There was a brief silence that made both of them feel uneasy. Beads of sweat started to form on Eric's forehead but he dare not move to wipe the running droplets away.

"And you know this how?" inquired the voice. As Eric listened he could make out an accent, it was a mixture of English and American but he couldn't quite put his finger which was most prevalent. Their boss was well-spoken and had a tone someone might associate with Oxford or one of the other great British universities.

"We know it from our source, Sir." The blond man replied briefly but to the point.

The swirls on the screen filled with soft waves as if the news had pleased whoever was on the other side of the feed.

"So we have someone on the inside of the department, this is good news," the face on the monitor said. "And as for Mr Steel, how do we know he has joined his family?"

Eric looked at the other man, who shot him an angry look in return. It was Eric's turn to continue: "We dropped a building onto him after we detonated several hundred pounds of explosives within, sir. The man is nothing more than ash."

The blond man's skin crawled as he heard sickly laughter from the monitor. As he watched, the screen became a mass of violent nightmarish shapes that seemed to claw at the glass.

"Then let us proceed with the operation, gentlemen."

And with that the monitor went dark and the room lights came on. The two men stood, still a bit shaken from the briefing, and faced each other.

"And now?" asked the mercenary.

"We do as THE MAN has instructed."

Eric shrugged and smiled, and the blond man shivered at the sight of his ghastly grin. They walked away.

FIFTY-SEVEN

THE MORNING WAS GREY and dull; each detective had their assigned buildings to check on, with them as backup a uniformed man riding shotgun. Their task was simple: check out the buildings from the addresses Jerry had given them. The Captain didn't like the fact that he didn't have the manpower to send detectives in pairs, but the department had been hit hard by cuts and now the loss of Steel made things even harder, however special units were on standby just in case they were needed. Brant certainly didn't want any more losses.

McCall had arrived at an old power station. The tall derelict building was shadowed by its twin that stood around a car length's distance away. Sam parked up and looked at the two foreboding old constructions. Built in the early 1900s they still held a presence of awe about them. The red brick showed signs of decades of wear and weather, and just the look of the gloomy places gave her an uneasy feeling. She sat

Rise of a Phoenix

at the wheel for a moment and scanned the area, and her grip tightened on the wheel causing the leather to creak under the pressure. McCall leant forwards and eyed up the buildings.

Officer Paris, a keen young recruit, sat beside her, completely in awe of the moment. He had heard stories of Detective McCall's courage and tenacity, but most of all her personable appearance, and he oozed enthusiasm.

"So what's our first move, Detective?" Paris asked, a childish grin on his face.

She turned slowly and shot him a look which soon melted the grin. He swallowed hard and sat back into his seat.

"We check the perimeter," she told him grimly. "When I'm happy we move inside."

She looked at him and began to regret her severity, but reasoned that this was not play time and he had to learn the seriousness of their predicament. He nodded, remembering what had happened to Detective Steel, and understood that she would be doing all she could to prevent the same thing happening again. He had never met Steel but from what he had heard the man was something of a legend, and everyone was shocked that he'd been killed.

Quietly they got out of the car and moved towards the buildings. A breeze blew down the street from behind them, almost as if they were being led towards the twin buildings. The one on the left was the first they searched but during her years of service, McCall had learnt to be thorough.

It had taken a good two hours to go through the rooms in the building on the left, but happily it was clear, so they proceeded to the intended building. Both their weapons were drawn as they approached the entrance; to save time, McCall had checked the perimeters of both buildings on their sweep of the left hand building. The entrance mirrored that of the other building: large metal doors that were sparsely covered with the last remnants of flaky green paint.

They approached and stood either side of the doors. Detective McCall stretched the muscles in her hands, causing a clicking sound due to compressed muscles that had held her weapon too tight for too long. Paris looked up at her, noticing the concentration on her face and he felt safe to be under her command.

She looked up and smiled at him. "You ready, Paris?" she asked.

He pulled up his weapon so it sat in his double-handed grip at head level, blew out a massive puff of air, then nodded.

The door creaked with age as she pulled it open. The noise echoed along the seemingly endless corridor. Stepping inside they could see the dark walkway bathed in large strips of light that beamed from the door-less rooms on either side of the hallway. They counted six rooms, each of which was no larger than a small office, but knew that all of them had to be checked.

Creeping forwards to the first two rooms, McCall and Paris stood at either side of the two entrances; they would take a room each and would follow this routine until they reached the door at the end of the long corridor. Finding that the hallway was clear, they then stood next to a large metal sliding door: it was grey and rusty, and looked heavy. McCall noticed that it somehow did not match the rest of the building. Judging by Paris's expression she could see that he was pumped up, full of adrenaline, which could inspire him in two ways depending on his personality. He could either be the bravest son-of-a-bitch on the planet, or he he might freeze on the spot. She breathed a slight sigh. *Time to find out*, she thought to herself.

Rise of a Phoenix

The younger officer grasped the door and waited for McCall's signal. Together they counted down from five. When they got to zero he swung the door open, allowing her to roll in and aim for cover. No sooner was she in than the door slid shut and a loud CLANG filled the large room to indicate that she was locked in. She banged her head on the crate behind her. Her hiding place was four large moving crates piled up to form an upside down 'T' shape. She cursed herself for trusting Paris's judgement until she heard his screams dying away. As she peeked over the barricade she saw around twenty men dressed in black tactical gear training weapons on to her position. Laser dots danced on the wood of the crates, just awaiting the word to lock on to her and bring her to a bloody end.

"Good morning, Detective," called out a voice from the floor above. The room was large with a walkway that ran around the upper floor, creating easy access to the first-floor offices.

This was obviously a large storage area for a large number of small items, or a smaller quantity of large things. She saw the man who had been speaking: it was a large blond-haired man, he looked like a mercenary. She sneered inwardly at the sight of him.

"Now, Detective," he went on. "Drop your weapon and come out if you please."

She laughed out loud.

There was silence for a few moments.

"I promise no harm will come to you if you come out," he went on. "I give you my word."

McCall felt as if she had no other choice but to comply. Hopefully the cavalry would come racing to her aid in time. At that moment she froze in place and her heart sank, realizing that her white knight in black armor could no longer come to rip her from the clutches of destruction, and a single tear fell from her cheek.

She stood up and held out the weapon which was balancing on her right index finger. Men rushed forwards and surrounded her, and one of them snatched the pistol from its perch.

"Have you missed me?" She spoke with venom, and he liked that.

He walked up to her, his face several inches from hers and he smiled softly. "Welcome," he said, then suddenly swung about and walked off as the guards bound her hands and led her towards a wooden chair that sat in the middle of the dusty floor. She struggled and fought, flooring two of the men, causing another to trip as they fell. Fortunately her legs were free, so she made for cover. As she was almost there McCall felt a sharp pain in the leg, and as she crashed to ground she saw a dart with multi-colored strands sticking out of her upper leg.

"You bastar—" she uttered.

The blond man walked forwards and looked down at her. He smiled proudly. "What a woman," he said as he watched the men carry her off to the chair.

FIFTY-EIGHT

THE MID-MANHATTAN LIBRARY was bustling with crowds of people. Students rushed here and there in search of project information, others just sat alone and read. A figure passed unnoticed, books and folders in hand; the person made their way to the archive vault, then went to a dimly lit part of the room and found a computer. Sitting down, the stranger began to type, feeding names into the database to find out any information on the orphanage where the murdered women had lived.

The computer monitor flashed with life as it brought up photographs and news cuttings from newspaper articles. There were stories of a mass rapist in the area, and another tale of a mother who had to give one of her twins away because of a house fire that had killed the husband, as she was unable to cope alone with the troublesome one of the pair so she had placed one of them into an orphanage. More photographs came up of the orphanage, some of the pictures were of the children who were all lined up hoping to be chosen for adoption. One group photograph had the three girls, standing side by side dressed exactly the same and almost looking identical. The shadowy figure stood up and moved to the printer, which was happily spurting out page after page of information. Once the person had collected all the sheets, they moved back to the computer and closed the pages down. Moving back into the crowds outside the library, the figure vanished.

FIFTY-NINE

MCCALL FORCED HER EYES open but they felt heavy. She was slightly disorientated and giddy from the poison that had infected her system after the dart had entered her leg. A splash of cold water suddenly brought her fully awake, gasping for air from the shock of the quick shower. She looked round and found herself tied to the chair she had seen just before unconsciousness. McCall closed her eyes to a squint, then slowly opened them, letting them adjust to the light and the effects of the drugs that were still upsetting her. Detective McCall looked round slowly, taking in as much detail as possible. She noticed that she was in the middle of the large empty floor space, and all that appeared to be in the room was her chair and a desk, which sat neatly under the large walkway she had seen earlier. Looking up, she saw that this structure traversed right round until it met with a large area in which there was another door.

The blond man who had been in charge of her capture sat on the desk and poured a glass of water into a crystal glass, picking it up as he walked towards her. He offered the glass to her lips, but she turned her head quickly. Stepping back slightly he smiled, saying: "My dear detective, if we were going to kill you we would not have tranquilized you, we would have simply shot you."

The prisoner saw his point and took a sip of the water. She looked up to the balcony and saw a procession of armed men taking up position above her, then her gaze settled back to her blond captor.

"Welcome, Detective," announced a strange voice. She tried to turn around to get a look at this new foe.

"What do you want with me?" she asked. "I must warn you they will be looking for me and Officer Paris." Her thoughts suddenly were of her back-up, feeling ashamed that up until now she had forgotten about him.

"Where is he?" she yelled. Sam desperately hoped that he was alive but she feared the worst. She was bluffing, pretending he was still around, aware that she had to try something.

"Really, my dear, I thought you were braver and more intelligent than that," he tutted.

"Well, can't blame a girl for trying." Her words brought a smile to the blond man's face.

"Firstly nobody will be looking for you for some time," continued the blond man. "And secondly we would like to know how much the police know?" Sounds seemed to come from all directions, and she struggled to pinpoint its source.

"Who are you?" she asked as her head weaved from left to right to catch a glimpse of the other person.

"My name is of no importance. However who or what I am is very important. You see, I'm a fixer; I fix things for people who require things to be done. You know, meetings, whether it be for business or death." The blond man smiled

Rise of A Phoenix

and shook his head. "Sometimes, it's both at the same time." She heard footsteps from somewhere but, again, couldn't pinpoint them.

"We are just parts in a grand scheme, you see, and so we move back to the question, what do the police know? I promise I will kill you quickly. If you don't answer me, well let's just say the boys haven't had a date for a while."

McCall struggled with her bonds to no avail.

"My dear Detective, just tell us what we want to know and it will be over."

She was afraid, knowing that whether she talked or not, either way she was dead. This time there was no Steel to come bursting in to save her, she was alone. From the left corner of the room she saw a shape coming towards her. Turning to look, McCall saw a tall thin man, who looked destitute. His hair seemed to be tousled and unkempt, as though he had just woken up.

As he grew nearer he took off his jacket and threw it to one side, then removed his raggedy tie and shirt.

"We have our parts to play, Detective." He walked past her and disappeared into a room just opposite.

She struggled to catch sight of him, just as his words echoed through the building:

"Even you, and of course the late Detective Steel."

Her head dropped at the mention of his name, and a flood of emotion swept through her. Anger, hatred, sorrow, even guilt. Then from behind her there was the TAP, TAP, TAP of shoes stepping on the dusty floor, and she looked to locate the sound and her mouth fell open. There before her stood Doctor Davidson.

"You?" she yelled. "How the hell are you messed up in this?" All she wanted to do at this point was to break free and kick his ass. Steel had said all along that there was someone on the inside, but the Doctor?

"Now, Detective, tell me what you know?" the doctor asked again, but she had the feeling that he wouldn't repeat it another time. To the side of them a cell phone chimed, they both turned to see the blond man take the call. "Yes, yes, I understand, yes, but…. What time?" He clicked the off button and put it into his jacket pocket, he waved for Eric to come over. Eric excused himself politely and walked towards his waiting colleague. The two men stood for a moment discussing something in a whisper. From what she could gather the discussion was heated, because their arms flew erratically flew in all directions. Finally they calmed down, and the blond man put a hand on Eric's shoulder and waved for the other men to follow.

"Are you sure you don't want…?" Eric raised a hand and flipped it in a *go on* motion, as he waited for the last of them to leave. Eric slowly circled the incapacitated McCall. Finally the heavy door shut with a loud CLANG.

"What now, Davidson?" The anger in her had made her oblivious to her fear, but in answer he just smiled widely at her and, reaching into the vest pocket of his suit, he took out a pocket watch. As he flicked the antique watch open she heard the tinkling chime of music. He looked at the time, smiled, then put back the watch.

"As it happens I have a very important meeting to attend," said Davidson. "So if you will excuse me, I'll be off. But don't worry I'll be back to continue our little chat." He was maddeningly polite and calm.

"Tell me what this is all about, Davidson!" she screamed at him as he turned to leave.

He stopped and turned to face her, and his menacing grin sent a shiver down her sweat-soaked spine.

"You really don't know do you?"

And in that moment of clarity he knew everything was back on schedule. He walked towards her and drew a huge revolver, whose barrel was a good eight inches, slowly from its holster under his left arm. She gazed in horror at the massive polished steel cannon he now wielded.

"What? Couldn't you find anything bigger than that?" she asked, trying to cover her terror.

He raised the pistol so that it was level with her head. McCall saw the menacing reflection of light reflected down the spine of the barrel. She stared back at him with scorn, as she watched him target her down the sights of the cannon. An evil smirk crept across his pale sweat-beaded face, and at the same time he was twisting the barrel and changing stance as if he was trying to pose for the perfect picture. Suddenly the sadistic grin vanished as his hand fell downwards and the shining revolver came to rest at the side of his leg.

"You know, my only regret is that Detective Steel will not be here to see me kill you."

McCall noticed the genuine look of sadness on the face of the tall thin man as he walked right up to her and knelt down. She was choked by the potent waft of cologne, body odour and deodorant, making her want to vomit.

"You see, detective, for me it's not about killing it's all about how it's done. Yes, sure, anybody can pick up a weapon and take a life, but for me it's about art."

She looked at him, slightly puzzled.

"You see for me the act of creating something wondrous is the reward."

McCall saw a spark of pleasure in his eyes as he spoke of

the act, as if he were a painter or sculptor creating a masterpiece, rather than some insane killer.

"So why kill those women, Doc?"

Her question seemed to amuse him. He stood up from his perched position with a large grin on his face. "You REALLY don't know anything, do you, Detective?" he said, crossing his long arms in front of his body and shaking his head in disbelief. He walked over to the desk and sat upon it, allowing his legs to dangle, swinging idly, like those of an amused and excited child.

"You thought we were on to you?" She asked. "You thought when we arrived it would be more of us?" She had questions, too many questions.

"The only one who was close to figuring everything out was Steel!" he answered. "But he couldn't say anything because he didn't know who to trust. Yes, poor Detective Steel, he will be missed." He held a false look of sadness that made her truly furious. McCall fought and struggled with the ropes binding her, causing him to stand and raise his weapon once more.

"Oh my dear Detective, you really do want to kill me don't you?"

She glared at him with a burning desire to see his head removed from his shoulders. She stopped struggling and composed herself; then she smiled and looked up at him.

"So Doc, since you're going to kill me anyway, why not just tell me what this is all about?"

He smiled back and shook his pale head, then he raised his arm and targeted McCall down the sights of the canon.

"My dear, this is not some film where the villain gives up the plot and then is foiled by the dashing hero just in the nick of time. No, I'm afraid you need to figure this one out for yourself." He looked up into the air for a second as if to think for a moment, then just as quickly his gaze returned to McCall and he aimed the weapon towards her once again. "Well, with whatever time you have left anyway." He smiled a sickly smile and drew closer towards her. His movements were slow and deliberate, almost as if he was dancing towards her.

"No? No ideas? Nothing?" His voice was filled with disappointment. "Well, tell you what, let's see if Detective Steel had any more luck shall we?"

Her face was filled with confusion until a familiar voice came from the shadows:

"McCall, are you OK?"

She nodded.

"Of course she is." The tall man sounded almost insulted by the very question. "Anyway, Detective, your theory if you please."

As he pulled back the hammer McCall saw the gun's chamber revolve, lining up one of the huge rounds with its polished barrel. A familiar voice echoed around the large room. McCall tried to pinpoint its source but the acoustics made it difficult.

"Well, to start with you are not Doctor Davidson, as much as I would have liked that to be the case, but no." She recognized the voice to be that of John Steel.

McCall stared up at the tall man in disbelief; he shrugged and smiled almost in an apologetic manner.

"In fact your name isn't even Eric," Steel continued, still remaining in the shadows.

"Go on." The tall man, who was now no longer smiling, held McCall in his sights, ready to end her life at a single wrong word or movement from Steel.

"You see McCall, long ago, let's say about thirty years, shall we?"

The tall man made a half shrug to acknowledge the assumption.

"There were two brothers, twins to be exact," Steel went on. "Anyway these boys grew up in wealthy surroundings and didn't have a care in the world."

McCall could hear the voice move round them, as if Steel was somehow circling them.

"Well, as these boys grew up the mother started to notice certain differences in the boys. Even though they were identical in appearance they were very different in personality. One was as good as gold, the other mischievous and dark. Years passed and life continued to be good until one day, when the boys were around seven or eight, there was an accident and part of the family home burnt down."

McCall noticed the tall man's grip tighten on the pistol's handle.

"They called it an accident but the mother knew that little Steven Brooks had somehow caused the fire that had killed her husband. Of course she couldn't prove this but she knew she must do something. So one of the boys had to go in an orphanage where he would be better looked after, allowing her more time to attend to her other son."

McCall looked up at the tall man with surprise. In turn he could see her evaluating Steel's words.

"Go on. Mr. Steel." The tall man spoke as if he was almost amused.

"Life was hard at the orphanage at the start. The boy was bullied and beaten by the other kids at first, apart from three girls that could have been sisters, they looked so alike. The girls took pity on the boy and cared for him, and oh how he learned to love these girls from afar. But life was hard, harder than any boy should endure, but eventually the other kids accepted him and he had a large happy family. However, because of his past the nuns made sure he was not available to be put up for adoption, so that no other family would have to suffer. As for the other brother he had an excellent education and the lifestyle of a prince, he was groomed for greatness."

McCall's face registered her comprehension and she almost felt pity for the man who stood before her, but one thing puzzled her.

"If you loved the girls so much, why did you want to kill them?" she asked him. "It doesn't make sense."

Dr Davidson never flinched; he just stared down the gun's barrel, cold and devoid of emotion. After everything Steel had explained, Sam McCall felt as if things were finally making sense. If this man had been through such hardship it was reasonable to suppose he'd become some kind of sociopath, certainly. But to kill people who cared for him? That was something else altogether.

"Unfortunately this story is a little more messed up than you think," Steel went on. "At first I thought about the brilliance of the murders: no clues left behind, nothing to fit the women together socially, only their past history, yes, brilliant. But then I began thinking that something didn't sit right."

There was a sudden silence, which made Steven Brooks, aka Dr Davidson, look up and around, his weapon following his gaze.

He rushed across to McCall and, as he stood behind her, he pressed the cold steel against her head.

"No more games, Mr Steel," he yelled nervously.

McCall could almost feel the fear in the man behind her, and she wondered what it was about Steel that frightened him so much.

"Come on, Mr Steel, you haven't finished. You come out now, or I paint this room with the inside of her head."

Then from a corner of one of the empty lower rooms something fell. McCall flinched in shock as the huge handgun was fired in the direction of the noise, her ears ringing from the loud explosion. From another corner came another clatter, like a bottle rolling on the ground. He fired again.

"What's wrong, Mr Steel?" asked Brooks. "Are you afraid to face me?" He was yelling upwards, hoping the acoustics would travel. As Brooks placed the gun's barrel against McCall's head, she felt the metal's warmth against her skin,

"Enough of these games, Steel. If you will not come out I will bring you out."

A clatter to his left drew his attention but he did not fire in the direction of the noise, he merely smiled an evil grin and eased back the pistol's hammer.

"Last chance!" he yelled at the disused room. There was no response. McCall's eyes widened as she felt the minute alteration of pressure against her had as the trigger was being pulled. The maniac laughed as he looked intently to his front. The hammer fell.

Sam McCall couldn't figure out why she had shut her eyes as she felt the sudden pressure being released as the hammer fell. It was as though not seeing anything would help in some way. Those brief seconds seemed like hours, during which so much passed through her mind.

She opened one eye and looked up to find the confused killer still looking around the room and also downwards at his gun.

Brooks had been keenly anticipating the appearance of a fountain of blood and bone, splashing vibrant color across the dusty floor. But instead of a loud crescendo of gunfire and the metallic scent of blood, brain matter and gunpowder, he had heard simply a dull crunch like the sound of a twig snapping underfoot. He looked down at his weapon to find a pencil jammed between the hammer and the breech. He was equally surprised to find Steel standing just behind him, smiling.

"Hi." Steel said before smashing his fist into Brook's face. The man stumbled backwards but before he could recover, Steel had side-kicked his left knee, bringing the man to the ground. Brooks raised the gun, only to be met by a kick to the hand, which sent the weapon skidding across the floor still with the pencil jamming the firing mechanism.

Steel stood before Brooks, who was on his knees. He held a large .45 automatic trailed on the man as he cut McCall free with his other hand. She stood up slowly, rubbing the marks the bonds had made.

"What kept you?" she said, trying to sound annoyed with him.

"Well, you know I like to make an entrance, plus the deli had a special deal on."

She smacked him in the arm.

"So, Mr. Steel, what happens now?" said Brooks. "You know that when you tell that touching story they will put me into an asylum and I will never be convicted. Who knows? I may even be out in about five years." The man grinned as he saw McCall's face do the calculation.

"He is right you know," she said, panicked by the very thought of this madman ever being on the streets again.

"Fine, we could just kill him and say it was the blond guy. Less paperwork," Steel said coldly as he raised his weapon.

Brooks's face dropped as he saw the massive automatic swing upwards towards his head. After studying Steel's life he knew what the man was capable of and that was what frightened him: he was more a monster than himself. McCall shoved the weapon out of the way and gave him a scornful look, only to have him smile at her.

"There is one problem with the story, though," Steel said as he put the handcuffs onto Brooks and put him into the chair.

McCall looked round at Steel curiously.

"What's that?"

"It was this asshole that had the good home. Davidson went to the orphanage."

Brooks smiled.

"Shame you can't prove that, detective," he replied, smirking. "As far as they know, I had a bad childhood."

McCall looked confused. "I don't get it. We just have to get the doc to tell his side." Then she saw the look on both of their faces.

"The doc is next?"

Steel nodded.

"But what if…?"

Steel raised a hand. "I have left word for him to be kept safe." She blew a sigh of relief, then her face lit up with a curious look. "So why the women?"

"Well, you know the first vic was a lawyer working on a big case?"

McCall nodded.

"Well it wasn't just a big case, it was a very big case. It was to do with arms smuggling, and if she was to disappear before she was able to make her argument to the partners it would be swept under the carpet. But there was a problem! It had to look like an accident or better still, the work of a serial killer, so naturally when Brooks learnt of the other women and his brother's connection, the pieces began to fit. I mean, what better way to hide a hit on someone than make it part of a triple homicide. If things went wrong his brother would be investigated, as they went to the same orphanage. Also he could 'become' his brother at the precinct to see what progress we were making. Brilliant, really."

McCall sat down, her head still buzzing from the mass of information.

"So why cut up the women?" She was perched on the corner of the desk, her hands splayed out to steady her. Steel smiled and walked round the back of Brooks to ensure he didn't have any lock picks or tricks hidden away.

"The thing about most professional killers is, they enjoy what they do. That's bad enough, but when they are psychotic that really tips the balance."

McCall had to agree that this was the strangest case and probably deadliest one she had experienced.

Somewhere outside sirens could be heard wailing, heralding the arrival of the cavalry. Steel smiled softly at McCall seeing her expression of relief. As they listened they could hear the welcoming cries of "CLEAR, CLEAR, ROOMS CLEAR." Suddenly the sliding door flew open and the distinctive urban camouflage uniforms of the teams burst in, weapons held high at their shoulders.

As the Captain entered the dimly lit room with the rest of the team in close pursuit, they were met by McCall and Steel, who were waiting by the entrance.

Faces full of confusion glared at Steel as though a ghost stood before them.

"McCall, are you OK?" Brant asked, quickly looking round the room. She nodded and smiled.

"I'm fine, no there's really no need to be concerned

about me." Steel spoke with an air of disappointment and hurt, as the Captain turned and scowled at Steel.

"Detective Steel, where the hell have you been?" Then he winked playfully at McCall. She smiled shyly then she followed Steel as they made their way towards a figure hidden in the shadows sitting on a chair. Doctor Davidson entered slowly, taking in the scene occurring around him, and then as he made his way towards Steel he froze along with everyone else as they gazed upon a familiar face. The Captain's jaw dropped open as he switched his view between the doctor and the man in the chair.

"Steel? McCall? What the hell is this?" His index finger pointed firmly at Brooks. As the team members looked at the two men the supposed strange behavior of the doctor started to make some sort of sense; the others headed off to the other parts of the building to try and find any clues as to the identity of the people who had abducted McCall.

After two officers were assigned to watch Brooks, Steel took McCall to the waiting paramedics outside, and as she sat down a tall man put a blanket round her shoulders and proceeded to tend to her wounds. McCall looked up at Steel and smiled. Her eyes were red from the ordeal but still seemed to glint with a sense of joy.

"Are you OK?" he asked.

She shook her head in disbelief at the question, still smiling, but broader this time.

"What's the matter? Is it something I said?" He seemed confused but then that's what Steel liked about her: he didn't get her; she was the mystery he would someday try to solve, but not just yet.

"Never mind, Steel," she replied, giggling to herself.

Steel left her and made for the large room to make sure

that Brooks was ready when the transport arrived. As he was just about to enter he saw the two officers coming from inside.

"Hey, why are you guys leaving? You haven't been replaced yet?" he asked.

The two officers seemed confused. "Actually, sir, we have. Two plain-clothed detectives said they were here to pick him up and they also suggested the doctor travel with them as a precaution."

Steel burst into the empty room then turned to the men. "When did they leave?"

One officer thought for a moment. "A couple of minutes ago," he said, realizing what had happened.

Steel rushed out of the building to try and catch any vehicle that was leaving the site, but was only greeted by a confused-looking Captain Brant.

"What's wrong?" The Captain looked calm, but his calmness would be short lived.

"Well, your guards just handed over the prisoner and the Doc over to a pair of detectives."

Brant exploded with rage, heading for the door to read the riot act until Steel stopped him.

"What's done is done, Captain, you can kill them later. First we've got to get those guys back."

Brant calmed slightly but made a mental note to put the men on traffic duty for a long time.

Tooms walked up, while Tony was still keeping guard over McCall. "Steel, man, we thought you were toast!" and with a friendly handshake Tooms noticed the mood. "Hey, what's up?"

The Captain almost seemed unable to reply.

"Well, our prisoner and the Doc are gone, someone took

them." Steel told him. Now Tooms realized the cause of the somber mood.

"So, we find them and bring them back." Tooms suggested.

Steel and the Captain turned to him and gave him a sobering look.

"You don't get it," Steel explained. "Firstly these men are twins, together, not a good thing, especially when one of them has made a dammed good job of impersonating the other." Steel sat down next to McCall and looked up at the group in front of him. "Secondly the killer will probably have his brother committed instead of himself if he can. That's my guess, anyway."

Steel knew they would be long gone by now so chasing them would be futile, plus, he had no idea which direction they went.

"I'll notify public transport and get his picture out just in case they skip," said the Captain. "Plus I'll send word to the border control."

It was something, but Steel just shook his head and looked at the floor.

"What's up?" asked Alan Brant, just before Tony made off.

"I don't think he will leave," Steel looked up at the Captain. "If anything he will try and take over his brother's life as a cover."

"But?" asked McCall, knowing all too well what the look on his face stood for.

"We messed it up. I still think he will go ahead and commit him, even take over his brother's life, but he won't do it in the city."

Tony nodded and shot off, knowing how urgent it was to put both the Doc and his brother's names down as fugitives.

Rise of a Phoenix

There was a buzz on Steel's cell phone and he reached into his small biker-style jacket and he looked down at the display. "Oh, that's not good," he said, putting it back into his pocket.

"What's wrong? Bad news?" McCall felt like making a joke but it didn't seem to be the time.

Steel stood up and straightened his clothing. "The big case that our first vic was working on, it was an arms trafficking case. The reason she was working late was to put her case together to show it to the board. Apparently it was big and could hurt a lot of people—big people."

"Sounds like a motive to me." The Captain popped a mint into his mouth, as McCall's face dropped in realization.

"An arms deal?" she asked. Everyone looked puzzled at her sudden outburst.

"What now?" asked Tooms. He had had a long week and this case was the most confusing one he had ever experienced or would ever want to experience in the future.

"Brooks kept on asking me how much we knew, he also said to the blond mercenary from the bridge that they were good to go." Sam McCall explained, her face brightening as the case at last was becoming clearer.

"So they kill the two others to cover up their actual intended kill: Karen," Tony's mind was working on the fresh data. "But that doesn't give us any idea where they will be." He was a good cop, but he needed data, something to work with. Now he had the few missing pieces for the puzzle and therefore he was happy.

"One of the addresses for the drop-offs was near where my dad was killed, did anyone check it?" McCall said.

The Captain looked at the map. "We had two officers take that but we haven't heard anything back as of yet. Do you think they will be there?" he asked, unable to know how McCall would handle going back to the place where her father had died.

"Yes. If not they'll be somewhere nearby anyway. At least it's a start," the Captain had to agree.

Tony came around the corner and put his cell phone into his pocket. "We are good to go on every way out of the city."

The Captain nodded, instructing: "OK, you four head up to that address, the teams will meet you there. You stay until they are ready, understood?" He didn't look directly at Steel, but Steel had known that last comment was for him, and he smiled to himself.

"If it's OK I have to stop off, get a couple of things first," Steel said, and with that the four of them took off in McCall's car.

"Where to?" McCall asked, looking at Steel in the rearview mirror.

"Head up town, I have a place." Steel replied. She nodded and pressed her foot on the gas. With a screech of tires, they took off. Tooms didn't know where they were going but he knew they need a little more firepower than the weapons on them—they needed an army. Luckily, they had one and as he dropped off to sleep in the back of McCall's car, the words his friend had said days before came flooding back to him:

"What I do know is, if you're in the shit this is the man to have at your back."

Tooms felt some reassurance from that thought, but he knew tonight would get bloody.

SIXTY

AS MCCALL DROVE THE street lights seemed to blur into one, and the sky above was a strange watercolor mix of blues and purples. The sun was setting, but this evening was not blessed by its normal fiery display. However, she did not take any notice of the scenery: McCall was transfixed on getting to that hotel and ending the crisis.

She looked in the rearview mirror and saw that Steel had fallen into a deep sleep, and she smiled. Just seeing Steel like that made him seem just a little more normal to her. The man had had so much shit thrown at him lately she was surprised that he could sleep so soundly.

Tooms, who was riding next to her, looked behind and saw that Steel had wedged himself into the corner while Tony was happily doing something on his cell phone; he turned back and pulled out his weapon. Sliding out the magazine he pushed down on the top round to check the pressure of the spring inside to be sure that there's be no loading problems. Happy that his clip was full and working, he reinserted the magazine and returned the weapon to its holster under his arm."I radioed through," Tooms told them. "The Doc is in custody, they found a car with him tied up in the trunk on the freeway, but no sign of Brooks or the two goons."

McCall didn't seem surprised at the news.

"Do we know what to expect when we get there?" asked Tony, who was now checking his back-up weapon. The baby Glock was ready to go, and replacing it back into his leg holster he felt a little better.She shook her head. "No not really, but I can guarantee one thing—"

Tooms turned slowly to look at her."—We are going to ruin somebody's day!" And with that she put her foot down on the gas and sped off with purpose.

SIXTY-ONE

IT WAS A BRIGHT summer's day with a light breeze that made the trees sway, and birds chased each other across a cloudless sky. In the grounds of an English grand mansion a party was in progress. Friends and family laughed and joked amongst themselves, children ran round playing, all dressed up in clothes their parents had forced them to wear.

The grounds were large with a long lawn in which a marquee had been erected to house the tables and chairs for guests to be seated later in the evening. Next to it wooden panelled flooring lay to serve as a dance floor, and above hung a string of lights in a cross pattern, held aloft by four large pillars. The grounds were enclosed by a wooded area as though a piece had been cut out of the woodland and the lawn placed into the gap.

Wading through the guests, waiting staff hurried carrying trays of drinks or canapés.

At the back entrance of the mansion lay a large gravelled area enclosed by a balcony of stone that stretched round from both sides of the house, only broken by the white stone steps. Music blared from two large speakers that stood close to the rear doors; on the floor trailed a cable to a microphone and stand—this stood beside a large stone vase that was part of the magnificent stone balustrades. Two men stood on the graveled area talking. One of them was tall and broad shouldered, and his thick black hair was starting to grey at the sides. The other man stood a few inches smaller and his build was slimmer than the others, his blond hair was cut neatly, and while the taller man had a beard this man was clean shaven. Both wore tuxedos as did the other male guests, and the ladies all wore new-looking cocktail dresses .

The smaller man gave the other a friendly pat on the left arm and hurried down the steps to a party of people who were deep in conversation. The tall man picked up the microphone and turned to the DJ, who was hidden behind a makeshift booth at the far end of the gravel courtyard. He tapped it, sending a loud screech through the speakers, making everyone wince. He smiled like a naughty schoolboy.

"Sorry, sorry!" His British accent was playful. "Hello everyone, my wife and I would like to thank you all for coming this afternoon, we are here to celebrate two things; firstly the latest blow to the gun trafficking this morning, when the special unit made a bust that was estimated to be valued at around four million pounds"

There was an explosion of noise as everyone cheered and clapped.

"But also, more importantly, the safe return of our son." He raised his glass to the crowd but his eyes were transfixed on a beautiful woman. She stood elegantly, wearing a white dress, her dark shoulder-length hair crowned by a diamond tiara. She smiled at him, her eyes full of pride and happiness. Next to her stood their son Thomas, who was a dark haired twelve-year-old who had his father's looks, and their daughter, a pretty thing no more than ten years old but looking like a reflection of her mother: they were even clad in the same style of dress. It was a little joke that they liked to play on the lord. The young Miss Sophie smiled at her mother and squeezed her hand, and Helen Steel looked down at her daughter and winked.

A waiter walked up to the man at the microphone and whispered something into his ear, causing him to smile.

"Ladies and gentlemen, it would appear the problem with holding a surprise party is that one never knows when the guest of honor will arrive. So seems the case, it appears."

The crowd laughed as the embarrassed host grinned and shrugged apologetically.

"However, I don't think he would mind if we started without him, what do you say?" Again, he raised his glass.

"I couldn't agree more, Lord Steel," said a voice from behind.

A tall blond-haired man approached. His large solid form was packed into a black uniform, and his greased-back hair glistened in the afternoon sun.

"Who are you, and what do you want here? This is a private party," said the lord, and the mercenary smiled and walked up to him.

"I'm afraid, Lord Steel, your party is over. And one more thing: my employer sends his regards." With that, the stranger turned to the crowd as if to make an announcement, taking the microphone from Lord Steel's grasp. He raised it up to address his hostages.

Suddenly from nowhere six shots rang out. The blond mercenary turned to see a large bald military looking man with a menacing grin on his face. His large gun was pointed at

Lord Steel, as he dropped to the ground. His wife and children had watched in horror as red eruptions exploded from his back until he fell to his knees, and, with a final shot to the head, he rested in a dark red pool that crept across the ground. Their shock was broken by the sound of automatic gunfire from the wood line. People were being cut down by random gunfire, women and men running for cover only to be slain by a loose round.

Helen Steel watched in horror as she saw a group of four men heading for the marquee, and moments later there were mixed screams followed by gunfire. Her eyes grew wide as she saw holes appear as projectiles were being punched through the sides of the marquee, then there was silence. She grabbed her children's hands and ran for the safety of the house. A woman dressed in black ran with them, her long brown hair flowing behind her.

The bald mercenary smiled as he saw them and shook his head, as the blond mercenary raced up to him. He grabbed the man by the arm and yanked him towards him.

"This was not the plan, you moron, now we have to finish this," he snapped at the bald guy. "But remember none of the families are to be harmed, the man wants them alive." The hairless man wasn't listening, so the blond shook him again, shouting: "Am I understood?"

He was answered by a false smile as he headed into the building with a group of other men.

A taxi pulled up to the long driveway. Inside a soldier sat listening to the driver go on about the state of affairs in far-off lands, and the passenger, weary from the long travel, just looked out of the window and gazed upon the green fields of his home. He wore his camouflaged BDUs, the creases on his sleeves stood up like blade edges. He had been away for a long time and now it was time to come home. He did not want any fuss, just a quiet time with his wife and the rest of the family, but he knew that his dad would come up with some homecoming event.

It all seem quite surreal to him being home, after spending so long in a land that was barren of luxuries or even trees and grass as he knew it, so he had to readjust his thinking. Was this a dream? Would he suddenly wake up and find himself back in the hell he had left? He slowly touched the car's window glass, hoping it would actually be there and it wouldn't fade away as soon as he laid fingers on it. He smiled as the feel of the cold glass sent a tingling sensation down his spine,

He rested his warm cheek against the window and closed his eyes. "Oh that feels good," he said, and the cab driver looked at him through the rear view mirror and shook his head. As they neared the house loud pops could be heard. Steel opened his eyes with a start and shot upright.

"Stop the car!" the soldier ordered, but the cab driver paid no attention.

"Stop this car now, God damn it!"

The car came to a screeching halt.

"What is wrong, you crazy man?" said the Indian driver, and the soldier got out of the cab and listened. Loud cracks echoed through the trees followed by screams: something was terribly wrong.

"Get the hell out of here and call the police, tell them there are shots fired at this estate, have you got that?" The driver nodded and sped away, leaving the soldier to dart into the woods.

Making his way slowly through the woods towards the rear of the house, the soldier had not gone far when he saw a figure all in black holding an automatic rifle; he was a sentry, put there to ensure that nobody got away. This was not a robbery, this was an execution. Looking round he crept forward behind the man.

The guard had been standing for what seemed hours, he had no real idea why he was here or who these people were. All he cared about was that he was getting a lot of money.

Suddenly there was a loud crack behind him, so he ducked down and trained his weapon. He could feel his heart pounding in his chest, the adrenaline surging through his body. He blew out a lungful of air as a large rabbit hopped by. He stood up and laughed and turned, then gasped as a figure stood in front of him and punched him in the throat. The mercenary dropped to his knees clutching his throat, a gargling sound emanated from the man before he dropped to the ground and the sound ceased.

The soldier stripped the man of his tactical vest and checked the ammo content of the rifle and the pistol: they were both full. He smiled an evil smile. "Payback time," he thought. The radios on his vest crackled to life as the teams were giving *sit reps*.

He knew he had to find his family, plus any survivors, and take as many of these bastards out as he could. Moving quietly and stealthily he made his way along. Before him knelt another man. The soldier watched the man looking here and there, sensing that the mercenary was jumpy and on edge and was aware that he could use this to his advantage. In front of the man stood a group of his colleagues, laughing as they shot at the feet of a couple of people, making them run back and forth.

The soldier, whose name was John Steel, crept between the mercenary and the armed group and then suddenly he stood up. The mercenary yelped in surprise and opened up with his weapon, and the soldier dived out of the way just in time as a hail of bullets slammed into the armed men before him.

The newcomer watched from his hiding place as a fire fight killed both groups of mercenaries. Grinning to himself, the soldier moved forwards and grabbed the dead man's ammo.

As he watched, the group of scared guests made it to the woods and disappeared to safety. He returned to searching the dead guard more carefully, which awarded him with a smoke grenade. He frowned as he surveyed the carnage before him. Who were these men and what did they want?

He had too many questions but now was not the time to ask them. He knew he needed to cut down their numbers, and if he could do that without being seen, then all the better.

After all, he reasoned, he was no good to his family dead. A large group of armed men stood at the bottom of the steps to the house, put there to make sure nobody got in or out. Steel tossed the smoke grenade playfully in his hand and hatched a plan. Moving carefully around the marquee to the end that was secured by guy ropes, he cut the canvas, using the knife in his vest pocket, and crawled in. The large tent was empty apart for a group of corpses who appeared to be huddled together. His anger raged.

There was cutlery on the tables and many of the candles were decorated with pretty bows. He undid some of the ribbon on these and pulled out the grenade, then took out one of the magazines from the pouch on his vest. Sliding out enough rounds to cover the green cylinder-shaped grenade, he began to strap them to the explosive, using the ribbon.

Outside, the group of mercenaries heard someone calling: "Help! Help me please!" The voice was fading and the herd of killers headed for the tent, fired up with blood lust.

Ten men entered the marquee in search of the wounded man, weapons trained in search of a target as they crept in deeper. The rear man walked backwards covering their retreat. He suddenly stopped as his foot was hit by something, and he tried to yell before the room was filled with smoke. The group started to cough and splutter from the fumes, their vision impaired, arms swaying, trying to find the edge of the tent.

Then, as the container began to get hot, the rounds began to fire off. Loose rounds flew all over, causing the group to stop and start to return fire, not caring that they couldn't see their enemy. Other men rushed to their aid but only found death as stray rounds burst from the tent. Men fell screaming, holding their wounds.

From inside the house the blond man came to the window and observed the madness. "Finish this before they end up killing each other," he said.

A large bulk of a man stepped forwards and removed the automatic grenade launcher from where it rested on his back. Taking the two grips firmly in his hands he placed three rounds into the tent. As the projectiles hit they exploded with tremendous force. There were several bright flashes, then the marquee was ripped apart, sending pieces of timber and fabric whirling in all directions.

Where the tent had been there was nothing to see but massive bulges of red and black flame. Burning pieces of debris fell from the sky in a shower of burning rain.

The man replaced his weapon, grinning as he did so. "Boom," he said, his tone deep and hollow. Joining the others they preceded through the house checking for survivors, looking especially for the four people who had run into the house earlier.

Rise of a Phoenix

"The mother, her two children and other women are not to be harmed in any way," said the blond mercenary. Then he stopped, forcing the men behind him to come to a sudden halt, as he turned to look directly at one man. He was of average height, clean shaven, and had an eager look upon his face. "Are we understood?" His stare became intense, almost burning through the man, who backed off slightly and nodded.

John Steel saw that the gardens were clear and had observed several mercenaries going into the house. He didn't know the strength of their numbers but he did know there must be survivors because everyone had gone into the house. Moving across the body-filled lawn he kept low but moved quickly.

Reaching the wall and the steps he chanced a quick look, finding there was nobody to be seen. Moving slowly up the stone steps he came across the body of a man, and was scared to see who it was. Looking closer, he found it to be that of his father. His head dropped down, and all he wanted to do was scream out, but he knew that would alert the guards and preclude any hope of rescuing the others. There would be time for mourning later.

He kissed his fingers and pressed them down on to the head of the man, then he looked up to the house and anger burnt within him.

Through the back door led into a large dining room. Beyond that lay the large hallway and stairs leading to the bedrooms. The soldier crept slowly towards the double doors of the dining room and slowly opened the door enough to take a look. In front stood a guard, and across from him at the foot of the staircase stood another.

Steel took note of the hallway with its large marble floor

and the dark wood main doors directly in front. A set of stairs that traversed the left wall was decorated with paintings of men and women, landscapes and animals; apart from the two guards he could see no one. He closed the door and sat down. He had to think and think fast. The radio that sat on his shoulder pouch squeaked and he quickly went to turn it off, and thought of a plan.

Getting up, he raced to the large speaker by the door to the garden, and taking the headset he placed it down by the large black box, then, taking some tape he had found in the DJ's tool kit he taped up the 'send' button on the handset, and then carefully taped the headset's microphone to the speaker.

He stood up and looked around; his face fell when he saw the microphone lying next to his father. Taking a deep sorrowful breath he walked over and picked it up. "Okay, you bastards want a party?" he thought to himself.

The mercenaries walked through the large house going from room to room. The blond man had decided to wait in the large office he had found, where the oak walls and floor were complemented with heavy looking antique furniture—this room appealed to him. He had given instructions for them to proceed and bring back any survivors unharmed, but he was worried about Travis. After all, these men were not soldiers, they were hired convicts and therefore expendable! That was if anything should go wrong. Unfortunately Travis was a murderer and rapist of the worst kind: he was an animal, simple and basic.

The blond man had given his junior an instruction for him to keep an eye on Travis, and well, if he did anything wrong, he would know what to do. The leader of the mercenaries walked round the room in awe of its splendor. He found a large wooden globe in a corner and opened it, and his eyes lit up at the sight of the fine brandies and whiskies, and he helped himself to a glass of the twenty-year-old malt. He walked casually to a massive wooden bookshelf. Dickens, Sun Tzu, Tolstoy, all the classics were there. The smell of old leather filled his nostrils as he leant forwards and breathed in the cultured atmosphere. Picking a book he sat down on the red leather chesterfield and set to reading, sipping the whiskey as he smiled and imagined.

Steel knelt by the door with his back to the wall, reaching up he pulled a combat knife from a scabbard on the shoulder of the vest he had taken. The long blade glistened as the rays of the afternoon sun caught its sharpened edge. As he knelt with the Glock .45 in one hand and the microphone in the other, he took a moment to think about the events as they would happen: turn the microphone on, throw microphone to the speaker causing feedback, burst through the door, headshot to both men, get ready for men to come down stairwell, take them out, get out of room and head up stairs in all the confusion. It was a sound plan, in his head anyway.

He mentally counted to three then, using maximum force, he threw the microphone towards the speaker he had placed by the open bay doors. Everything turned to slow motion as the missile sailed through the air and landed with a clang that shot through the loud speakers, and, in turn, through the earpieces of the mercenaries. The men grabbed their ears in pain as the feedback came full force, incapacitating them for a few moments.

Steel swung open the doors and fired. Both guards took a round each, one to the back of the head and the other dead centre between the eyes. Steel watched as five men rushed down the stairs to find out what was wrong with the speakers. Steel cut them down with the pistol, and he watched in satisfaction as each of the men slammed against the walls of the stairwell as the impact of each round punched through them, leaving bloody smears.

Time to move, he thought, only stopping to pick up the dead guard's pistol, then rushing up the stairs with both weapons pointing in outstretched arms, he reached the upper hallway and knelt down behind a wall at the top of the stairs, waited for a second, then shot over to the first room.

The blond mercenary bolted out of his seat and ripped the earpiece from its place. Racing out of the door he made for the stairwell, picking up his men as he went. He had found five men recovering from the sudden blast to the eardrums, but they were okay, well, fit enough to kill someone anyway.

As he peered through the crack of the partially open door, Steel made out six men rushing downstairs. He knew could take them out, but he did not know how many more there were or where they were: no, he had to leave them and press on. Going down the long corridor, he checked room after room until he reached the end; there was nothing. He smiled to himself: if he found nothing then neither had they. Steel looked up towards the attic; he had to get to the attic.

The blond mercenary and the others rushed into the dining room and found the microphone next to the speaker.

He switched it off and threw it onto the lawn. Looking round he noticed the headset and speaker unit taped to the speaker, and ripping it off, he stood up.

"The boy is here," he instructed. "Find him. And I want him alive."

The others nodded. The head mercenary looked at the small microphone from the headset and smiled, he glanced up at the house and cast a view from left to right, trying to ascertain where his quarry might be. "Welcome home, John Steel," he muttered.

but never thought that as an adult he would be doing the same thing. The bulk of his body plus the extras made the journey fairly uncomfortable. Reaching the top, he used the knife to bore a small hole in which to see the attic. The attic was long and dark with only the light from the small windows in the roof above. It was large and spacious. Dusty boxes of long-forgotten things stood on top of one another, and as he looked he thought that only true fear would bring someone here; there was nowhere to hide, he thought.

He saw that it was clear, and, lifting the sliding door carefully, he stepped out. Dropping to one knee he drew one of the pistols, realizing that he would have to make it to the other side to satisfy himself that there was nobody here. Walking slowly and carefully he inched his way down towards the end, if nobody was here then they must have used the dumb waiter to go down to the kitchen or basement and then out from there. Moving slowly, his eye caught a shape in the distance. It was only a few feet away but the dark made it seem like miles,

Keeping down, he waited for his eyes to adjust, then he closed his eyes and took several deep breaths. Slowly he opened them and saw that it was a women lying there. Her face was not visible but he knew who it was and he felt that he could not move.

The blond mercenary went back inside the house and found that the others had regrouped in the large hallway; he walked up to the large man and nodded.

"What happened boss?" asked the other man.

"We have a homecoming after all it seems. I thought he wasn't due back for another week, but never mind, what is done is done. Right, first things first." The tall blond man looked at the group. "Where the hell is Travis?" he asked.Everyone looked round and shrugged.

"God damn it. Okay, find that psycho before he gets us all killed. Now move!" The men split off, and he grabbed the large man's arm and shook his head at him. "No, my friend, you're staying with me." The big guy smiled and reached down to take the strangely configured combat shotgun from one of his dead colleagues. As he pulled it up the dead man's hands still clutched the weapon, refusing to let go, and this made the blond mercenary laugh as he watched his friend struggle with a dead man. "He was always fond of that, never left his side, even more so now it seems."The big man looked up and shrugged.

"Leave the weapon, my friend, it seems the dead have claimed it, and it's not wise to annoy the dead." The large mercenary let the weapon and the body drop, more because of fear of disobeying his superior than anything. The big man was part gypsy and grew up on his grandma's tales of the old country and the legends and myths and curses. The blond mercenary had befriended him in the service. They had both joined the Foreign Legion many years ago but had later found a better employment.

The basement was cool and dark. A mother and her two children scurried across the floor to the wooden coal-cellar door. As Helen Steel reached up she realized she didn't have the key. She looked round at the small nail embedded into the wall next to the double doors, but it held no key, and she cursed the gardener, as she knew he had often forgotten to put it back. A noise behind them caused the trio to find a hiding space, which wasn't difficult, as the cellar was long with many rooms branching off it. They listened intently as someone was moving from room to room in search of their prey. The little girl hugged her mother. As Helen looked over to Thomas she could see both fear and anger burning in his expression. She grasped his hand and squeezed it for comfort, and looking up at her his mood lightened a little. Helen looked down and felt a glimmer of comfort in her daughter's eyes.

A sickening voice echoed down the hallway, saying: "Come out, I won't hurt you." A snigger came next, and she trembled.

Helen noticed some old barrels leaning up against the far wall. Grabbing Sophie and Thomas she hurried quietly towards them and, lifting one of the lids off, she placed the terrified children inside.

Sophie clung to her mother, knowing she was protecting them with her own life. "Now," their mother told them. "You stay in here and don't move, okay, no matter what you see or hear. You don't move until the police arrive." She stared into the glassy eyes of her child, knowing this would be the last time she could do so, then she kissed Sophie on her forehead and Helen took off and passed a necklace to the child. It was a golden locket with a picture of them all. The long golden chain swayed as her hands shook with emotion.

Sophie grasped the necklace and held it tightly to her, and she stared upwards, fearfully.

"Thomas," she told her son. "I need you to look after your sister, okay?"

His watery eyes stared back at her.

"But—" She kissed his forehead to stop him saying anything else.

"You have to be brave. No matter what, you stick together, promise me."

The two children reluctantly nodded.

"I love you, both of you and I always will, remember that," she said and, tears rolling down her face, Helen replaced the lid.

As the two children listened with eyes firmly shut, they could make out the heavy breathing of a large man: he panted and snorted like a rhino, and they huddled together in the barrel and tried to make themselves as small as possible. The snorting brute came nearer and nearer, his feet shuffled on the floor. Thomas in his imagination conjured images of the Minotaur from the Greek myths. Then a noise of someone running alerted the beast and the children heard it follow.

Sophie shook with fear, her body soaked with perspiration; Thomas held her close, comforting himself as well as reassuring his sister.

Helen Steel managed to get to the dumb waiter and quickly stowed herself into it. She had to go up to the attic and get Elisabeth. The four had parted their ways so Helen could force the large bald man to follow her, giving Elisabeth time to hide or get away, and in turn Helen and the children would get out through the coal cellar doors.

Moving towards the sound of the footsteps the brute found himself at the dumb waiter. He banged a powerful fist on the wall as he saw the elevator moving upwards, then a calculated evil grin came onto his face and he made for the stairs.

Steel moved slowly towards the woman, his legs felt heavy, almost impossible to move. Suddenly he crashed to his knees, kicking up a cloud of dust that hung in the pools of light. His face twisted with the pain of seeing his sweet wife lying there motionless. Steel reached out a hand to grab her, his powerful fingers clawing at the distance between them.

Forcing himself up he dragged himself towards her, tears streaming down his face. His mouth moved but no sound would come from his lips. He was only feet away now but it seemed like miles. Again his body smashed down upon the ancient floorboards. He did not care anymore who found him, he had come here to save her and he had failed. He reached forwards and touched her hair, but his outstretched fingers were unable to grasp her. His body contorted by emotion, he was unable to move, his mind in shock. Carefully he brought his clenched fists up to his face and blew out several deep breaths.

Closing his eyes he reached forwards, and as his hands fell upon her body he cried out. The animalistic howl wailed through the house, causing the mercenaries to stop and look at one another.

"The attic!" shouted the blond mercenary, "and be quick!" He was racing up the stairs, and the others followed.

Steel knelt on the ground holding his wife's body close to him; his tears flowed as if they'd go on forever. In front of him, out of the shadows, ran a figure. The tears blurred his eyes, until a familiar voice broke through his consciousness. It was his mother.

"John, behind you!" she screamed.

A gunshot echoed through the attic. Enhanced by the open space it was more like an explosion. As he watched, his mother was hurled sideways from the impact, blood and flesh painting the large beams behind her.

Steel watched helplessly as his mother tried to claw her way towards him, reaching out an arm, then he noticed the angry exit wound in her back. The sounds of her wheezing, and struggling for breath burnt into his ears. Then there was a new sound, one of heavy footsteps.

There was laughter, then three shots rang out. Steel looked down, his body still numb from shock and saw the exit wounds in his body. And then, as he looked down, he saw his wife's eyes open just before the next shot rang out.

He heard her scream and then there was silence. He felt the pain of every hit his body had taken. Looking down he saw Helen's her eyes open, then the cold stare of emptiness filled them. As he watched he saw the last spark of life leave her body just before the next hit. Before he slipped into darkness Steel smelt the foul body odor of a large man, and the sound of the man's breathing filled his ears.

"What the fuck have you done, Travis? Santini will have our fucking heads for this, you animal." The blond Merc was maddened by what he saw. Steel slipped into darkness just as the man laughed and walked off, and his laughter grew louder.

Steel screamed then woke up. McCall pulled the car back under control after being scared out of her wits by his yell.

"What the hell was that, Steel?" McCall barked.

"Sorry, bit of a bad dream," Steel replied, trying to calm everyone.

"Really, you think." Tony was readjusting his seating position.

Then as Steel looked out of the window he felt clarity. For the first time ever he had nearly finished the dream.

"We have to go somewhere before we meet the Captain and the others," Steel said, leaning forwards.

"Where are we going?" asked McCall, somewhat suspicious and a little bit curious.

"A place I have got," John Steel replied. "We have to pick up some stuff."

"Where to? You got a bat cave?" Tooms joked, but the smile left him when he saw the expression on Steel's face.

"Trust me, look, you will all thank me. If we live, that is."

All three of them gave Steel a nervous look.

SIXTY-TWO

THE NIGHT AIR WAS warm and menacing and clouds covered the sky. In a multi-story parking complex men in dark uniforms hurried about loading large reinforced carrying boxes into several white vans. On the floor above stood a tall man with blond greased-back hair. He had overseen the labors of his men and now he just wanted to look down upon the city. Soon their business would be concluded and there was nothing to stand in their way. He had heard of the demise of Detective Steel and it saddened him slightly—he had heard so many tales of the man's valour that he seemed almost like a legend.

He wore a black suit but underneath it a strange high-necked collar fitted tightly around his throat. The material was the same as the other men wore, but he had had it constructed so as to be more elegant. The breeze blew past his face and he closed his eyes and breathed in the evening air. Life was good, he thought, as he opened his eyes just in time to see down below a black Mercedes pull into the parking lot.

Two men with long jackets were in the car as it stopped. As the window rolled down a faint whining sound emitted from the its motors, and a gloved hand came out of the vehicle's window and flipped open a pass. The large guard waved at his colleague to open the barrier, as the large yellow-and-black metal barrier was raised, and the large guard spoke into his radio, saying, "Sir, Mr Smith has just arrived."

The blond man smiled. "Very good."

As the Mercedes travelled along the winding path, the driver dimmed the lights of the vehicle, until they reached the floor where the men were busy loading up the vans. The vehicle stopped next to one of the armed guards, and the window came down.

"Where is he?" requested Mr Smith nervously. The guard pointed upwards then continued with his patrol.

As the black car got to the designated floor it slid into a parking spot. Four men, including Smith, got out and made their way to the man. Smith noticed he hadn't even turned round, he just expected.

"Good evening, Mr Smith." said the man.

"Good evening, Mr Jones," he replied, waving the others away.

"Your report, if you please." Smith came up and stood beside him. Smith was at least several inches smaller than Jones. They both looked out over the shimmering view before them.

"The cop is with Mr Williams, they are er... having a conversation."

Jones nodded with a smile. "I want no mistakes, Mr Smith." His voice was stern and deep.

Smith nodded. "Don't worry, Steel is gone, the other cop is otherwise engaged, shall we say. I can't foresee any problems." Smith was nervous but didn't wish to show it.

"Then let us proceed."

Jones turned to Smith and put his left hand onto Smith's right shoulder and nodded. Walking away, Smith took that as a sign for NOW. With a screech of tires the convoy set ventured through the maze of the garage until they reached the exit, then one by one the five cars and seven white vans set off into the night.

SIXTY-THREE

McCall followed Steel's directions, which led them down several back streets and darkened empty blocks, until eventually they arrived at an old rundown building. McCall observed that in front of it were three roller door entrances.

"What is this place?" she asked, terrified at what they might find. Steel grinned and took something from his jacket pocket. In his hand he held what appeared to be some kind of car remote control device. Pointing it towards the building he clicked a button and a small red LED light blinked three times, then with a loud metallic bang, the middle door started to roll up.

"Can you drive in, please?" His words were calm and somewhat amused, probably in anticipation of what they were about to find. As the car rolled slowly into the large space, Steel got out and walked over to a small panel on the left-hand wall, which was obviously a control centre for something.

Rise of a Phoenix

Inside the car the others looked at each other nervously. It was dark, apart from the blue glow from the vehicle's stereo system. Steel selected the fire-alarm button, lifted the fake cover and, holding the remote, pressed another button. A hidden key extended out of the side of the small remote device. Inserting the key into the slot under the fire alarm, Steel turned to the others, nodded, then looked up. He turned the key, and instantly the roller doors came down. And then they began to move: downwards.

"Hey, where the hell are we going, man?" yelled Tooms in a sudden panic. "Don't tell me you DO have a bat cave?"

McCall grinned sarcastically, but that soon faded when she saw Steel's unnerving grin. All the while, the elevator gave a clang of ancient gears.

The Captain and the special weapons teams had arrived at the hotel. Black vehicles screeched into position and armed men in black tactical gear burst out of them and moved to the building, weapons held at the ready. The two teams divided: one would cover the back, the other would breach the front, but any action would have to be performed simultaneously. The Captain looked down at the cell phone strapped to his belt, picking it up he saw the caller ID was that of McCall."McCall, where the hell are you people?" he demanded. "We are all set up and ready to go!" Brant's voice was quiet but brash."Hi, Captain we just had to pick up one or two things from Steel's place," she replied. "According to my satnav we are about fifteen minutes from your location, Sir, and we will be there as soon as we can."

Then they closed the conversation, as the team's commander signalled that they were ready for the signal from the teams. Captain Brant looked up at the old hotel, and his eyes suddenly grew wide and watery. His heart sank as he realized where they were.

"Alpha in position," came the voice came over the speakers in the tactical truck. Inside the command vehicle, they had audio and video feed from all members of the team.

"Bravo in position," the Commander replied. "Okay, we are good to go, on my mark… mark." The two teams used the large metal battering rams to disintegrate the two doors, then the teams moved quickly, making a lot of noise. Team One proceeded straight upstairs while Bravo cleared the lower floors. "Clear, clear," both teams reported the building safe for the Captain and the others to proceed to enter. Then there was another message: "Sir, we have something on the second floor." The captain froze for a moment. "In what room?" he asked nervously. "Room 207." The Captain's eyes closed tightly: *not that room*, he thought. *Of all the rooms not that one.*

McCall and the others suddenly felt a surge of panic come over them. Tooms leapt out of the car and, as he ran towards Steel, he stopped and his mouth fell open. As they approached the bottom, lights began to flicker on, starting at the entrance and finishing at the end of a long room.

"What in the name of—" Tooms stopped talking and just stood and stared as did the others. The room was around twenty feet long and twelve wide, the walls were coloured a sterile white and double-sided shelving ran down the centre. The place looked more like a grocery store than anything sinister, but instead of tins of beans and sweetcorn, the shelving held arms of all kinds. This was no hideout, this was an armory. Each shelf held a different type of weapon, next to which different accessories were laid out, including scoped and suppressors. These were arranged so as to match the guns they pertained to.

Tooms drooled as if he was a child in a candy store as he slowly wandered around, then he grinned as his eye caught a glimpse of the black Ford F-150 Atlas vehicle. "Hey, Steel," he called out. "I thought this was just a concept vehicle?"

Steel just shrugged as he headed towards a metal locker, saying: "We can expect to be outnumbered but I don't believe in being outgunned."

McCall stood, her mouth open, nodding her head in agreement. "Steel, what the hell are you getting ready for, the third world war?"

Steel walked up to a locker that contained several black canvas kitbags, and picked them up and threw them to the others.

"If you can carry one of these you should take it," he told them. "What's in these bags might make the difference between us walking out or being getting carried out."

They all knew that the shit was going to hit the fan, and now they felt they had an edge.

"What's the plan?" asked Tony, who was picking up MP7 9mm machine pistols and some 5.56 mm assault rifles and shoving them into his bag.

"We find them, and we bring them down, any way necessary." Steel seemed calm as he spoke.

The others packed what they could and put several extras in the trunk of McCall's car. Steel held a long heavy-looking canvas bag, which he carefully placed in the trunk of his own Ford F150 Atlas along with his other equipment.

"What's in the bag, you planning on fishing?" joked Tooms.

Steel smiled. "No, a spot of hunting may be in order though." And with that the trunk was slammed shut. They were ready.

Captain Brant walked up the stairs slowly. To him, everything seemed to be happening in slow motion. He passed a group of team members in the corridor, and he seemed to see through them as if past and present were colliding. People's voices seemed garbled, as though they were speaking from a sealed container, then one voice seemed to get clearer, bringing him back to reality: "Sir?" he said. "Sir?"

Brant shook his head as a team member grabbed him. "Are you okay, sir?" asked the man, clearly concerned.

"What?" said Brant. "Yes, I'm okay, it's nothing."

Both the leader of the team and one of its members looked at him oddly.

"Eight years ago I watched my partner take a sniper's bullet in this room," the Captain explained. "So do you think I have a problem with this place? Damn right I do. Will it affect my judgment?. No it will not."

Then his voice and stature changed, it became more aggressive, more like his old self. "So what have we got?" he asked, sliding his hands into his pockets.

"We found a note, Sir, it's addressed to you."

Brant looked firstly at the officer, then using a gloved hand, took the piece of paper. It simply read: *Captain Brant; sorry we missed you hope to get you next time.* This was written in red wax crayon letters, scrawled as if done by a child. Brant took the note and gave it to the officer, who then bagged it.

As Brant entered the room, a chill ran down his spine as if a ghost had passed straight through him. The place hadn't changed in all these years. Brant looked around and sighed, then he felt a presence in the room. He closed his eyes and turned, and, as he opened them, he hoped that he was wrong in his assumption of who the newcomer might be. He was not.

There holding on to the doorframe stood Detective McCall, and she looked pale and sickly. The team member rushed to her, saying, "Are you okay, Detective?"

The Captain shot him a sorrowful look. "Son, the man who died was my partner, but he was Detective McCall's father." The team member felt awkward and left.

"You okay, Kid?" the Captain asked, and she nodded, taking in the full aura of the room. Steel and the others walked in. Steel looked at the room and picked up on McCall's pain.

"God, this place hasn't changed in eight years," said the Captain. "I'm quite surprised the new tenant didn't spruce up the place."

Steel looked up in surprise. "What new tenant? This place has been empty for eight years."

"Really?" The Captain's words sounded hollow as Steel turned to face him. "So who cleaned the place? There's no dust or anything out of place."

There was an awkward silence before Steel turned his attention to the window.

"So this place looks exactly as it did eight years ago, yes?" John Steel asked.

The Captain nodded.

Steel had an uneasy feeling and carefully walked to the window, then he turned and faced the others. "Sam was explaining you were looking for places where the men dropped off the packages. If there was some sort of deal going down this place is too cramped, and there are no escape routes." Then he turned to face the window once more. "But that place is perfect."

In front of them there was a large multi storey car park.

"But why keep the room just as it was?" Brant asked, looking puzzled.

"To mess with you," Steel answered. "Don't you see this is what he does? He gets inside your head and plays with your mind." The Englishman turned his focus back to the window.

"That must have been where the shooter killed my dad?" McCall stated it as a question.

Captain Brant nodded. "After the shooting we did a canvass and found nothing."

Steel looked closely, realizing that the closed walls of the car park gave it perfect cover. "I don't know what, but my gut tells me something over there will dictate our next move."

The SWAT commander corralled his teams and gave them new strike orders: if something was going down his team had to be the first ones in.

"Tony, can you get the footage from these cameras? I want to know who came in and out," requested McCall, looking up at the CCTV cameras covering the entrance to the lot.

"What you thinking, McCall?" asked the Captain.

"Well, we can get an idea of how many and which direction they went in if they left," She reasoned.

Steel watched as Tony raced off down the street.

The teams had their orders and were ready to move in. But as far as John Steel was concerned, something did not sit right, and the Captain could read the discomfort on his face.

"What's up, Steel? Man, you have that look, and I don't like that look."

The SWAT commander was just about to give the order to go.

"Tell your teams to stand fast, something's not right with this," Brant said.

Rise of A Phoenix

The Commander regarded him with a confused expression, saying: "Listen, if you have some information we should know about it."

"It's just that the man who is doing all this is thorough and calculating," Brant commented. "He would know we would come here just like he knew we would be at the warehouse."

The Commander stood up from his chair. "So, Mr Steel," he snapped. "What do you suggest we do, sit on our asses?"

Steel shook his head and thought about the layout of the building. He turned towards the Commander. "We need your copter again."

The Commander thought for a moment. "Do you think this place is rigged?"

Steel's body stiffened, making himself stand more upright. "Sir, I think this place is a loose end and this man doesn't do loose ends."

The Captain and McCall both nodded at the Commander, who thought for a moment, and then turned to the man next to him at the desk. "Get the copter ready and get me E.O.D will you?" The young man gave the thumbs up and got onto it. "Okay, people, what's your plan?"

SIXTY-FOUR

IN A CARGO DOCKYARD stood a massive metal beast of a ship, and the yellow of its security lights picked up the edges of its black weathered hull. Down below at the dock a convoy of vehicles rolled onto the concrete, and the six vans and four cars raced up to the rally point. As the procession stopped, men dismounted the vehicles and surrounded the convoy. Everyone held their positions until a figure ventured down the gantries, the lead car door opened and Mr Jones got out, looking at a man who was approaching. The man was shorter than Mr Jones but he had broad shoulders and long black hair tied back in a ponytail. He wore a short beard on his massive jawed face, and his eyes were dark, appearing to be almost black.

He approached and Jones went forwards to meet him, and the men embraced like brothers. "My friend, it has been too long," said the pony-tailed man in a middle eastern accent.

Rise of a Phoenix

"Mr Moses, I believe your ponytail is getting longer," said Jones.

Moses stepped back. "Mr Jones, I do believe you are getting uglier."

The pair laughed and walked for a bit. "We have the merchandise if you care to inspect it?" Jones waved at some men, who quickly started to unload the cargo.

"Has he sent word yet?" Mr Moses seemed uneasy talking about 'The man'.

"No, we haven't heard anything for a while, so I presume it's business as usual."

Mr Moses felt the need to change the subject. "So, I heard you had an interesting guest?"

Mr Jones smiled at the thought of what his employer might be doing to Sam McCall. "Yes, her father was a bother and it seems to be a family trait, and as a bonus we've got Steel as well. No matter, that business is resolved, it's just a pity I missed it."

Moses seemed surprised. "How did you get Steel out of the way?" he said in astonishment.

Jones laughed. "Mr Smith dropped a building onto him. Apparently it was delicious to watch." Both men laughed, realizing that there was nothing to stand in their way, not now.

Jones caught a glimpse of Mr Smith's approach. Smith waited at a safe distance until the pair's conversation ended.

Mr Jones turned towards Smith, who made his way forwards, while Mr Smith passed over his cell phone and Mr Jones listened to the person on the other end.

"Are you sure of this?" Jones said, looking up at Smith while he took in the information. Moments later the call was over.

Jones threw back the cell phone to Smith. "Well, Mr Smith, it appears we will be having guests; they have found the garage so it's only a matter of time. Tell the men to prepare for intruders."

Smith squared his shoulders and made his way to the men at the convoy.

"Problem, Mr Jones?" asked Moses.

Mr Jones just grinned.

SIXTY-FIVE

THE BOMB SQUAD HAD made a search of the lower levels and, sure enough, they had found enough explosives to turn the building to rubble.

"We were lucky, Captain," the young sergeant explained. "We found shape charges in strategic places, the things were on a remote so once activated, BOOM!" He used his hands to drive home the point

Sergeant North thanked the bomb squad commander and gave Steel a gracious nod. Steel reciprocated in the same way.

"The thing that I don't get is," McCall asked Steel, "is how come we are always one step behind on this?" The Captain gave Steel a penetrating glare, but Steel did not flinch

McCall had noticed the exchange. "What? What am I missing? What the hell are you not telling us, Steel?"

The female detective was mad. It was true enough that she was tired and she had been through so much these past couple of weeks. However she had not had a building collapse on top of her, as Steel had—the English detective still hadn't offered an explanation for his escape. She felt that all of them deserved an answer to her question.

"The reason Steel kept everything closed up was because he thought that someone in the department was, well, less than trustworthy." Captain Brant said.

McCall shot Steel an angry look. "So we are not trustworthy?"

Steel stood there motionless for a moment, then said: "It wasn't you guys I didn't trust."

She bit back a retort, her eyes blazing with fury. "Who then?"

"I don't know yet. Listen, I trust you guys, in fact you're the only people I do trust at this point." His words were evidently sincere.

Sam McCall knew nothing about his past, but she realised that something unimaginable must have taken place to give the man this kind of paranoia.

"Captain, we are ready to go up," a man from the SWAT team confirmed as he walked up to the group.

"Okay, let's get these bastards!" Brant's words were harsh and filled with conviction. The group put on their body armour and prepared to go in. The Captain remained at the operations van while he watched his people move forwards, the plan being that each detective would accompany a team. The SWAT commander didn't like this idea, but he knew that every officer was more than capable of taking care of themselves.

Four teams would venture into the building, taking and clearing a floor each.

"How are we looking, people?" asked the teams' commander.

"Alpha clear, Bravo clear, Charlie clear, Delta we may have something on the top floor, over."

The Captain and Sergeant North looked at one another,

and North turned back round to the com set and asked: "Sit rep Delta".

The speaker crackled for a moment then came the report: "We have a white van, no visible movement from within. Over."

North thought for a moment. "Okay, all teams verge on Delta's location, close the net from all sides. Out."

He leant back in the chair and ran fingers through his hair in frustration. "What now?" he asked.

Brant looked at the head cam feed from Delta, and, sure enough, a light coloured van was there with the windshield facing forwards.

The Delta team members were kneeling behind the curved wall of the rampart; a sniper had his weapon trained on the vehicle and the leader kept watch, while the others kept low and ready. Steel came running up the rampart towards the team, saying: "Hi guys, car trouble?"

The leader gave Steel a 'Very funny' look, and Steel crept forwards slightly and took out a strange set of binoculars. "What you got, Steel?" asked the leader quietly.

Steel rushed back again. "North, pull your teams back! Right now!"

All the teams froze, taking cover as they waited. "What's the matter now, Mr Steel?"

Steel's back slammed against the wall of the concrete as he slid down. "Sergeant," he began. "How hard were the building explosives to find and remove?"

The E.O.D sergeant leant forwards and picked up the microphone. "Well quiet difficult, we had to use—"

Steel butted in: "—Given what we know of these people's expertise how difficult was it?"

There was a pause.

"Given that," the sergeant replied, "I would say relatively easy."

North tapped on the desk with his pen. He knew that Steel was making sense but did not want to admit to it. "All teams return and cover the exits, Steel come to me, if you please."

All the teams confirmed the orders with a "Roger that." Steel and the other detectives ran back to the command vehicle where the three chiefs were waiting.

"Okay, Steel, what have you come up with now?" The SWAT commander did not like Steel much, that was plain to see. From McCall's perspective it appeared to be a massive testosterone battle, but Steel was unaware of it, which in her view made it more fun. North was greener than green and for him this operation was like his personal toy train set, and Steel was not a welcome player. North could see that Steel had had some type of training but didn't know what kind. Sure, the advice Steel had given up in the past was spot on but now he was making him look bad.

"The van," Steel said intently.

"The van, yes it's a van, what about it?" North snapped.

Steel was starting to get annoyed with the sergeant; he had noticed that his ego was overriding his judgment as far as Steel was concerned. "Sergeant, everything for this guy is about tying up loose ends, so I think either something is in the van, as it was in the warehouse, or it's in the building itself. And hey, if he can kill some cops in the mix all the better; look, these people, whoever they are, like to leave breadcrumbs for us to find, then lead us into a trap. Well, as I see it, this is an entire loaf."

"Okay, what do you suggest?" North put on his sunglasses, trying to look superior.

"Send in the bot, get the copter to scan it with everything. My gut says something is wrong."

North nodded reluctantly. "Okay, we'll try it your way."

With a cloud of dust the copter was moving off towards the car park building. The open walls allowed a perfect view for the cameras as it hovered past making sweep after sweep. Using infra-red, x-ray, they scanned it with everything.

"Okay, what we got, Son?" asked North, coming up to the technician who was flying the four rotor beast.

"Problem, Sir," the pilot answered. "First we have this." He showed a scan, which showed what appeared to be boxes underneath each wheel.

"What the hell is that?" asked McCall, staring closely to the picture on the monitor.

"They are anti tank mines, TMA-2s." Steel's voice was soft and full of alarm.

"So no problem, we get E.O.D to blow it and we move on." Tooms declared. He was now getting tired of the games.

"Tell that to the guy in the back," Steel said, pointing to another cam that showed heat signatures.

"Who is in there, do you think?" McCall asked, stepping back from the table.

Steel shrugged. "I don't know, but if these guys are clearing house it's someone who can talk and probably has a lot to say."

SIXTY-SIX

IT SEEMED LIKE HOURS since Tony had arrived at the station, after spending ages chatting up the cute woman at traffic. He had got the footage they needed and a phone number, so he was now a happy man. He stretched in his seat. After viewing hours of footage on the screen in front of him he had to be close, he thought. He needed coffee, but, just as he was getting up, he saw the back end of a van leaving the complex. He cursed himself and rewound the disk. There, driving down the road was a convoy of cars and vans.

"Got ya," he said, thinking out loud. Now that he knew he had to plot a route of where the vehicles might be heading, he could get some coffee. As he turned he saw Detective Jenny Thompson standing behind him, and he jumped in surprise, startled to see her. "God, you scared me," he said, laughing. She smiled and came closer.

"What you doing?" she asked, seeming interested. Jenny leant forwards to check the screen.

"We—that is I—found the vehicles they used to take the stuff from the garage."

She turned her head slowly, her face just inches away from his. He closed his eyes, enjoying her perfume,, all manner of exciting thoughts running through his head. He opened them and gazed directly into her face, lost in the moment. Hours of sleepless nights and all the extra work combined to make him want to forget conventions, grab her and make love to her right now, and her expression told him that she felt the same way, as she licked her lips provocatively. She wore red lipstick that glistened as the lights from the monitor's screen flickered. He was feeling hot.

"Isn't it warm in here?" she said, smiling, then undid a couple of buttons of her top. His eyes felt looked deeper into hers, then something inside of him crashed him back to reality.

"Sorry, Jenny, I have work, and so do you."

Her mood soured as Jenny refastened her buttons.

"Sorry, Detective," he tried to apologies. "But we have to find where these trucks are going."

Steel had found himself a nice comfortable car's hood to lie upon as the bickering commenced about how to get the man from the truck.

"We just go in, open the door, he steps out, simple," yelled McCall.

Tooms shook his head. "We can't. The mines are probably set in place so any change in weight would trigger them. Why don't we just hook up the van to another van and drag it?"

Detective Steel smiled as he lay there with his arms crossed.

"No, we can't do that either, we don't know how secure the structure is," added North. "We have to do something, we are losing time, people, we may have a clue or evidence in there, and we just have to do something."

The Captain was out of patience.

"We do like Tooms suggested," Steel said good humouredly. Tooms gave him the thumbs up for backing him. "However, we use a helicopter not a car. We attach it and then rip it out through the opening."

Everyone looked at him as though he was nuts.

"Really?" North had his arms crossed in defiance of the idea. "And who will go and rig it up?"

"Well, I appear to be the only one dumb enough so I guess it's me." Steel replied.

North smiled at the idea.

SIXTY-SEVEN

AT THE PRECINCT TONY had found the destination of the convoy. He had ascertained that it was to a cargo docks to the north. Several minutes of computer checks had revealed that the vehicles were rented to the Captain of a container ship out of Europe, the *Eisen Wolff*. After getting in touch with the port authorities, he was waiting to find out the destination and place of origin.

Tony pondered on why Jenny Thompson had come on to him, concluding that it might just be the effects of stress. After all, everyone had been working around the clock since this whole business started and Jenny's new post, as detective, had to have some sort of confidence-boosting effect. He smiled to himself, flattered at the thought she might be interested in him. Suddenly the phone on his desk gave off its loud ring, shocking him back to reality.

"Detective Marinelli." He listened to the voice on the other end and scribbled down some names and an address, then thanked the caller for the information and put down the receiver. He stood up and grabbed his coat.

"Hey, Jenny, I'm going back, you stay here just in case something comes up," he told her.

She looked at him, puzzled, and said: "Don't you want me to come too?"

She seemed genuinely keen, but Tony knew that deep down she was too inexperienced for this kind of operation. "No, I need you to stay here. If we need feet on the ground somewhere else you need to get the other teams that are on standby and get there. So you could do that quicker from here." She faked a disappointed smile and nodded. He returned the smile, but deep down he knew he never wanted a repeat of this case ever.

SIXTY-EIGHT

AS THEY WAITED FOR the helicopter on the roof of one of the high-rises, Captain Brant had a bad feeling. He knew that Steel could handle himself, he had read the man's service file and it scared the hell out of him, knowing what this man had been through and what he was capable of. However, the rest of the team was not so indestructible, and he could see that the more crazy things Steel managed to get away with made the rest of the team a little more reckless.

Brant reached down to his vibrating cell phone. On the screen he saw the ID was from Tony's cell.

"What's up, Detective?" Brant looked up and saw the flashing lights from the CH-47 Chinook.

"Captain," came Tony's voice on the phone. "We found that the convoy has gone to a shipyard in Brooklyn, they are off-loading some sort of cargo in special containers. Sir, I think they are weapons."

Steel noticed the expression on Brant's face and he knew that something was wrong. "What's the matter, Captain?" Steel asked as several men were strapping him into the harness.

"We got a location for the convoy, they are off-loading cargo onto a ship at the Brooklyn shipyard," Brant told him.

The SWAT commander smiled grimly. "What we waiting for? Let's go."

Brant and Steel looked at the commander, completely perplexed by his words.

"Really, let's go!" he repeated.

Steel was still standing there, arms outstretched like some weird mannequin.

"Sergeant, aren't you forgetting something?" Brant asked.

Steel shook his head. "Look, he's right, you all go, all I need is E.O.D and CSU."

Brant slapped him on the shoulder. "You really are a crazy son-of-a-bitch, you know that?"

Steel just nodded and got ready for his ride.

"One question," asked McCall. "Where they going to land?"

Detective Steel just laughed and ran over to a man kneeling down in the middle of the roof.

The Captain watched Steel run over to the winch cable that hung down and strap himself in, then with a roar from the engines the bird flew off with crazy-assed Steel hanging from underneath. Brant watched with his heart in his mouth as the craft neared the car park building. The bad feeling he had had was not bad enough, he thought to himself.

Detective Steel span round to watch the fleet of police vehicles leave the location. *Good,* he thought, at least they would be safe from any blast. But then he remembered the dockyard and the possibilities there.

Rise of a Phoenix

He turned to face the oncoming building, aware that he had more pressing things to worry about. The helicopter turned and was flown neatly towards the opening where the van stood. Unhitching himself, John Steel put the hook onto the middle of a long lashing strap. Putting down a rucksack he produced two large magnets which he placed onto the sides of the van. With great care he then attached the lashing strap. All was in place. He knocked softly on the side of the van, saying: "Hi, we are going to get you out. Now listen carefully, you need to hold onto something at the front of the van if that's possible. You may feel a bit of a tug but don't worry about it, it will be fine."

Steel looked up and made a prayer sign.

"Who are you?" yelled a voice from inside the van.

"Oh no one special," answered Steel. "Just hold on. Okay?" And with that Steel ran like he had never run before.

"Echo One this is Phoenix, proceed in figures ten over. Copy that."

John Steel had realized that he had not really measured how long it would take to make the run from the second floor to the exit, but it was too late for that now, and so he just ran and hoped for the best. He heard the noise of the chopper pull away but he still had some way to go, in fact he was only on the first floor. There was nothing for it, so he headed for the nearest opening on the opposite side.

A massive explosion shook the building, the concrete came down in slabs. the size of Sudan's As the pilots looked the building crumbled from the centre, leaving a cloud of grey mist. Below them hung the white van. They had made it, but they saw no sign of Steel.

"Hello, Charlie One this is Echo One, we have the package," were the words that came over the radio. The Captain held his breath. "Echo One any sign of Phoenix?"

There was a moment of silence. "Negative, we do not have eyes on Phoenix, sorry."

McCall and the rest sat open-mouthed shocked as the Captain concluded with: "Roger, take package to CSU and return home. Good job, boys."

Brant put the handset back onto the dash. "He will be okay, the son-of-a-bitch has more lives than a room full of cats, he will be at the meeting place, you'll see." Everyone could see he needed Steel to be there, just to show that there was still hope for them to get out of this mess alive.

Around a mile from the port the police convoy stopped and made plans. Tony had gone back with Thompson to meet up with the others. Before arriving, Tony had obtained the plans of the ship and the ground plans for the shipyard.

Laying the plans for the vessel onto the hood of his car, Tony explained that Blackheart Industries from England owned the *Eisen Wolff*, and the Captain was a man called Moses who was originally from Egypt.

Sergeant North looked at the plans for the moment. "Okay, this is the plan," North said. "Alpha will clear these buildings to the left here, and here, then move to this location." Underneath the ship's plans lay the ground plans, showing several large buildings with a view of the ship.

"Bravo, you will take the right, clearing here and here, then stand—fast here." Sergeant North pointed out a small workshop to the rear of the ship. "Charlie, once Alpha and Bravo have cleared these buildings you then become top cover for when they board."

The team leader nodded.

"Delta, you will move up as soon as they both reach this position." North pointed to the two entrances to the lower decks under the bridge house. "Your objective, to secure the bridge." Their team leader looked at the plans quickly and gave the thumbs up.

Since everyone knew what they had to do, all teams gave a "Roger that," reply.

McCall looked around. "So what do we do?"

North looked at her. "Stay here. You and your people aren't SWAT so you're out."

McCall felt the onset of a burning rage. Captain Brant felt her frustration but knew that North was right.

"Sorry, Sam, this is his ball game," Brant told her.

She felt the swell of the sergeant's ego as the Captain said those words.

"What about Steel?" Sam McCall asked.

North looked puzzled. "What about him? We don't even know if the man is alive but even if he is, he isn't SWAT so he is out as well."

McCall felt herself wanting to punch the smile off his arrogant face.

"Now if you people don't mind, we have work to do." North made a shooing gesture, as Brant turned to join them.

"Thank you, Captain," North said to the Captain, unable to suppress a grin.

"What are you thanking me for? Don't thank me, North. You wanted it you got it. Thing is if you fuck this up it's all on you. We are only Homicide, remember, it's not our ballgame."

So saying, Brant turned and left a gob smacked Sergeant North.

The SWAT teams had made it to the fence line just beyond which lay their first objectives. Knowing there would be someone watching the main gates, their only option was to go through the fence. Alpha team sat ready waiting for Bravo to give the thumbs up, and on the signal a member using a can of dry ice spray made a large circle on to the fence. There was a hissing noise followed by a crunching as if eggshells were been walked upon, as the solution ate through the metal. The fence was then easily kicked in at that point, opening up a breach. As both teams crept towards their first targets, North watched and listened with anticipation.

"Alpha Phase One complete, Bravo Phase One complete." North smiled as he heard the news, and looked at his second-in-command. It was time to move. He was now oozing with over-confidence as the two men rushed for the large building that overlooked the container ship.

On entering the building, North and his comrade found the stairwell to the operations room. Moving in slowly, the senior man looked round. All the power was off inside so they would not be illuminated. He pointed to a large table near to the right-hand wall. The other man nodded and unpacked his backpack. As he laid out laptops and microphones, he began to set up the mini command centre. There was a flicker of light as the screens came on line.

"We are on, Sir," the second-in-command said.

North smiled as he looked through his tactical binoculars. "All teams sound off." He gave the order.

There was a crackle of static on the line, followed by: "Alpha ready, Bravo ready, Charlie ready, Delta ready."

North took a deep breath, then said: "All teams go."

As he watched, Alpha and Bravo teams took the ship from both ends and converged on to the bridge house, moving fast and professionally, until finally all three teams were at their target point.

"All teams breach when ready," he ordered, and with that the teams disappeared from view.

A loud sound of metal-against-metal echoed through the

Rise of a Phoenix

Operations Room and North recognized it as the top slide of a pistol being released. He closed his eyes in anticipation of the inevitable shot. But instead of a gunshot, pain and death, there were merely two loud thuds as bodies hit the ground.

The two SWAT members looked round to see two men on the ground, each of them with a knife buried in the back of his head. North looked at the empty door way and screamed: "Steel!"

McCall and the others were sitting there feeling restless. Tooms was cleaning his pistol, while Sam McCall just paced up and down the room. Captain Brant looked up as she came up to him.

"Captain," she asked, "couldn't we just?"

He looked at her. "Just *what*, Detective? We are Homicide not Special Weapons. Besides we don't have the firepower, we have just a couple of hand guns and whatever we have in the trunk."

Tooms smiled. "He doesn't know?" His voice was full of excitement, as the Captain glared at them.

"I don't know what?" He followed McCall to her car's trunk, and as she opened it his eyes lit up. "Holy Mother of… You've got to be kidding me. I take it this was what you had to stop off for?"

In the car's trunk, their armoury lay before him. "Okay," he conceded. "We got the tools, but it's still SWAT's show. Until North fucks it up."

The Captain put down the AR-14 rifle he had been examining to answer his cell phone. "Brant," he snapped, his mouth dry from excitement. He listened to the brief statement and then put the phone away.

"Detective, be careful what you wish for," he said to McCall.

She looked puzzled.

"That was Steel just now. The son-of-a-bitch made it out, and we have to go in."

They got into their cars and made for the entrance.

High above the dockyard a lone sniper sat in a crow's nest observing the entrance to the area, ensuring that no unwanted guests could come to back up the SWAT teams. For him the boredom had set in long ago, and all he had to do was look through his scope from time to time.

Then from one of the buildings there was a flash of light and movement. Using his scope he homed in to find a TV set had been left on playing a porno film, and the sniper pointlessly looked around as if someone may be watching, then looked back to the window.

As he zoomed in to watch, he was suddenly surprised to see another sniper aiming his weapon straight at him. Before he could react, the .338 round had penetrated the glass of his scope.

After Steel had been looking at the puff of red where the man's head used to be, he packed away the powerful MSR sniper rifle and moved off.

One down, lots more to go, he thought to himself.

Pulling their car up by the SWAT vehicles, McCall and the others crept out of the vehicles and moved around to gather the weapons from the trunk. Taking out the canvas bags they prepared themselves for what was ahead. The Captain had ditched his Remington pump-action, and swapped it for an automatic shotgun, thinking to himself, *don't mind if I do*.

Finding the left-hand entrance that the teams had created, the group of police moved quickly from building to building. With Tooms taking 'point' (leading) position, he took them through shadows and as close to cover as he could, until they reached the building where the SWAT leader had set up. This time moving slowly and quietly, they continued on up the stairwell. McCall could not help but notice how everything appeared to become larger, as the light diminished. Beads of nervous sweat collected on her brow.

Tooms crept up the stairs checking the corners, and all his military training came flooding back to him.

"God, I miss this, bro." he muttered.

Tony smiled, noticing that his friend and partner was in his element. Finally, they reached the floor. Just beyond the door in front of them lay the corridor to the Operations Room. Tooms's heart was beating hard in his chest, and the rush of adrenaline was intoxicating. Opening the door slowly he saw flashes of light from monitors lighting the hallway. Edging forwards they reached the room. Tooms stopped and raised his fist to signal stop, and everyone crouched down as he moved forwards. McCall saw him stand up and wave them in

There on the ground lay two men in black, both with knives embedded in the backs of their heads.

"Is it them?" Brant asked, using his boot to roll one of the blood-soaked men over onto his back. "Unfortunately no. Looks like someone bagged the bad guys."

Tony squinted outside, saying: "Yeh, I wonder who?" Then he pointed to the corpse that was hanging from the crow's nest.

"Ouch." McCall said, and stopped looking through her scope at the headless man and concentrated on the looking at the main deck of the massive ship below them. "I found Steel, he's on the main deck," she said excitedly, and re-slung the rifle. "Okay, people, let's go and help the man. Tooms, you happy with taking point?"

The big man grinned and took off.

Deep inside the ship Alpha Team entered a large room, and the only light they had was from their weapon lamps. "Oh my God," Said the team leader, who stood motionless as he realised they were in a room full of missiles. "All teams converge on my location, we have a problem."

Bravo and Delta confirmed the request. Moments later the teams entered the room.

"Jack, what the hell is going on here?" someone asked.

The team leader shook his head. "I don't know, man, but what I do know is" His speech was cut short as the door was slammed shut. The three team leaders rushed forwards. "What the hell, who the hell was on guard?"

Then they looked down outside the door to see a man lying unconscious. Two men dressed in black picked him up and threw him into another room. The trapped team's only hope was that the Captain and his crew had made it down to the shipyard.

Brant and the others had made it to a stack of crates next to the gantry, and two armed men stood between them and the hostages. McCall and Tooms moved forwards, their silenced Beretta ARX160 rifles held ready for contact.

"Police, put down your weapons," McCall shouted while Tooms covered her. The two guards turned and lifted their weapons. There was a dull popping sound, as Tooms shot one and McCall took the other, then the two guards dropped to the ground. Moving over to the two bodies McCall checked but found no pulses.

"Hey you!"

The voice came from behind them. Two armed guards knelt ready, weapons trailed on their targets. McCall and Tooms were fully in their sights, so they put down their weapons and raised their hands. McCall heard no sound, she just saw each man lunge forwards as a round took away their faces and pushed their lifeless bodies into the water below. The two detectives both exhaled the litre of air they had held in anticipation of being shot.

Gathering up their weapons, Tooms waved to the others, who followed them up the gantry to the main deck. Once there, the containers stacked one upon another meant that there was plenty of cover from the mass of mercenaries who were no doubt waiting for them.

Tooms took point and McCall followed, and the group moved tight and stealthily. As Tooms crossed one corner, a large man grabbed him, and was about to plant a large blade into his head. But there was the sound of a dull thud and the man fell, blood oozed from the wound in the back of his head. The Captain spun round as four mercenaries rushed towards them. Dropping to one knee he opened up on the men, each of whom spun off their feet as hot metal pellets made contact, ripping through flesh and cloth.

The police unit moved as one through the maze of containers. Suddenly McCall looked up and saw three mercenaries on top of a container, their weapons at the ready. With a burst of fire she ripped into them, sending sprays of red body fluids into the night air, as the men's bodies went reeling over the other side. The others swung round, weapons trained on the targets, but it was too late. McCall smiled, saying, "Too slow, boys."

Crouching behind some metal containers, they spied their target. The entrance to the bridge and the lower decks was not far from their position. McCall's cell phone vibrated in her pocket. After taking it out the text on the screen simply read: *Have found hostages, come to lower decks. Steel.*

McCall put the phone away but felt puzzled. She looked up to find Tooms had the same look of confusion.

"What's wrong with you two?" asked Brant.

Tooms looked around them. "Why does Steel need our help?" he asked.

Tony seemed confused by the question, but the Captain then had a spark of insight. "He doesn't need our help," Brant told them. "Hell, the guy did this sort of thing for a living—oops."

McCall and the others looked at him in surprise. "Did *what* for a living?" she asked.

Brant realized his slip and tried to cover up his gaff. "Ask me if we live, hell, ask him if we live."

McCall and the others now had a really bad feeling. "Okay, my question is why does he want us on the ship?" she said.

Tooms was now feeling even less happy.

"Well my question is why you are getting texts from me when I didn't send any."

They all looked round, amazed to see Steel standing behind them holding the massive sniper rifle. "Steel, what the hell is going on?" McCall asked.

Steel walked up to her. "Hi, can I get your phone please?" She gave it to him with a puzzled look. "They are tracking you through your phone. All of you have to get off right now."

Brant walked up to Steel, asking him: "Where is everybody?"

Steel put McCall's cell phone away. "The teams are downstairs, and the sergeant and his second are back at the van, so everyone get off, right now."

McCall shot him an angry look.

"Sorry, Sam, but no you can't help, you'll slow me down."

Rise of a Phoenix

Steel's words were cruel but also accurate. He had to move quickly and someone alongside him would get in the way, she realized that. Steel swapped weapons with Tooms. "Sure you can handle that?" he asked, grinning as Tooms shot him a sarcastic look. Reluctantly they obeyed the Englishman and headed for the side. As they moved off, Steel grabbed the Captain's arm. "Sir, this boat cannot leave these waters." He shoved a manifest into the Captain's hands, a list detailing all kinds of weapons.

"This ship is heading for the middle east," Brant was so angry he was practically foaming at the mouth. "So this whole thing was about arms smuggling?"

"No," replied Steel. "It was about money."

Steel made his way down the metal stairs, the darkness shattered by the dimly lit red lights. He had to find the teams and fast, but first, he had to even up the numbers. Soon he found a room full of crates, and he smiled at the irony of the situation. Making his way inside he took out McCall's cell phone and hid it deep within the room. He found a spot in the shadows at the end of the corridor and waited.

He did not have to be there long before red beams of light cut through the dimness of the corridor. They were here, at least twelve heavily armed men. He smiled as he watched them go into the room one by one.

"Where are they?" screamed one of them.

A short man took out an electronic tablet and watched the display turn into a map of the boat. Touching the screen it zoomed in on the room.

"They are here," he said, "Or at least her cell phone is."

"You dumb ass," said another man, who came round the corner of boxes holding McCall's cell phone. At that moment the door slammed shut and there was a creak of metal as the brace went on. The imprisoned men rushed forwards, firing as they went, hoping to wound or kill whoever had locked them in.

"Great," said the man with the cell phone, throwing it into the corner, and hearing it disintegrate against the wall.

SIXTY-NINE

INSIDE THE OPERATIONS ROOM Brant and the others watched as the ship gave a bellow of smoke in preparation to disembark. Brant picked up his phone, looked at it for a brief moment and then shoved it back into his pocket.

"Find me a secure line," he ordered.

Everyone looked for a landline phone that was still functioning had not been ripped out.

"Will this do?" asked Sergeant North. They all turned to see him and his second-in-command. He was holding his cell phone in an outstretched hand and looked guilty and ashamed.

Brant took the phone from him. "This was nobody's fault but theirs, so let's have no guilt or recriminations, let's just get our people off there, and get these sons-of-bitches."

The Captain then called the commissioner and told him of the situation. He also fulfilled his promise to Detective Steel, grimly explaining that it was vital to stop the ship by any means necessary. They all looked at Brant, fully understanding what that meant.

"He will get those men and himself off that ship before anything happens," assured Brant. "I know he will."

They all nodded and sat down on whatever they could find. The situation was out of their hands now and there was not a damned thing they could do to help. They watched helplessly as the ship got underway. "God speed, Steel," the Captain spoke under his breath.

Steel raced down corridor after corridor until he heard the sound of banging. At first he thought he was close to the engine room but this sound wasn't that of mechanical discord, this was an almost purposeful tapping. As he got closer he could hear the yells of trapped men. Knowing it wasn't the room he had trapped the morons in earlier, he knew it must be the SWAT teams. Wrenching open the door, the men drew back seeing only a shadow, until one man put on his flashlight, and there stood Steel.

"Any one order room service?" Steel joked.

The men rushed forwards to greet him. "Daniels," someone called out. "They took him somewhere."

Next to their room was a broom closet with no handle, and with a huge kick the team leader of Alpha had found his man, who was still unconscious.

"We have to go now." Steel told them. He could feel the engines getting stronger, and He knew Captain Brant being a man of his word, would do as Steel had asked, meaning that very soon all manner of hell would be raining down on this ship.

Looking through his binoculars Tooms saw men in the water. Adjusting the focus to zoom in, he identified them as the missing SWAT men.

"Well I'll be damned, he got them off, the bastard did it," Tooms declared.

Rise of a Phoenix

Everyone cheered, and Brant turned to the room full of people. "We've got to get them out of the water."

Leaving their equipment, they all rushed down to the dock to assist the half-drowned men. Finding several small boats they set off to get as many as they could, leaving McCall and Tony on the bank.

Steel was last to leave the cabin. He could see the city lights sparkling brightly in front of him, and as he broke out of the doorway two powerful hands grabbed him and tossed him like a doll. Hitting the deck, he rolled and ended in a crouched alert position. In front of him was a large man with blond greased-back hair.

"So, Mr Steel, it appears my men didn't find you after all."

Steel Smiled smugly and tilted his head in a defiant gesture. "No, I guess they didn't."

The two men sized one another up. "You are full of surprises, Mr Steel," began the blonde-haired mercenary. "I must say, my employer finds you most interesting."

This was a new piece of information for Steel. It seemed that these were not just mercenaries making a quick buck, this was an entire organization: the organization his father was trying to root out. The people who had killed his family all those years ago. He glared at his enemy. Even with his eyes covered by the sunglasses, Mr Jones could sense the clear cold hatred.

"Oh, you'll never guess just how many surprises I've got lined up." As the Englishman spoke there was a rumble from down below. Then a massive explosion ripped a hole in the side of the vessel.

"Oops," said Steel. "You're not the only one who can play with explosives."

Jones lunged for Steel, who simply rolled out of the way. Another explosion rocked the ship knocking both men off their feet. But Jones was quick and he forward-rolled to Steel's position and smashed down with one punch to the face and then an upper cut to the stomach.

Detective Steel spat blood just as the large man grabbed him by the collar and lifted him off the ground.

"Well, Mr Steel let us see how un-killable you really are," Jones snarled.

Just then another explosion rocked the ship, knocking them off balance. Steel head-butted his adversary then, as Jones dropped, Steel brought his knee up to Jones's groin. The large man bent forwards in agony, only to be met by Steel's knee to his jaw. Jones spat teeth and bloody saliva. Quickly snatching a blade from behind his back, he swept forwards, slicing a nick into Steel's torso.

Steel looked down at the rip in his top, and saw the faint line of red that stretched across his muscular stomach.

"So, Mr Steel, to the test, who is the better man?" Jones shouted.

The Englishman looked around in amazement: this man wanted to have a knife fight as the ship was being ripped apart. Steel rushed for the side. Suddenly instinct told him to drop down, just as a twelve-inch blade whizzed past his head.

"I knew you were a coward." Jones said.

Steel stood up and faced the man. "There is a difference between bravery and stupidity. At this moment staying on board an exploding ship is going into the realms of being friggin nuts."

Jones gave an evil grin. "Don't you want to find out who is the better man?"

Steel shook his head. "Not really." He moved away

"Or to find out who killed your parents? You never did find that out, did you?"

Steel turned, this time slowly, his teeth bared.

"Now we shall see." Jones produced a boot knife. "Come, my Lord. let us do battle."

McCall looked through the binoculars to see the two men fighting. "My God," she called out. "It's Steel and some monster of a man. They're fighting."

Tony looked at her, confused, and took the binoculars from her. "Is he nuts? Don't he realize that thing's going to go blow up any minute?"

In front of them the boats were being filled with members of the SWAT teams, while others clung to the sides.

Explosion after explosion ripped the ship to pieces, shards of metal being sent flying with each eruption, but the men battled on. Jones was surprised by the sheer power and anger that drove this beast. Now he realized that what had left the mansion all those years ago was no longer a man. Jones knew for the sake of the organization that Steel had to be put down.

The two men faced each other. Jones saw that Steel had scars all over his body, but it was not fazing him. For the first time in his life he felt fear. He now understood all the stories he had heard about the wrath of the Phoenix and now he knew just what it meant.

"Come on, Steel," he taunted. "If you still have the strength."

He gripped the knife tighter. After seeing him attack again and again he knew Steel would rush headlong and try to dodge the knife and get in a couple of punches, but now he was ready for him. With anticipation, he watched Steel start his run up. Jones gripped the knife tightly and braced himself: this time he would leave the knife strike for last.

As Steel grew near, he hit the deck and slid, knocking Jones to the ground. As the blond man's back slammed against the deck, Steel knelt on his arms and gave him six massive right hooks to the face. Blood flowed freely and the sound of crunching bone filled his ears.

Detective Steel stood up, panting and breathless. "Come on, you gutless wonder, come and get me if you're able. I'll make you bleed for my family, I'll make you all bleed."

Then Steel was knocked backwards by a massive explosion. Once the smoke had cleared he saw pieces of metal had pierced the deck and something had decapitated his enemy. Steel smiled at the irony that the man's own weapons had caused his death. Turning, he jumped into the water, just as the ship was vaporized by a final, incredibly powerful explosion.

From the vehicles everyone cheered. They had made it, and it was all over. However, McCall and the others didn't cheer, instead they ran down towards the dock, intent on knowing Steel's fate. McCall ran, her heart pounding as she picked up speed. Her arms pounded like an old locomotive, and her eyes were transfixed on the harbor, hoping to catch a glimpse of him coming out of the water.

A loud cracking sound filled the air, and then something hit her. At first, it did not register until she found herself falling down. The others hit the deck, taking cover behind crates and machinery.

"Sniper" Tooms shouted as he watched McCall spin and hit the ground hard.

"Sam, are you okay?" called out the Captain with tears in his eyes as he looked over to where she lay motionless and feared the worst.

Two badly injured hands broke the surface of the water

and grabbed the sides of the harbour wall. Pulling himself out of the sea, Steel rolled onto his back and gasped for air. His head fell to the side as the rest of the ship continued to erupt, reminding him of the Fourth of July celebrations

He sat up and saw someone lying on the jetty. Standing up, he slowly moved forwards, and his heart began to pound frantically in his chest. The closer he got the more he could see of the woman on the jetty, and memories of all the women from his past merged together in his mind. Just a couple of feet away he dropped to his knees as the strength left his legs. Brant and the others helpless to do anything in fear of joining their colleague. McCall was bait and Steel was the prize and they couldn't do a damn thing to help either of them.

On his hands and knees the battle scarred man crawled towards McCall's limp body, leaving bloody trails of battle on the ground.

The Englishman reached out a hand to grasp her pale flesh but the few feet between them seemed like a chasm. Tears cascaded down his face making his facial wounds sting, as he crawled closer and closer, his body numb from memories of past conflicts. From here, he could smell the mix of sweet perfume and the metallic tang of fresh blood. Brant and the others watch in trepidation as Steel picked up her limp body and held it close, doing all he could to squeeze life back into her shattered form.

Steel kissed her forehead, and as he rocked her back and forth he spoke softly in to her ear. "It's going to be okay, you will see."

This was a broken man the police officers saw before them. Never could they have imagined that after all this he would crumble. Only the Captain knew that he wasn't there with McCall. He was back in the attic of his ancestral home with his wife as she lay dying .

A smell wafted onto the breeze, a smell of bad deodorant and body odour. And a laugh that he had not heard for so long suddenly pierced his ears. Steel faced forward, and as he listened, he heard the click of a revolver's hammer being drawn back. A blink of an eye was all it took.

Brant and the others never even saw him toss the blade. But in that blink of an eye the large bald man was on the floor, holding the gushing mess where his trigger finger used to be. The chromed weapon had tumbled from his grip. Steel didn't really know if someone or something had guided the knife or it had just been blind luck, but there was an added bonus, as the .50 calibre revolver span towards the ground, firing as it fell, and blowing off the man's left foot.

Steel stood up and walked towards the bleeding man. He was almost in a trance, unable to hear the others calling him. He reached down, grabbed the man by the collar, and started to drag him towards a tool shed.

"Steel, what the hell are you doing?" yelled the Captain. "You're a cop for God's sake!"

They watched him turn round and for the first time they saw him without his glasses. His emerald green eyes stared back at them looking lifeless, soulless, sending a chill down their spines.

The Captain saw something hit the ground in front of them and, in horror, he saw Steel's badge lying there.

"I'm not a cop anymore," he yelled.

And they watched, frozen in fear as he dragged the screaming man into the shed. There was a loud bang as the door shut and locked, followed by a bone-chilling scream.

SEVENTY

AS SHE LAY IN the hospital bed listening to the sounds of people walking up and down the corridors, the squeak of safety shoes on non-slip floors, ringing phones answered by loud-voiced nurses, Sam felt safe but disappointed. All of her colleagues had been to visit and her room looked more like a flower store, and Get-Well cards littered a small table next to the door, a testimony to her colleagues' affection for her.

However, John Steel had not been in. After all the times he had just appeared from the shadows, why couldn't he turn up now? The one time she needed him and he was not there.

Sam turned as Tina entered, holding a bowl of cherries and a card.

"Hi, honey, how you feeling?" Tina asked as she watched McCall trying to sit up.

"Uh uh, you lay right where you are," Tina told her, seeing the pain in her friend's face.

"So, any word from *you know who*?"

Sam McCall shook her head, even though it hurt to do so.

"So what's the last thing you remember?"

McCall closed her eyes for a moment. "Steel dragging some bleeding guy into a shed. They say that he killed Steel's family, he never mentioned anything."

Tina smiled. "Well, he never really gave anything up. Now I know why."

The silence was broken by Tina's cell phone vibrating in her bag. Taking it out she saw it was from the precinct.

"What happened to Steel after that?" Sam asked.

Tina put the phone away. "He threw the guy to the Captain, nobody knows why, hell if it had been me I would have killed the bastard!"

They both laughed, a breeze blew the curtains and Tina walked over and closed the window. "You need anything, babe?"

McCall shook her head and smiled painfully. Tina kissed Sam on the forehead and left.

"I couldn't do it."

A voice from the shadows at the other end of the room startled her.

"Steel?" she called out.

He walked out of the shadow and there he was, larger than life. Her expression ranged from pure joy to astonishment.

"What do you mean, you couldn't?"

He sat in the chair next to the bed. "After years of searching for them in the end I couldn't bring myself down to their level. You taught me that, Sam, thank you."

She winced in pain, as she tried to smile.

"Look on the bright side," he said encouragingly. "Next time the guys are showing off their scars you can beat them hands down."

McCall tried not to laugh. "What about you?" she asked.

He stood up. "I'm still with the unit but I have some leave so I'm off back home. I've got some loose ends to tie up."

A worried look suddenly came over McCall's tired looking face.

He walked up to her and stared into her sparkling blue eyes. She returned his gaze, wishing he would take off those damned glasses so she could look at him properly.

He edged closer and she could feel the warmth of his breath on her skin. She closed her eyes and tilted her head forwards. Her lips open slightly to catch the kiss, but his mouth landed softly on her forehead. Sam's eyes opened as a solitary tear rolled down her cheek. Raising his hand to catch the tear she brushed her cheek against his hand. He smiled and stood up.

Walking to the window, he turned back to her.

"The ones who shot you are just pawns, you know that. They have been chasing me for years." She managed to sit up.

"You don't have to run anymore," she told him as he smiled at her reassuringly.

"I was never running just waiting. But it's time to bring the fight to them." He walked forward and placed a blue rose on her pillow. Picking up the flower, she inhaled the perfume. She felt a sudden waft of cold air that made the curtains of the bed space opposite billow. She watched him put his right hand over his heart and then take a small dignified bow. As he did so he moved back into the shadows of the dark room.

With a scream of pain, she reached for the light switch, only to find the room empty. McCall winced in pain as she got up and moved to the window. Looking out upon the night, the breeze was refreshing against her skin and the moon was as full and bright as a winter's morning. Holding up the rose, she once more inhaled its sweet scent. He was gone for now but she knew deep down that one day he would be back.

In the darkness of Steel's apartment, the priest watched Steel pack a suitcase. Their mood was sombre and conversation short.

"Where are you off to?" the clerical man's words disappointed and intrigued him. Steel took a handful of black suits that still hung on their hangers and carefully placed them into the sturdy suitcase.

"I have to go to London to follow up a lead."

Gabriel stood up and walked towards the window. The orange glow of the city's lights seemed soothing, and he could see why Steel preferred to have the lights off.

"A lead? From who?" he asked. He saw Steel smile coldly and knew then he did not really want to know.

Steel turned towards his friend. "SANTINI, It's not a 'He', it's a 'They'."

Gabriel nodded; it made sense that the organization had a name.

"And what about your partner, did you tell her you were going?" He saw in the reflection of the large glass window Steel stop folding a shirt and nod slowly. The Englishman had a sorrowful look on his face.

"She will be fine, they all will."

Gabriel turned and made his way towards his friend. "And you John? Will you be okay?" The priest's voice was soft but held a stern tone to it.

The other man looked up and smiled. "You know me, I am always fine. Look, I am just going to find someone an old friend asked me to look for. There won't be any trouble. It's a simple quick there, quick back, No problem."

Rise of a Phoenix

Gabriel reached down and picked up the black-and-white photograph. The picture was of a woman in her late thirties with long hair. He turned it over and read the name *Tarrasa Benning*.

"Who is she?" Gabriel asked, putting the photograph back in its place. Steel picked up his glass of whisky and moved towards the dresser.

"I don't know who she is, but I know she has answers, and I have a lot of questions."

He reached into the draw and pulled out a large .45 automatic. After pressing a small button next to the pistol grip the weapons magazine slipped out effortlessly.

Pulling back the weapons long top slide he checked that the chamber was empty, and then quickly let it go forward using the weapon's inner spring. The almost fiery orange light from the city's illumination cast a strange reflection on the weapon's dark steel, making it seem as though it was glowing with heat.

The top slide had sideward angled recesses cut into it, which revealed the polished bear steel of the barrel. Steel pressed down on the top round of the single stack magazine, then reinserted it into the weapon then placed it back into the draw. Carefully Steel took out some folded shirts from the same draw then placed them into the case before closing the draw and then the case. A cold shiver ran down the priest's back. He could see that the old soldier had returned.

The Phoenix had risen.

Printed in Great Britain
by Amazon.co.uk, Ltd.,
Marston Gate.